The
LAST
RESTAURANT
IN
PARIS

BOOKS BY LILY GRAHAM

The Summer Escape

A Cornish Christmas

Summer at Seafall Cottage

Christmas at Hope Cottage

The Island Villa

The Paris Secret

The Child of Auschwitz

The German Girl

Lily Graham

The
LAST
RESTAURANT
IN
PARIS

bookouture

Published by Bookouture in 2022

An imprint of Storyfire Ltd.
Carmelite House
50 Victoria Embankment
London EC4Y 0DZ

www.bookouture.com

ISBN: 978-1-80314-001-8
eBook ISBN: 978-1-80314-075-9

For Fudge, darling friend, sorely missed.

PART ONE

1

GILBERT

The old antiquarian bookstore was a sliver amongst the larger pastel-coloured shops on the leafy Parisian street of Rue Cardinet. It was called Librairie d'antiquités de Géroux but was, nonetheless, as much a part of the Batignolles village as the Saturday farmers' market, the square, or the tourists retracing the steps of impressionist painter Alfred Sisley.

The only other building that seemed as much a part of the furniture was the abandoned restaurant on the corner, like one of those unfortunate heirloom pieces that tends to clash with everything. Most people believed it to be cursed or haunted as a result of what had happened there during the Occupation, when the former owner had poisoned all of her customers one night. A fact that had turned to legend over the intervening years.

For instance, some swore that when the wind changed or a new season approached you could still smell cooking. When the leaves from the plane trees turned gold, rumours swelled of cream and port and roast chicken. Delicious at first, then as the day grows, turning acrid and sour. And when the wisteria bloomed, whispers flew of apricots and butter and *clafoutis*, similarly mouth-watering in the beginning, but then growing sickly sweeter by the evening, till you needed to breathe through your mouth to escape the decaying scent of rotten fruit.

Nonetheless, this, too, brought the tourists.

The idea of lingering phantom scents annoyed Monsieur Géroux, the owner of the antiquarian bookshop, on good days, and made him spitting mad on others. Now in his mid-sixties, and with hair tending more to salt than pepper, he despaired at how events that were monstrous enough in their cold, hard facts, turned, over time, to myth, like in some gothic romance.

It had been over forty years and Monsieur Géroux still got nightmares about it. And now, that infernal restaurant was still finding a way to cast a shadow over him.

The bell tinkled as he slipped into his store, pulling the door closed behind him with a sigh. Usually, when the familiar scent of old books, wood and nostalgia enveloped him, he felt a sense of relief, of home. Today he felt dread.

Thanks to that letter.

It had arrived the day before, seemingly innocent in its smart white envelope and officious-looking typescript, until it revealed itself to be an invitation from a law firm to speak about *that night*. The worst of his life, when his brother, Henri, was poisoned and killed. For an awful moment, after he read the letter's request, he thought he might burst into tears. He'd fled his shop, heart pounding in his ears, needing to be anywhere but there.

He'd spent the evening walking along the river Seine, trying and failing to get the contents of the letter out of his mind, taking in none of the sights that usually offered calm. The narrowboats with their potted rooftop gardens and their canine sailors, keeping an eye out from the bow. Lovers walking arm-in-arm, perhaps to place a lock on one of the bridges. Shop vendors displaying their wares along the banks, their stalls full of bric-a-brac, records, or books – the latter he could never resist perusing, perhaps with a hot crêpe wrapped up in wax paper in one hand, dripping hot sugar and lemon down his chin, while he browsed, forever hopeful that he might find that rare gem that he might be able to sell on in his own store.

But the calm hadn't arrived nor the joy and he hadn't been in the mood for crêpes.

He let out a sigh now, as he approached his shop. He tried to uncrumple his face, like a piece of paper, with the palms of his hands. He'd barely slept, the past rising up to torment him all through the night. The memories poking at him with ephemeral fingers that he twisted away from and tried to ignore, like that letter.

But he couldn't.

His hand shook as he flicked on the brass light switch and the store interior was illuminated. The walls were painted olive green. There was a wooden floor in a herringbone pattern, floor-to-ceiling shelving in green-painted wood, olive again, and a window seat with mustard-coloured cushions. Against one wall were several glass cabinets filled with rare books; some grew curiously fashionable in his circles of trade, depending on the market. There were first editions, some he would never sell, others he'd been trying to flog for a decade or more. There was even a good champagne from '68 he was saving for the day he finally sold a particularly ugly American first edition of *Lolita*. Though some days, he wondered which one would go first, him or the book. At times this amused him, others not so much. The open shelves were full of second-hand books that weren't quite as valuable, but proved slightly more popular. Though, as the dust might argue, not popular enough.

In the middle was his desk, an old-fashioned behemoth that had once belonged to his grandfather who had been a headmaster at a local boys' prep school. It looked suitably austere: if it were a face it would have a very firm chin and Charles Dickens sideburns. It had faded green padding set atop the mahogany, and on top of this were several books, neatly stacked and in need of repair. Monsieur Géroux winced, though, when he saw the mess he'd left behind the night before, seeing that his tools were still laid out from where he'd been busy with a book repair, the glue bottle left to dry. Globules of the stuff were now marring the surface of his desk.

He prised off the bits of glue on the desk – as well as the cap that had formed at the opening of the bottle – with a fingernail, only to sigh when he saw the abandoned paintbrush he'd been using to rebind the leather cover stuck to the desk, the bristles as hard as rock. Even with a good soak in hot water it was likely ruined.

He was annoyed at himself.

'Coffee,' he decided. Even on a bad day there was coffee, which was always a small good thing.

Monsieur Géroux collected small good things. The unexpected sound of birdsong, a half-price sale at the bakery, a smile from a passing child. Storing them in his mind for later, when needed.

There were days he felt every bit of his advancing years, like that morning when he'd felt as tired as the lines and shadows beneath his eyes would suggest when he'd shaved off the bristles on his face. But there were days, too, when he caught a glimpse of himself in a passing window and suffered a momentary shock when he realised that the old man looking back in the glass was him. He still thought of himself as a young man with rusted brown hair and freckles.

At least the freckles were still there. He hadn't liked them when he was younger, but he was fond of them now. Funny how that happened.

He went to light the tiny gas stove in the kitchen to the left of the store, hidden away behind a painted door, also olive green. He sometimes worried he'd overdone it with all the green.

He ran the hot water tap and put the brush in a glass jar to soak. Then he spooned thick black grounds of fresh Italian coffee into his cafetière, breathing in the scent before he put it on the stove to simmer.

He would deal with the letter later, he decided, firmly, after he had cleared up and completed his tasks for the morning. It felt better to give his worry an appointment, and a small part of the calm he'd been searching for since the evening before finally grew inside him, like a small green shoot.

He took his coffee to his desk and began to sort out the mess he'd left for himself the evening before. He switched on the radio to France Musique, a channel with an emphasis on jazz and classical that was his usual morning company. The haunting strings of the prelude of Bach's 'Cello Suite No 1 in G Major' filled the air as he took a fortifying sip of his tar-thick coffee and began to work, applying glue to a new brush and beginning to repair a poetry volume.

Outside, the cobbled street was beginning to fill as this corner of Paris woke up. Shop doors were opening, the closed signs switching to open. People walked past, their hands clasping a *pain au chocolat* as they made their way to work, or a warm baguette to take home from the bakery at the end of the lane. Children were laughing, and jumping off and on the pavement en route to school. There were old men shuffling their way to their favourite café further on, with its bistro chairs spilling over the pavement, where they would while away the morning with a coffee, a toothpick, and a front-row seat in which to watch the world roll around them.

Monsieur Géroux, however, saw none of this as he continued with his repairs.

The radio station had moved on to the soothing melody of

Pachelbel's 'Canon and Gigue in D Major' when he heard a familiar scratching at the door sometime later.

'My first customer.' He went to open the door, his mood lifting. 'Well?' he said, lips twitching.

There was a small whine and something that looked like a hairy brown carpet slunk inside on three legs.

'And where have you been, Tapis?' he asked the creature, as if it would answer and tell him of his adventures.

The animal blinked up at him with amber eyes half buried beneath wiry fur. Monsieur Géroux made a tutting sound, then went to fetch the old thing's breakfast.

Tapis was a dog, but he lived the life of a cat. Monsieur Géroux swore that he'd once seen him waiting at a traffic light. Other shopkeepers on their street swore that they'd seen him roaming the night with a pair of cats who appeared to be doing his bidding, like some furry mob boss. Monsieur Géroux wouldn't have been surprised.

Tapis ate his breakfast, then settled down for the day in the window seat. Monsieur Géroux watched the dog fondly for a while before he moved on to the next book he needed to repair, only to realise he hadn't actually finished the first one, and he had left globs of glue all over his desk. Again. He closed his eyes and prayed for strength. He was still distracted because of that letter and it was no use pretending otherwise.

He sat drumming his fingers on his chin, then gave in at last, opening up his desk drawer to retrieve it and read it once again.

19 Avril 1987

Dear Monsieur Géroux,

I am a paralegal at the law firm Lefauge et Constable. Recently we had a development with one of the properties we manage – a former restaurant on the corner of Rue Cardinet and Lumercier that used to trade under the name Luberon. We were finally able to locate the last remaining relative of the former proprietor, Marianne Blanchet. French law dictates, as you may know, that we cannot sell a property until we have identified all potential inheritance claims.

I understand from our records that you are familiar with the establishment I am referring to. This is why I am reaching out to you.

In our files regarding this property, I discovered that you were listed as a contact because you submitted testimony to the authorities forty years ago. As one of the few people alive with knowledge of what truly happened there all those years ago, would it be possible for me to put our client in contact with you?

Our client, Sabine Dupris, was not aware that she was a relation of the former owner, and the news – as well as the discovery of the incident that occurred there – has been most distressing, as you can imagine. She has many questions that remain unanswered. Questions we are unable to answer, regrettably. You are, of course, under no obligation to speak with her.

Sabine Dupris has given us permission to share her details with you, which are below.

Best regards,

Julie Dupont

Monsieur Géroux paused over the word 'incident' with a grimace. *A nice euphemism for murder*, he thought, grimly, wondering if they gave lessons to lawyers and paralegals on how to write such things.

He frowned, continuing to the part that read *our client was not aware that she was a relation*, and despite his promise to be stern with himself, felt his heart soften, knowing that none of this could have been easy to discover.

He read again the words, *under no obligation*, then pursed his lips at *young client rather distressed*. Knowing that despite those assurances, an obligation was most assuredly implied, one that may as well have been circled in red ink. This was a letter not so much written as *designed* to pull at his heart strings.

He didn't have to give in to it, though. He could just shove the letter back in his desk drawer and ignore it. He had provided information to the authorities about what had happened in that restaurant forty years ago, and as far as he was concerned, that had been that. What this woman was asking was unthinkable... to dredge up all those memories and to tell some relative of Marianne's what she had done?

All those people she poisoned, *intentionally*.

To speak of the murder of his brother to some stranger. Like he was what – giving a history lesson? She was likely young; the young haven't yet learned how real the past is, just a whisper away the older you get, and sometimes too real to face.

Monsieur Géroux pinched the bridge of his nose, and put the letter down.

The details that this client had searched were still available on the public record. He didn't need to relive it so that he could provide insight into some forgotten family history. Or attempt to make sense of the insensible – as he would never be able to answer the one question she was bound to want to know more than anything: why? Why had Marianne Blanchet killed all those people?

He didn't *know*.

And it haunted him still.

The thing was, surely what he had to say, what he *hadn't* put on record, was even more distressing? Because it would just lead to more questions he couldn't answer. The only one who could was Marianne and she was dead now, thank goodness. Executed for her crimes.

Still, he was, as the paralegal had so cleverly pointed out, the only one alive who remembered what had happened and could speak about it.

For a moment, his brother Henri's face floated before him. When Monsieur Géroux died there would be no one else to remember him either. It was this more than anything that changed his mind. Henri deserved to be remembered, especially by Marianne's family, after what she did. At the bottom of the letter was a name and number. His fingers trembled as he picked up the telephone.

2

SABINE

Each of us is told a story about how we begin. One that starts with the people who come before us, providing the foundation on which we build ourselves. Yet when that story shifts, unexpectedly, so do we. Our lives becoming feet made of clay.

For Sabine Dupris that moment arrived with a phone call.

She was standing barefoot in her tiny kitchen with its pale-blue wooden cabinet doors filled with tiny floral swirls that she had lovingly painted herself. Madonna was singing about 'La Isla Bonita' on her small radio, and she was transported not to a Spanish island but outside to where a pair of robins were finally making use of her home-made bird feeder. They didn't seem to mind that her carpentry skills were a bit of a work in progress.

She clasped her hands beneath her chin, and bounced on the balls of her feet in glee, then the phone rang and everything changed.

A young voice introduced itself as George Constable, a lawyer she didn't recognise, someone who claimed to have news regarding her mother's estate. Sabine frowned. Considering that her mother, Marguerite, had died two years before and had spent her last years living with Sabine and her husband, Antoine, this came as something of a surprise.

'Are you sure that you have the right person?' she'd asked, all thoughts of the birds wiped from her mind.

'Quite sure. You are Sabine Dupris, née Allard, daughter of Marguerite Allard, née Marchant, yes?'

She nodded, her throat turning dry, then realised he couldn't hear her and said softly, 'Yes?'

'I think it would be best if you came to see us so that we could explain properly – it is a bit complicated to discuss over the phone.'

The following afternoon, Sabine made her way to an office in Montmartre. Outside, well-heeled customers were making the most of the early spring sunshine.

In the fancy office upstairs, she was shown to a waiting area which consisted of three orange chairs beneath a giant framed poster of Monet's water lilies that ran along the entire wall. She caught a hint of her reflection in the mirrored glass, and saw with a pang that her dark, curly blonde hair was listing to the side from where she'd shoved it up into a bun and there was kohl smudged beneath her eyes. She was just twisting her hair back into its knot, when a young man in a new suit came out to greet her. He looked fresh out of law school. Tall and gangly with large brown eyes and hair that seemed intent to flop over his forehead, despite the amount of hair gel he'd enthusiastically applied to the rest of his mane.

'George Constable,' he said, extending his hand, then adding, 'Junior,' as her eyes drifted up curiously towards the sign above their heads where the name of the firm was etched in black on silver metal, Lefauge et Constable.

She smiled. 'Sabine Dupris.'

He nodded. 'If you'd like to follow me,' he invited, gesturing to a meeting room around the corner, surrounded by glass. It felt to Sabine an odd space for a private meeting, like she was on display, a curiosity in a jar.

'Coffee? Water?' he offered.

'I'm fine, thanks,' she said, taking a seat. It was orange. She sensed a theme. Then she thought darkly that no amount of cheery colour was likely to make much of a difference to their clients. It wasn't like people chose a lawyer for the good times. Well, perhaps the rich did, she mused.

He took a seat opposite her, and lit a cigarette, offering her the pack.

She shook her head.

He shrugged, '*Bon*.' Then opened a file, and shuffled some papers. Eventually, he started to explain why he'd invited her to come, while long streams of smoke billowed from the cigarette in his fingers.

He began a complicated monologue about inheritance laws which sounded exactly as if it had been recited from a textbook. Perhaps it was still fresh in his mind, she thought, then reprimanded herself for the thought; she was probably not that much older than him, at twenty-nine.

As he spoke, the cigarette turned into a long spool of ash. She wondered when he would ever tap it off, distracted.

When she didn't respond, he grew increasingly nervous. He played with his blue-and-grey-striped tie for a moment and some of the ash landed in his lap. He swore softly, and she hid a grin while he patted his trousers, at last putting the cigarette out in the ashtray.

He had a different accent, she thought, not Parisian. Normandy perhaps? He carried on describing inheritance laws and her attention drifted again for a moment, but was brought sharply back when he started to speak about the winding path it had taken them to find her mother, Marguerite.

'I must say, though, because she was adopted, I was worried that would make tracking her down nearly impossible.'

Sabine drew a sharp breath.

'What?'

He mistook it for enthusiasm for his skills at research, perhaps, and nodded. 'I thought your mother's adoption records might be sealed, but, thankfully, that wasn't the case. Which means that we were able, at last, to find her after nearly forty years, and now, after her passing, well, you...'

Sabine stared at him with a frown, noting the serious brown eyes, the whites within, tending slightly to yellow, perhaps from the smoking. His suit, which now had a mark of ash on the trousers, was expensive, as was this office – it couldn't be cheap having one in this part of the city, she thought. It didn't seem like the kind of place that would be involved in some elaborate inheritance scam or joke on some poor, unsuspecting soul.

Sabine worked at a library; it wasn't like she had much money to be scammed out of, surely they would need a likelier mark? She'd heard of these things happening to people, those who discovered that they had inherited some piece of land or property, only to discover it was all some nefarious plot to swindle them out of their money. It didn't seem like the kind of place to play that kind of joke. Even so, it felt like one.

'I think you must be mistaken,' she said, pulling a face.

He shook his head and repeated a summary of what he'd told her five minutes before.

He stiffened. 'I assure you, all the checks have been made. Your mother was the legal owner of a commercial property in the Batignolles, Paris, which she inherited from her mother, your biological grandmother, Marianne Blanchet. A former restaurant, it seems. I daresay you may even know of it... it has a bit of a regrettable reputation, unfortunately.'

Sabine frowned, trying to reconcile all of this in her mind and failing. He was clearly confusing her with someone else.

'No,' she frowned, 'what I mean is you must be mistaken because my mother was *not adopted*.'

He stared at her in some consternation, eyes widening in realisation. His voice grew oddly slight, like a balloon with a puncture. 'Oh, I see.'

Sabine continued. 'I knew my grandparents, when they were alive. My mother looked a lot like my grandmother, Aimee Marchant,' she said, with emphasis.

His hand shook slightly as he took a fortifying sip of water, his eyes glancing for a second around the glass walls as if beseeching someone, anyone, to come in and help before returning, reluctantly to look at her. 'It must have simply been a coincidence, madame, as I – I'm afraid to say that she truly was adopted. We have all the paperwork, including your mother's birth and adoption certificates. There is no mistaking it, I'm sorry.'

Sabine just stared, forgetting to blink.

'You mean to say, well, that she didn't know either?' he asked, filling the silence.

A swarm of insects were buzzing in her ears. Sabine could only shake her head. Finally, she managed. 'Can you show me... these... certificates?'

He nodded, then looked down at his file, and began to shuffle through the paperwork again until he came across two certificates, one for her mother's birth, the other her adoption.

The colour drained from Sabine's face as she located them. Even upside down, the names jumped out at her. *Marguerite Blanchet*. The same name on both, followed by the names of her grandparents, Aimee and Édouard Marchant, now deceased, on the adoption paperwork. It was all there in black and white.

'Can I have a copy of this?'

He nodded. 'You can take the originals. I'll make a quick copy for our records.'

Then he got up to go do that, rather quickly, as if desperate for an escape. He returned a few minutes later and handed her the documents. Then he offered her a coffee again. This time she accepted. Though, really, she wanted something stronger.

She stared down at the paperwork he handed her, she couldn't seem to make sense of it.

'Is it possible she knew but didn't tell you?' he asked, after he placed a cup of coffee next to her left elbow.

Sabine's eyes shot up and she stared at the lawyer, her blue eyes turning dark.

'Why wouldn't she tell me? My mother told me everything, she was my best friend.' Tears smarted in her eyes, and she dashed them away in a mix of embarrassment and anger.

He remained silent for some time, his skin mottling to a rising red-and-white tide. He swallowed, looking like he wanted to run back to the print room. 'Well, perhaps she didn't want you to know, or perhaps she herself was not told? Either way, under the circumstances, it is possibly due to the same reason.'

Sabine blinked. 'What *circumstances* – what reason? Why wouldn't she want me to know?'

He frowned, hesitating for a moment, unconsciously leaning slightly away from her. 'I can only make a guess. You see, your grandmother – your biological grandmother, that is – was the owner of a restaurant that was once called Luberon.'

He took out a small envelope from the paperwork in front of him, shook it open, and something old, made of brass, landed on the gleaming desk. It was an old-fashioned key.

'Luberon,' she repeated, in confusion, staring at the key, but thinking of holidays in Provence with her grandparents – of charming hilltop villages, sun-drenched stone villas, vineyards, lavender, rolling countryside, the sea...

She thought about that moment often in the months that followed. The moment before she knew. Before he corrected her and everything changed.

'It was a restaurant,' he said, indicating the key, 'based in the

Batignolles village, Paris, on the corner of Rue Cardinet and Lumercier. It's abandoned now.'

'It's still there?'

He nodded.

'Can I go see it?'

He frowned. Then nodded, pushing the key towards her. 'You may,' he hesitated, adding, 'It isn't derelict but I would advise caution – it has been empty for some time and we still need to do a full building survey, but it's not the safety that is the real concern.'

'It's not?'

'No. Well, see, I'd be remiss if I didn't tell you the full story; if you go there, of course, you are bound to find out. So I must warn you. As I said, to this day it holds something of a dark reputation. During the war, when the city was under occupation, the restaurant's owner poisoned and killed all her customers one night.'

The colour drained from Sabine's face. 'What? How?'

'Deadly nightshade,' he said, and for a moment she wondered again if he were pulling some kind of a joke.

He continued. 'It led the authorities to surmise it was a planned execution. Several Nazis were killed, along with two local Parisians.'

She blinked, horrified.

'What happened to her – afterwards, do you know?'

He nodded. 'She was executed.'

Sabine stared. 'I can't believe I never knew any of this.'

The lawyer nodded as if he were wondering the same thing. 'And you're quite certain your mother had no idea?'

She looked at him in utter disbelief. 'That she was the child of one of the most evil women in Paris and just – what, forgot to tell me? I hope not. I hope she had no idea, if truth be told.'

3

GILBERT

She was a scribble of a woman with curly blonde hair, bunched on top of her head, huddled in a red-and-black-check coat, several sizes too big. Curiously, she had on two different shoes, one green, one black.

Monsieur Géroux frowned as he considered if it was some new fashion. It didn't *seem* like fashion. More like she had got dressed in the dark, but who was he to say? Perhaps that was fashionable now.

When she straightened up, though, Monsieur Géroux forgot all about her attire, he forgot every word he'd ever learned. Her eyes were the blue of a paraffin flame. It was like seeing a ghost. Except he was the one who turned pale.

'I'm Sabine – Sabine Dupris,' she said, small, red lips stretching into a disarming smile, taking a hesitant step forward and holding out a small hand, only to wince and try to rid it of what appeared to be a smudge of white paint. 'We – we spoke on the phone,' she continued, becoming more hesitant, when he didn't say anything, but continuing to stare without blinking and making no move to take her hand.

It took some time for the sand to leave his throat and for him to find the words, like dregs at the bottom of a jam jar that he scraped out. He went to shake her hand but she'd already withdrawn it. 'Yes. Um, welcome,' he added, hastily, though he wasn't sure that she actually was. As he continued to stare he realised her eyes weren't exactly the same as Marianne's. They were slightly darker and the gaze was not quite as piercing. But the shape of them, combined with the lines of her face, was achingly similar. It was a gut punch and he swallowed.

'You have a sweet dog,' she said, like an offering.

'He isn't really mine.' She frowned and he explained. 'He's his own creature.'

She smiled as if she liked the thought of that.

'Thank you for seeing me,' she said. 'I can't tell you how much I appreciate it.'

'You look like her,' he said, the words tumbling out of him, like runaway coins.

'I do?' she breathed.

He nodded, then bit his bottom lip. 'What I have to say – well, it isn't going to be easy.'

'I didn't think it would.' She nodded, running a hand over her messy top knot, wincing as she felt how much it teetered to the side like the leaning tower of Pisa. 'Ever since I found out that my mother was adopted, my head has been in a spin. It's like I haven't been able to find firm ground,' she admitted. 'Especially considering the reason why she was given away. I mean, I suppose, no one wanted her to know what *her real* mother had done.'

It took a moment for her words to sink in.

His spine turned to glass.

He had of course seen the resemblance but he assumed the girl was some distant relation, a great niece perhaps.

'Marianne had no children,' he breathed.

Sabine frowned. 'She did. My mother, Marguerite. That's how they tracked me down. Like I said, I had no idea she was adopted.'

He stared at her, while his stomach dived. 'I had no idea, either. She never s—' He stopped himself; since when had Marianne ever told him the full facts? Everything with her was a collection of half truths and puzzles. Even back then it had tormented him. It was just like her, he thought, even now, to keep surprising him, even in death.

Sabine frowned, finding herself blushing. A small thought seemed to flit across her face and she began to ask, rather clumsily, 'Um. Are you – erm, implying that you and ah, her... were in a relationship?'

Monsieur Géroux started to change colour starting with his neck, and spreading to his ears; a bright pink. His eyes widened and to her surprise he let out a short bark of laughter. 'Oh no.'

At her frown, he half laughed, half smiled. 'I would have liked that... back then,' he admitted. 'Most would have, she was beautiful. But I was much younger than her at the time. I was barely fifteen, and she was in her mid-twenties. All I meant really was that I knew her in the years when my brother, Henri, and I worked in her restaurant and we were very close. Or at least I thought we were. Perhaps she was pregnant and she didn't say anything, maybe she gave birth after—'

'After she fled the restaurant you mean? I assumed, well, that the authorities would have found her quite quickly afterwards ... and killed her.'

'Perhaps, it's just a thought, and I don't know how long exactly it took for them to find her – all I know is that it wasn't immediate, it took a few weeks, or months even, before they tracked her down... she could have given birth during that time.'

She nodded, then frowned. 'Was she involved with anyone before then?'

A shadow passed over his eyes and he said, 'Not that I knew of.'

Sabine wondered if there was something else to that. Something he wasn't saying.

He went to put the closed sign on the store door, then invited her to take a seat at his desk, pulling out a chair for her.

'Coffee?' he offered.

Sabine realised he was probably stalling, as he looked nervous enough, but she was tired, and hadn't been sleeping much since she found out her mother was adopted. She looked down at her feet, and saw that she had put on two different shoes. She closed her eyes in embarrassment; she'd been in such a flap at the idea of coming here and finding out about her biological grandmother. She'd found it impossible to fall asleep and when she did at last, just before dawn, she woke up ten minutes before she was supposed to meet the bookseller. Hence her dishevelled appearance. 'A coffee would be great, thank you,' she said gratefully.

'Milk, sugar?'

'Just black, thanks.'

He nodded.

As Monsieur Géroux made the coffee, she looked around the shop. The dog went to make himself comfortable in the window on a cushion and she followed to give him a scratch behind his ear. His fur was a mixture between soft and wiry.

'What's his name – the dog?' she called.

'Tapis.'

She smiled. He looked a bit like an old carpet. It didn't diminish her affection for him, which grew with every moment that he stared at her with his rum-coloured eyes, lifting a paw to invite her to carry on patting him.

When Monsieur Géroux brought the coffee, he snorted. 'I see you have yourself another victim, Tapis,' he said. 'He has a bit of a fan club.'

Sabine smiled. 'Well, I'm definitely in it now.'

Monsieur Géroux was staring at her. 'I almost didn't phone you,' he admitted.

Somehow that didn't surprise her, considering how wary he appeared at first. She was sorry for that, though, for putting him through this. But he was her only chance to find out what really happened.

'I can imagine. I mean it. I really do appreciate you taking the time to speak to me. It can't be easy to talk about.'

'No,' he admitted, with a deep sigh. 'Other than the authorities, I don't think I've ever really told anyone, apart from my wife and even then, there were parts I left out.'

'Oh, you're married?'

'I was, she passed away five years ago.'

'I'm sorry.'

He nodded. Took a sip of his coffee. 'Thank you.'

'I can't imagine what it must have been like, going through the Occupation. My own grandparents – adopted grandparents,' she corrected with a grimace, 'barely spoke of it. But I remember how my grandmother always used to speak of the change in my grandfather, after he came home.'

Monsieur Géroux nodded. 'A lot of the men were like that – the ones who came home, they weren't the same people who'd gone off to war. It can't help but change you. But then the ones left behind were hit just as hard, in other ways, and we changed too.'

He looked up at the ceiling and then made a funny sound, like a snort.

'What?'

'I'll never forget the day they marched into our city, these strangers, with their uniforms and cold faces, declaring our city theirs, while the government left us to fend for ourselves. Many of our friends left, but we had nowhere to go. We were prisoners in our own homes, every freedom we had taken for granted changed, as we now answered to them. When I met Marianne, she was the only source of light for me during that time.'

Sabine blinked. Shocked.

He nodded, scrubbing his face with his hands. 'See, that's one of the reasons it's hard to speak about.' His lips trembled. 'I *liked* Marianne. She was older than me, probably a good ten years, but she was full of life. The world for me had gone grey but it was like she was in colour. I was living with my mother at the time, who was very ill and my little brother, Henri...' he closed his eyes and his lips trembled as he said his name, 'who was a handful, rebellious... and it fell on me to take care of us all. See, my father was off fighting, one of the poor unlucky souls sent to defend one of the lesser-protected borders near the Ardennes Forest, which the Germans, to everyone's shock, used to enter France. He was killed on the fifth day of their invasion, so we were told. So few men were there to put up a real fight. It was thought that the Germans would use the highly defended Maginot Line and that there was no other real route to France. It is a mistake that in many ways cost us the war.

'By the time Paris was occupied in June 1940, we had grown poor – about as poor as you could be back then, without actually starving, no one had money or interest in antiquarian books back then, and we were forced to close. This was my father's,' he explained, waving a hand to indicate the shop, 'before it was mine. Like many others, I was grief-stricken and hungry, and finding it hard to have anything close to hope at a better future, until I met her.'

'How old were you?'

'Twelve. Too young to enlist but old enough to feel like I wanted to fight – to do something. But times were tough, I couldn't just abandon my brother and mother to go fight, I had to try to make a living, to do my duty and carry the family, like my father would have wanted. I answered an advertisement for a kitchen-boy-cum-handyman, and that's when I met her. Your grandmother, Marianne. She held the interview herself, in an empty building around the corner from my home that she was trying to get permission to convert into a restaurant.'

Sabine stared and then suddenly gasped in realisation. 'She opened the restaurant *during* the Occupation?'

'Yes.' He nodded. 'While everyone else was either closing theirs down, or escaping to the Free Zone, or had theirs commandeered by Nazis – in enforced collaboration – she decided to open up her own establishment.'

It sounded even worse when he put it that way. Sabine blinked. 'Why? Why in Occupied Paris?'

'It's a good question. Many people assumed it was mercenary – the only ones with the money during that time to visit a restaurant were the Nazis, of course. But I never got that sense from her. The way she phrased it to me was as a sort of act of defiance. That while soldiers' boots were running roughshod over our streets and elsewhere, and the war was busy tearing things down, she would build something instead. Something for our people – the ones left behind.

'She told me that she was going to negotiate – not collaborate with them – in order to ensure that her neighbourhood didn't go starving. She would feed the officers good, wholesome food in a welcoming environment and the only thing she would ask in return was that she was able to feed as many neighbouring families as she could at affordable, subsidised rates.

'By this stage, the city had been occupied for a year and despite the rations, people were often going to bed hungry. Later, the citizens would condemn anyone who collaborated with the Nazis as the worst kind of traitor – but I've never seen it that way, so black and white. Thousands of women and children were left alone, the men gone, apart from the young or the very old. Their government literally abandoned them for Vichy, the ones who survived did so based on their wits, they shouldn't be judged so harshly.'

'I agree,' said Sabine.

He looked at her in surprise. Even today there were those who would argue with him, red-faced and outraged at such an idea.

'It's easy to think what we would have done, in times of peace and prosperity, to think we'd be brave and so full of integrity, to starve rather than collaborate. But there were children to feed, and the elderly to care for – the truth is most of us would act exactly the same if it ever happened again. We'd put on a smile if it meant we could keep ourselves and our loved ones alive. Humans don't really change, even if we like to think we do.'

He nodded. 'Well, that's what I thought too.' Then he laughed. 'I figured, actually, I could do both – work for her, keep the Nazis happy, and also work for the Resistance – distributing pamphlets.'

She stared at him in awe. 'Really?'

'Yes. I joined one of the student rebellions a few months after we opened the restaurant.'

'Wow – that's incredible. What was it like in the beginning when you first started to work there?'

Sabine couldn't imagine how terrifying it must have been working in an Occupied city, with German soldiers everywhere. In a war, while your whole family relied upon you, at just fourteen.

'In the beginning, it was just her and me, really, working all hours to get the restaurant opened; painting, doing repairs, but it was all under their supervision, and that added an extra layer of stress.'

'I can imagine, it sounds like a lot of work.'

He nodded. 'It was but I was happy to do it, the days went past fast. To be honest after that first harrowing year of Occupation, it was a relief to have something take up so much of my time. But it was more than that.'

'What do you mean?'

'Well, like I said, I was fourteen,' he explained with a half smile at his former self. 'She was easy to like, easy to be around, and for a long time, I thought that I was in love.'

4

GILBERT

The hand-painted sign for the new restaurant, opening in a week's time, sparkled in the late-summer sun. Luberon.

Fourteen-year-old Gilbert Géroux was sweeping the front step when he overheard two older women whispering loudly. One was tall and thin with dark hair and a sour expression, the other had a wispy cap of mouse-coloured hair and her expression was equally bleak.

It looked like they had just come back from the market, with their string bags, which were woefully slim. Before the Occupation, their bags would have been full of all manner of things from the rich pantry that was France. Cheese from Normandy, tomatoes from Brittany, olives from Provence. Today, even from this distance, through the gaps in the string, Gilbert could see they were sparse, tired pickings, a thin bunch of carrots, a turnip and a potato, most likely wizened and with plenty of eyes.

He could hear them talking as he continued to sweep. Their voices becoming loud, like they meant him to overhear.

'They say *she* had special dispensation,' said the tall one. 'To turn it into a restaurant.'

The one with the wispy hair grunted. 'Yes, everyone else is starving, their businesses going under and she's opening up – it's little wonder how she achieved *that*.'

The tall one sniffed. 'Shameful, shameful. And the fact that she's going to serve provincial fare, here, it's like a double insult.' Then she laughed at her own dig.

'What do you mean, provincial fare?' asked her companion.

'Heard it from my neighbour, Madame Da Barra, apparently *she* told Madame Da Barra herself. Bold as brass, she was, when Madame Da Barra asked about it. Wants to only serve "wholesome, country fare", she said. Like that slop they serve in rural Provence – just stews and such mostly. Luberon,' she scoffed, dripping scorn. 'Here? I ask you.'

'Oh,' said the shorter woman. 'I can just imagine how much those sauerkraut and potato boys will love that.'

'Oh yes. She should have just saved herself the trouble and called it The Happy Collaborator.'

The two laughed, and then finally walked on.

Gilbert shook his head, his fists balling at his sides, then threw his broom onto the floor, making his mind up that he was going to go there and give those two clucking hens a piece of his mind – Marianne had only opened the restaurant for their own good! How dare they turn their noses up at the simple country fare – it meant fuller bellies at cheaper prices, any idiot should see that. What was wrong with a good stew anyway? It made sense! Like they could all afford meat and seafood now?

Besides, Marianne's plan had worked – shortly after she was given permission to open, she had managed to negotiate better deals and prices for the locals as well as a very favourable rate for produce.

Yes, technically, it was a 'collaboration' but a full belly was nothing to scoff at in these times, and as Marianne herself had pointed out a full belly meant you lived to carry on the fight – starvation and rebellion was a war waged only on oneself.

As he stepped into the street to give them a talking to, a paint-splattered hand moved to encircle his wrist. He whipped around to find Marianne behind him.

Her long blonde hair was tied up in a blue-and-yellow silk scarf and she was wearing a pair of navy overalls, yet somehow, she still managed to look beautiful. Her lips were cherry red. She'd told him that she would only start giving up when there was no more lipstick to be had. Though she'd winked when she said it. She wasn't winking now, but gazing at him curiously with those intense delphinium blue eyes.

She gave him a smile, and a dimple appeared at the corner. The only thing that showed on her face that she had overheard what those women had said was a slight blush creeping on her cheeks and neck.

'It's not worth it, Gilbert. We need them to come around, and you can't force that.'

'But how can they "come around" if they don't understand?' he said with a frown. His freckles disappeared as his face turned red in annoyance.

'The locals will come around, just give it time. Something like this,' she said, pointing to the building behind her, 'a restaurant that is being opened with the help of the Germans, well, it's not an easy thing for them to just accept overnight. Their pride is one of the only things they have left. We need to acknowledge that and try to show them we're actually on their side. Our job is to win their trust, slowly. We need patience,' she said, with a wink.

Despite his intentions, he felt himself giving in to her smile. Besides, what she said made sense. He didn't know how she could remain so calm, and rational; his anger was like a living thing, so close beneath his skin.

While so many Parisians looked tired, seeming to carry the

weight of the war on their shoulders, walking with leaden feet, tired of the rations, the curfews, the occupied forces, and the daily indignity of it all, Marianne Blanchet seemed to step lightly. To smile, frequently. He couldn't quite figure out why it was different with her, but perhaps as everyone else seemed to have almost given up hope, she seemed full of it. And it was infectious – he couldn't help wanting to be around it. Like a flower turned to the sun.

He had probably fallen in love with her after the first ten minutes of meeting her, and it had only got worse the longer he knew her.

She looked at him with concern. 'You look tired, Gilbert. Your eyes have big circles underneath them – when was the last time you took a break?'

He shrugged, then gave her a crooked smile. 'When was the last time you did?'

Her grin widened. 'Touché. Tell you what – help me paint the last two skirting boards, and then we'll have some coffee and maybe even an early day? Sound good?'

'If you want.'

Just then, the sound of booted feet beat a tattoo along the cobbled street, and his mouth turned dry. He would never get used to the sound of approaching Germans, the fear it instilled was primal. Even Marianne, so calm, so collected, had tensed. Together they turned slowly to find a group of Nazi officers marching towards them. He saw, for just a second, the strain show on Marianne's lovely face, but then she smiled, and it vanished.

One of them, more senior than the others, and bigger – standing at over six feet, with huge arms and legs, his dark blond hair shining in the sun – was one they'd both met before. He'd helped sign off on the restaurant as it fell under his jurisdiction. He was charming and friendly, and sometimes – to your detriment – Gilbert was sure, you could even forget he was a Nazi.

His name was Otto Busch, and he came forward with his arms open wide, a huge smile splitting across his tan face.

'Madame,' he greeted.

Gilbert picked up the fallen broom, and stifled a sigh. He could forget about that coffee now.

As he approached, Busch let out a low whistle of amazement at the transformation to the building. He looked young for his rank and he was. He had risen quickly, due to his ability to be ruthless – something he'd told them himself the first day they met him, with a great smile of pride. The idea that the Nazi army could consider him ruthless, even by their standards, was somewhat chilling, Gilbert had thought.

As Gilbert looked at him he was struck once again at how deceptive appearances could be. He looked like a fresh-faced farm boy, no trace of the apparent ruthless soldier about him, for now anyway. But he was careful to keep such thoughts to himself, schooling his features to be wary, but welcoming.

Not that it mattered, the officer only had eyes for Marianne.

'Madame Blanchet, you've moved fast,' observed Busch. 'I'm impressed – just look at that beautiful sign.'

'Well, that was young Gilbert's work – he's an artist – if it wasn't for—' she hesitated, 'his mother's illness, he would have gone away to art school. I'm lucky to have him.'

Gilbert could guess that she was about to say *if it wasn't for the war.*

It was a good save. The Germans did like to pretend they were here for other reasons, besides the war.

'That's good work,' said Busch, looking at him properly for the first time. 'Your mother is ill – that's terrible. Has she been to a doctor? Perhaps there is something I can do to help?'

Gilbert didn't like being the source of Busch's attention, even for this. 'Erm, she did see one but it was a while ago.'

This was months before and it was getting harder and

harder to get her heart medicine, there was a shortage of everything – including doctors.

'Mmh. A lot can change over time,' said Busch, who turned and started speaking to one of the other officers in rapid-fire German, issuing a demand, so it seemed to Gilbert.

An officer with dark hair and a sunburned nose answered with a salute. '*Jawohl!*'

'Give him your address,' Busch told Gilbert.

Gilbert looked startled.

'Don't worry, boy,' said Busch. 'We'll just get a doctor to visit her. I know a good one, leave it to me.'

With mixed feelings, Gilbert gave his address. It would be wonderful to get his mother help, but at the same time, he really didn't want Nazi officers in his house... He tried to keep the thought from showing on his face. But Busch didn't notice.

Marianne and Busch were standing very close to one another, speaking of other things.

Busch was marvelling once again at how much had progressed with the building – the outside which had been badly worn had been repainted, flower baskets had been added, filled with pink geraniums. The sign had been hung and the clean windows gleamed.

She smiled. 'Well, we couldn't have done it without your help.'

He waved his hands. 'It's nothing,' said Busch, dismissing her thanks, 'I just signed a few papers, spoke to some colleagues, it was easy to convince them that a new restaurant was needed here, madame, you are just what we need, agreed?'

There were enthusiastic calls of approval from the group.

Gilbert felt slightly ill. Especially when Busch left his large, meaty hand on Marianne's shoulder, and he wondered for a moment how easy it would be for him to hurt her. He resisted the mad impulse to flick it away.

'Well, I am in your debt. You will always have our best table,' she said.

Busch clapped his hands in delight. 'Well, that sounds like a good deal to me.'

Gilbert looked away, Marianne wasn't being overly friendly but it still gnawed at him, her somewhat subservient tone. The fact was, Busch could have had the best, or in fact every table of hers, every hour of the day, whether she wanted him to or not. Everyone knew that. The pretence annoyed him. But many of the Nazi officers treated the city as if they were on holiday, and were their special guests. If they were, they had long outstayed their welcome. The veneer of respectability slipped sharply when anyone was stupid enough to show displeasure at this idea, however, paying for it dearly with violence, imprisonment or their life.

'I'm honoured,' he said.

'It is our pleasure,' she said, only to sigh and turn to look back at the restaurant, as if reluctant to part with such fine company. 'I'm afraid, though, that duty calls, sir. Gentlemen,' she said, nodding at them all, 'we must get back to work, if we're to open in a week.'

His pale eyebrows raised. 'Can we be of any help, madame? I know you only have young Gilbert helping you, is that correct?'

Gilbert wondered where he expected her to get more help – from the struggling, half-starving women of Paris? Or the properly starving senior population who got so few rations it was a crime against humanity? Perhaps the Jews – most of whom they'd managed to drive out. Or from the capable men who were forced to trade their lives, hopes and dreams to fight against a madman's ideology on the battlefields?

Marianne however just nodded cheerfully. 'Yes, just Gilbert – but he works harder than ten grown men, I swear! I am the one who has the better deal, for it is like having a small army myself – I have to force him to go home or to take breaks.'

'Ah, youth,' said Busch, admiringly. 'But still, let us help, madame,' and he called several of the men who were awaiting outside. 'Change of plans, we're going to help Madame Blanchet this afternoon. Anything she needs to get this restaurant ready in time for opening – do it.'

There were a few looks of surprise. But they immediately gave their assent.

'Just tell us what you need, madame,' said Busch.

Marianne and Gilbert shared a quick look; there went their easy afternoon. Gilbert lingered for a moment in the street as the officers trooped inside, Marianne at the helm and beginning to direct them onto tasks. Busch was smiling, rolling up his shirt sleeves.

Several passers-by watched along with Gilbert. No doubt news of *this* would spread far and wide.

He heard a hacking sound and he turned to see an old man in a dirty coat with a venomous look in his eye spit on the ground. He held up two fingers with the back of his hand, then walked on.

Gilbert sighed, then went to help, thinking that despite what Marianne seemed to believe, they might need a miracle before the local people accepted this restaurant.

5

SABINE

Sabine had been listening to Monsieur Géroux recount the first days of opening the restaurant in awe, and was shocked to find that over two hours had passed. She needed to catch a train.

'Oh, monsieur,' she said, with regret. 'I'm sorry, I need to get to work, my shift at the library – well, it's already started.'

Monsieur Géroux blinked, looking at his own watch in his surprise. He seemed shocked too. 'Is that not the way?' he mused. 'I wasn't, you know, looking forward to discussing the past, and when I did finally start, I find I can't shut up. Forgive me – and I didn't even get to... well, you know.'

He meant that they hadn't as yet got to that awful night, when everything changed, and Marianne poisoned all her customers.

Sabine waved her hands. 'No, this was better,' she said, meaning it. 'It's so much more than I could ever have imagined – to get a real feel of what it was like back then. Look, I hope this is not presumptuous of me, but if you find you still want to share, I'd love to hear more. Perhaps I could take you to dinner – maybe Thursday night?'

Monsieur Géroux nodded. 'You know,' he said, in more of the same, shocked voice, like he was surprised at himself, 'I'd like that.'

Sabine was glad.

'Should we meet at Pistachios at seven?' Pistachios was a fashionable local bistro, that was covered in wisteria in spring and was famed for its *cassoulet*. This was according to the entry she'd looked up in her *Michelin Guide* for France; it was well-thumbed, and she and her husband, Antoine, often made weekend trips to restaurants and villages based on its recommendation.

'Perfect. The *cassoulet* is good, so I've read.'

She smiled, wondering if he did the same thing.

In the afternoon, Sabine was sorting through the returns at the Montparnasse library where she worked, and putting them back on the shelves, when Antoine came past.

He was tall with gangly limbs, big brown eyes and an easy smile. He worked ten minutes away; he couldn't wait to hear what had happened. 'So – what did he say?'

Katrine, the other librarian, saw and mouthed, 'Ooh la la,' at her, and despite the fact that they'd been married now for five years, she blushed. Antoine made it worse by leaning forward and giving her a lip-smacking smooch for Katrine's benefit. Sabine's colleague laughed uproariously, stopping only when a customer gave her a silencing look from one of the tables near the back.

'Tea break,' said Sabine, pulling Antoine away, to a local café around the corner for a quick takeaway. 'Can't be long – I was already late this morning.'

Antoine was the only person Sabine had told when she

found out about her grandmother. She'd tried to keep it to herself but he dragged it out of her after her meeting with the lawyer.

When she'd finally told him, she'd been hesitant. 'I want to tell you, but I'm afraid of what you'll think.'

His eyes had bulged. 'You can tell me anything, my love – gosh, even if you killed someone I'd still adore you.'

Sabine had issued a short, barking laugh. 'Funny you should say that.'

Antoine had looked shocked. 'What? You really did kill someone?'

Sabine had shaken her head, 'No, not me...' and proceeded to tell him everything.

Antoine was a good listener. He'd kept any potential gasps to a minimum, apart from when she told him her mother was adopted.

'You can't be serious – Marguerite? But she looked like your grandmother Aimee!'

'Right!' she'd exclaimed, she'd thought the same thing. 'But no; the lawyer showed me the paperwork, she was definitely adopted.'

And when Sabine had told him how her biological grand-mother had killed all those people, he'd swallowed, and looked at her with such empathy. 'How awful for you to find that out.'

Later, he'd said, 'I'm not excusing anything but those were dark times, maybe there was more to the story.'

Now as they sipped their takeaway drinks outside the library, watching as people walked past, wrapped up against the spring chill, he asked about her visit to Monsieur Géroux, and Sabine filled him in on everything that had happened.

He looked amazed. 'It's incredible. I mean, it's so horrid what she did, of course, but to actually hear an account from someone who knew her – amazing.'

Sabine agreed. 'It makes her, I don't know, more real somehow. Though that's hard too. I mean, yes, what I'm hearing is a young man's memories of her, but I can't help liking her so far – isn't that awful?'

Antoine shrugged, took a sip of his tea. 'Not really. I mean, people aren't made of just dark or light, we're all shades. Look, there's no guarantee you will ever truly know why she did what she did or got the full measure of her, but at least you'll get more of a real glimpse of who she was.'

Sabine nodded, looking off into the distance as she remembered meeting the bookseller. 'What's surprised me the most, though, was finding out that she had given her baby up for adoption after she opened the restaurant.'

'What?'

Sabine nodded. 'Well, that's what Monsieur Géroux surmised. He said she didn't have a child when he knew her, though he couldn't be sure if she was pregnant when she killed those people. That happened near the middle of the war, I think, 1943.'

Antoine frowned. 'When did she die?'

'I'm not sure, the lawyer said she was executed afterwards, but he didn't know how long afterwards.'

Antoine's eyes widened. 'If she fell pregnant, before she killed those people, if it was a Nazi officer, it might count as motive... she might have gone on the run afterwards, had the baby and given it up.'

Sabine sat back; it took a moment for her to register what he was suggesting. She couldn't believe it hadn't occurred to her. This was what Monsieur Géroux had been speculating too, wasn't it?

'You think one of them got her *pregnant*?'

'Or possibly rape – it could explain the poison. Perhaps it was revenge?'

Sabine blinked. 'Perhaps, the lawyer said she'd killed several Nazis, but two of them were locals, Parisians. So I don't know...'

He shrugged. 'It's just a theory – I mean, there's an easy way to see if it's a possibility or not.'

'There is?' she asked in horrified awe.

He nodded. 'Check Marguerite's birth certificate – the year she was born. If it was before the incident, it's likely that your grandfather wasn't a Nazi.'

Sabine blew her cheeks out. 'Oh God, Antoine.'

She hadn't considered that her history could get any worse.

Sabine walked home the long way. It was market day, but she wasn't in the mood for fresh honey melons or her favourite cheese from Boulogne-sur-Mer in the north – officially the smelliest in France, and the reason they had their own tiny cheese fridge, despite the impish size of their flat.

She avoided going home. Not because she didn't want to see Antoine, but because she knew that in a box in her wardrobe were her important documents, and one of those was her mother's birth certificate, which the lawyer George Constable had given her when she'd asked.

It was the first thing Antoine would have done. But Sabine was known for putting thing off. Sometimes for weeks and months.

She blew out her cheeks, considered going for a drink to delay the inevitable, then decided to just get on with it.

When she got home, she poured herself a glass of wine, and then sat on the living-room floor with the box where her mother's documents had been put.

She took a big, fortifying sip, before opening the box and searching until she found the birth certificate. She took a deep breath then turned to look at the date of her mother's birth.

Marguerite Blanchet, born in the Abbey de Saint-Michel, Lamarin, Provence, 15 June 1938

Mother Marianne Blanchet, father Jacques Blanchet.

'Oh,' she breathed aloud, in relief. Her mother was born before the war. Her grandfather was French.

But soon her relief that her grandmother had perhaps not been a victim of rape and her mother's life born out of something so dark, was replaced with confusion once more. When Antoine had theorised that her mother was born in 1943, shortly after Marianne had killed that restaurant full of people, including the Nazi officers, it had seemed to offer an answer. To provide a motive of sorts – although one that wasn't perfect as it hadn't explained why she'd killed two local Parisians, but there could have been a reason for that... perhaps they'd seen or hadn't helped her or some other explanation.

Sabine was right back at the start. She stared at Marianne's name and frowned. 'Why did you kill all those people?'

6

SABINE

PARIS, 1987

At four in the morning, Sabine was starting to second-guess her decision – one she'd made in the early hours of the morning – to come and see the restaurant for herself. But she was here now. At the corner of Rue Cardinet and Lumercier.

She didn't think she was really going do it until half an hour before when she'd taken the metro. Paris was hushed. The only sounds that could be heard were from the bakery down the end of the lane, and the droning call of insects.

She took out the old brass key from her pocket that George Constable had handed her reluctantly before he'd told her what her grandmother had done.

Now she was here, and was beginning to understand his reservations. In the sunshine, when the street was a riot of bloom and colour from wisteria and the bright flower boxes, pretty pastel buildings and cobbled streets filled with people, it was hard to imagine such a horrific incident taking place, but now, in the dark and cold, hours before dawn, her imagination didn't have to stretch very far.

She put the key in the lock. The door was jammed shut, the wood swollen from years of neglect. She gave it a push with her shoulder, and it began to inch open only to suddenly give way and for her to go tumbling inside.

Inside it was like spilled ink and deathly cold. No light or warmth had touched it for years, thanks to the boards on the windows. There was also a faint smell of damp. She held a finger under her nose, then took out a torch from the bag at her shoulder and shone it around.

There wasn't any furniture left behind, save for a fallen chair and a table that was full of empty wine bottles. She shone her light on them, and then walked over to investigate, picking up one of the bottles and removing a layer of dust from the label with her fingers. The bottle was green. A Bordeaux from 1932. She shook her head in awe.

As she walked away, wiping her fingers on her jeans, she stepped on something that crunched. She frowned, then shone the flashlight down. It was a framed poster. An old-fashioned illustration of a woman from the Twenties lounging on a chair with an affronted-looking cat looking toward the viewer. It was sweet and a little funny. She could imagine that perhaps posters like this had adorned the walls at some stage.

She walked around, beaming the light across the faded walls, and she could see the remnants of faded pastel green paint along with decorative wainscoting. The torchlight revealed that once, long ago, it had been brushed with gold paint. She edged closer. Pretty, she thought. At the bottom of the skirting board, something unexpected caught her eye. It was a small row of crayon daisies like a flash of spring. She inched closer with a frown.

A child had sat here, long ago, and drawn these, she realised.

It was a sobering thought. The idea of a child, here, made everything feel more real and more horrifying, somehow.

.   .   .

Her torchlight revealed the outlines of where tables had once stood, and she could get a sense of how the restaurant might have been laid out, with seating for around six to eight tables, she thought, at a guess.

An open hatch in the wall let you glimpse inside the kitchen at the back. Sabine made her way there, being careful with her footing. The lawyer had said it wasn't derelict but that didn't mean it was safe. Who knew if some of the floors would need to be replaced?

The kitchen was smaller than she would have expected. The stainless-steel counters languished under several generations of dust. On the wall was another framed poster, this one of a fat Persian cat wearing a chef's hat, with a curly moustache and looking rather smug. It was kitsch and cute, and not quite something she expected from a woman who had ended up killing all those people. It did, however, fit a little with the image Monsieur Géroux had created of Marianne in her mind. It was hard to meld the two.

She shone the light around the rest of the kitchen. She began to open up the cabinets, seeing nothing there but old pots and pans. She lifted one out, it was stainless steel and huge, then turned it around to see the label, but it was badly scratched. She put it back and moved on to the drawers, which had a few leftover utensils, including a big soup ladle and a wooden spoon, but were mostly empty, apart from the occasional mouse dropping. She wiped her hands on her shirt in distaste, pulling a face at how filthy she'd become. Then, sitting on her haunches, she began to rifle through the rest of the bottom cabinets. Like the drawers above, they were mostly empty. There was a wad of old newspapers, which she took out curiously. They were water damaged, though, and unreadable, which was a pity. But at the back, behind the space that she had cleared of newspapers, she saw a slip of paper sticking out.

She tried to pull it free but couldn't get a grip. From where it was wedged it looked like it was stuck in the drawer above. She stood up, then opened the drawer, but couldn't see the paper. She frowned, then pulled the drawer out. It was wedged in the casters. She gently pulled until she finally prised it out. It looked like an order slip used by restaurants. She recognised it from her years of waitressing at a small bistro to help pay for her studies at university.

She looked up and saw that on this side of the open hatch there were several hooks – most likely this was where orders were placed for the attention of the kitchen staff.

The paper was faded and dirty. But she could see that instead of an order there was a small note, though a scuff mark appeared to obscure the first line. It might have been a name or a letter or just a splodge from a bubbling pot.

The days are short, but hours can seem long, H. She needs to spend these last ones with her boys. That's an order.

M.

Sabine looked at the note and frowned. Was this from Marianne?

She put it in her coat pocket, then carried on her search through the kitchen. But apart from a mouldy box in the corner that contained yet more empty wine bottles, there was nothing.

Sabine made to leave the kitchen, only to pause as she looked at the silly cat poster. She drummed her fingers against the dusty counters, thinking about whether she should take it or not. It was cute and would look fun in her own kitchen. But a part of her wondered if that was macabre somehow? Taking something from here...

Marianne had been a person too, a grandmother, even if she never lived to see it. It was also the only thing Sabine would have of hers, besides the little order slip.

She stood on her tiptoes and took it down. It was full of dust, and she would need to give it a good wash. If it ended up being too morbid to keep, she'd just dump it in a bin somewhere later, she decided.

At least now, though, she'd seen the place for herself, and assuaged her curiosity – although, as usual it had led to more questions than answers. It looked like an ordinary restaurant. Despite the years that had passed, she could see that it had once been a charming space – it didn't look like a site where people had been poisoned. If there had been any ghosts here, they had moved on. There certainly weren't any phantom scents from the kitchen, either, apart from rat droppings, that is.

She could return the key to George Constable and be satisfied that despite the rumours and myths... it was just an ordinary, sad place. There was nothing here to suggest why Marianne Blanchet had done what she did.

When she got back to her flat, she found Antoine waiting for her. As soon as she let herself in he was there, like a puffed-out brown chicken, circling around her.

'Where did you go? I woke up and you were gone!'

She winced. 'Sorry. I just needed to get some air.'

He frowned, then raised a brow. 'You just decided to get out of bed at the crack of dawn to walk the streets with this—' Then he looked at the poster, and snorted with laughter. 'What the hell is that? It's brilliant. Is that for me, to apologise for leaving me all alone with no note?'

She grinned. This was why they loved one another.

'It's a bit of a long story.'

'I assume so if you're coming home with it at five thirty in the morning.' Then he raised a brow; clearly he'd guessed where she'd gone. 'Did you go to the restaurant?'

She nodded.

He shook his head. 'I'll make us some coffee,' he suggested. 'Then you can tell me about it.'

She squeezed his arm in gratitude, thankful that he didn't moan that he'd wanted to see it too. Which she knew he had. This first time, she'd felt, had to be done alone.

Antoine took out some frozen *pain au chocolat* from the freezer and popped them in the oven to heat through, then put on a strong pot of coffee.

Sabine took the framed poster to the edge of the sink which she filled with hot water and dishwashing liquid, dunking a sponge into the soapy liquid and scrubbing at the dusty, sticky glass. She had to go over it a few times, the water turning black, but eventually the old glass gleamed.

She stared at the cat with the chef's hat for some time and then decided it wasn't too macabre to keep. It was sweet.

She put it on the counter while Antoine checked on the pastries, which were ready. The air had started to fill with the scent of warm chocolate.

When they had cooled down a little, she took a bite and her teeth sank into the buttery, gooey chocolate parcel and she groaned in bliss. She was starving, and tired, and the sugar helped, though she'd probably pay for that later with a crash. She poured them both a large mug of filter coffee, and they sat down at the small kitchen table and she told him about the restaurant and what it had been like to see it.

'That was from the kitchen,' she said, indicating the poster.

His eyes widened. 'You took it from there?' he breathed. He may as well have said, *the scene of the crime.*

She winced. 'Yeah, I mean, I know it's probably a little twisted, but I like it.'

Despite his tone of surprise, he shrugged. 'Things only get

twisted if you make them – there's probably hundreds of these posters all around the world. Liking it doesn't mean anything.'

She hoped not.

7

GILBERT

Monsieur Géroux redid his tie for the third time, only to swear softly. It had been years since he'd worn one. Or his good suit. Was it too much? Should he just wear his familiar tweed jacket with the tan leather elbow patches?

He put on the suit. Then stared at himself in the mirror and sighed. He looked like an undertaker. Or like he was going to a funeral. Which, to be fair, was what he usually used the suit for nowadays. It used to be weddings.

Tapis watched him from the foot of the bed, burying his head in his paw and making a soft whining sound.

Monsieur Géroux sighed. 'It's awful,' he agreed, taking off the suit and putting on his familiar navy chinos, white shirt and tweed jacket.

Tapis put his head to the side as if he were reconsidering his earlier statement.

'Pah!' said Monsieur Géroux. 'This is what you get now.' Then he bent down, slipped on his shoes and made to leave. 'You staying or coming?'

The dog yawned.

'Suit yourself.'

Outside the air was cool, but no longer cold. Summer was heading their way. He passed a flower shop, where the proprietor was just taking in the day's specials. There were peonies, their blooms hot pink and large. Lisianthus, soft and delicate. And those old-fashioned pale pink roses his wife, Annie, used to love so much. He loved this time of the day in Paris. It felt so alive. People bustled past wearing their best clothes, the air full of perfume. It had been years since he'd had evening plans too.

Was it strange that after all that dread he'd felt at meeting someone from Marianne's family, he felt relieved? Like he finally had someone to talk to about it all.

Still, they'd only cracked the surface. What he had to say wasn't easy – to say or to hear. But it was like breaking a seal, now that he'd done it, he wanted, strangely, to keep going.

Sabine was waiting for him on a table spilling onto the pavement, sitting on a rattan chair facing the street. Her long, curly blonde hair was loose and she was dressed in a mid-length coral dress with a denim jacket and matching coral ballet flats.

He was struck once more at the resemblance between grandmother and granddaughter.

Here in the soft lights of the bistro, she looked even more like Marianne. It was like seeing a ghost. His hands trembled slightly and he grew awkward. For a moment, he felt again that earlier trepidation, that earlier dread. But it was gone as quickly as it had arrived. She stood up when she spotted him, reaching over and giving him a kiss on both cheeks. 'How handsome you look, Monsieur Géroux.'

He found to his consternation that he was blushing.

'I've ordered a glass of merlot – can I tempt you?' she asked.

'Please.'

He felt the need for a drink, that was certain.

She hailed a waiter and soon afterwards, he was sipping a

glass of house wine. Something he would usually be too proud to do, fancying himself as something of a connoisseur. It wasn't bad, to be fair. But it wasn't exactly good either.

He worried that they wouldn't have anything to say – or that they would be awkward together after the last time, when he'd spoken so much, and shown his vulnerable underbelly too quickly. But it was just like the last time, helped even more so by the bad good wine.

'I went to see the restaurant,' she confided, in lieu of any small talk.

He nodded, but curiously didn't seem that surprised. 'I doubt you can see much, though, the window glass is filthy.' Though you could still see where someone long ago had scratched the words, *collaborator and murderer*. In that strange order. He didn't mention that, though.

'No,' she said, eyes wide. 'I mean, really see it. I was given a key.'

Monsieur Géroux's eyes bulged and he gasped. 'You mean you actually went inside?' He swallowed. 'H-how was it?'

'Cold, dusty. But I could see a little of what you were talking about – the way you described it. The paint is faded but you could see how pretty it must have been. I even found this line of daisy chalk drawings at the bottom of the wall.'

Monsieur Géroux paused as he took a sip of wine. 'D-daisies?'

She nodded.

He frowned, then his eyes widened in amazement. 'Oh my goodness, I think I recall that, actually. It was a little neighbour girl we knew. Lotte, her mother, was my mother's dear friend, our neighbour, Fleur Lambert. She took some time to come around to the idea of a restaurant opening there, even one that would have very favourable rates for locals. In the beginning it was just the officers who attended. The French who came were often collaborators from elsewhere, invited by the Germans.

The locals took some convincing to attend. Fleur was one of the first.'

'How long did that take – and for others to come around?'

'A few weeks. The Germans believed they were helping by running a series of articles to spread the word – but it did more harm in the beginning than good.'

'Articles?' Sabine breathed, shocked.

'Oh yes. They had a paper called *Pariser Zeitung*, it provided the news briefing in German with supplements in French. It served as the only source of information for the French about the Occupation. It even provided some updates from unoccupied Vichy – where the government had fled. It was reported to us as if they were a foreign nation. Well, as you can imagine, to many of us by then, feeling abandoned, they may as well have been.'

Sabine just stared at him in shock. 'What was the news-paper like?'

'Full of praise for the French.'

Sabine blinked. 'What?'

'Yes, see, in the early days of the Occupation, the Wehrmacht – the German army – had been forceful and forbid-ding. They'd tried the stick, which hadn't worked as much as they liked. So they tried a new tactic instead.'

'The carrot?'

He took a sip of wine, and nodded. 'Indeed. It was swollen with flattery. They praised all the businesses and institutions that collaborated with the Germans. Waxed poetical about the beauty of the architecture, the people, and the belief that together they were building a new Europe. I mean, it was such a weird time. I know now it's impossible to imagine a restaurant opening up during a war, during an occupation. But the Germans treated France as a kind of jewel in their crown – many of them acted as if they were there on a kind of colonial holiday. Francophiles, charmed by our art, literature and culture – they wanted us to keep putting on our shows, keep running our nightclubs and dance halls.'

She sat back and listened in horror as he began describing what the first few months of life were like back then, during the Occupation, when the new restaurant, thanks to the press from the *Pariser Zeitung,* became a roaring success, with the Germans that is.

As she sipped her wine, their world began to fade as she was transported to a very different, and very dark Paris.

8

GILBERT

PARIS, 1942

'Have you seen this?' asked Gilbert, making his way into the kitchen, where Marianne was busy chopping up vegetables. A mushroom bourguignon was simmering on the stove. There were baskets overflowing with vegetables: tomatoes, aubergines, cauliflower, potatoes, turnips – seeing such a bounty, it was hard to imagine they were in the midst of war. Except that, of course, it all came from the invaders. Gifts from Luberon's admirers, chiefly Otto Busch and his friends. The dishes she made for the locals included a lot of legumes and other starchy carbs as opposed to meat; it was designed to be cheap and filling. Not that any locals had come by just yet, even with the extra rations and discounts.

On the small wireless, the sweet sound of Lucienne Boyer was singing, '*Parlez-moi d'amour*', and Marianne was humming along as she prepared the evening's meal.

She dipped a clean spoon in the pot, and scooped some of the rich liquid. 'You must try this, Gilbert, tell me what you think?'

He took the spoon from her, tasted the rich broth, then closed his eyes in bliss. She was a magician. 'Mmh, it's wonderful,' he moaned, picking it up to take another spoonful.

'Tut, tut, no! Use a clean spoon, Gilbert!'

He did so and she turned to him and frowned. 'Seen what?'

'Oh... this,' he said, handing her the latest edition of the *Pariser Zeitung.* 'You're in it.'

To his shock, she didn't seem surprised, though she winced slightly. 'I know. It was Busch's idea. It's not going to win me any favours with the locals, though.'

'Probably not,' he agreed, and opened it up and began to read out the article, which was titled, 'Food like my grandmother used to make.'

'The owner of the new restaurant in the charming village of the Batignolles in Paris has a wondrously unpretentious attitude towards food in that it should be good, but wholesome too. In a city that is known for its metropolitan sophistication, which has always looked down at anything deemed provincial, Blanchet's attitude is refreshing – she is bringing the countryside to Paris, she says, by cooking the kind of food her grandmother used to make in Provence.

'"When I was little, she ran a small farmer's café restaurant in her village, and she served just one meal a day: lunch. As a customer, you almost never knew what you were going to get, it was part of the charm. People came because they enjoyed the surprise and the good food. No one was ever disappointed – not so that I ever knew anyway."

'One couldn't for a moment imagine other nations, like the one across the pond with their "toad in the hole," ever being so adventurous. It is a quintessentially French trait, this bold and brave approach to their love of good food. And now, just like her grandmother's café in Luberon, there is no menu, just a long line of people who come to Madame Blanchet's restaurant knowing

that whatever she decides to make that day is likely to be wonderful.

"'In this city where a menu can be as long as your arm – and yet some people just order the same thing over and over again – I want to give my customers something surprising."

'Well, we can safely say – mission accomplished. Well done, Marianne Blanchet, and all hail Luberon.

'It is rather flattering,' said Gilbert, which was something of an understatement. 'And there's a picture of you too.'

Marianne laughed, scrunching her small pretty nose as she pulled a face. 'It makes my teeth ache – it's so sugary,' she said. 'But I couldn't exactly say no, I mean look,' she said indicating the bounty, 'these have been sent from officers, with cards wishing us well.'

Gilbert snorted. 'Most likely they've seen your picture and your promise that you aren't going to make anything fussy.'

Marianne's lips twitched in amusement, but she shrugged. 'It'll be good for business, and anyway, first we need to feed the sharks in order to feed the minnow.'

He rolled his eyes, then grinned. That was such a Marianne thing to say.

Just then there was a sound of booted heels coming into the kitchen, and both of them tensed for a moment. They turned to find Otto Busch standing in the entrance, a folded-up newspaper beneath his arm. He looked positively jubilant. 'Ah, madame! Everyone is talking about your restaurant! Why, I wouldn't be surprised if it was as popular as some of the ones in the centre of the city.'

Marianne smiled, and it was the force of a thousand suns. Gilbert hated that she used it on the German. 'You think so? I just want to make real food, nothing too fancy.'

He laughed, throwing back his head and revealing his perfect teeth, especially his sharp incisors. 'But that's why they'll come! Everyone's talking about it. Ha! Even I was congratulated for helping to cultivate such a jewel – but it's easy when you have a diamond. That's what you are, madame, a diamond!'

Gilbert had to work hard not to cringe. His mother, Berthe, always said that his face was like a map of his internal world, displayed there for all to see. She'd meant it as a warning. He hadn't quite figured out how to stop it, so he often spent a long time examining his shoes. Luckily, Busch hardly ever noticed him.

Busch continued, enthusiastically, coming forward without invitation to sample the stew. He kissed his fingers to his lips. '*Magnifique!* Most of our boys, well, they're more familiar with bratwurst and potato salad than fine cuisine, and if they discover country-style fare like your *cassoulet* and hearty stews, they'll be over the moon.' Then he tapped his nose, and winked at them both, smacking a hand onto Gilbert's back. Gilbert let out a squawk that seemed to please the General, who laughed, while he said, 'But don't tell them I said that, eh, they are trying very hard to be sophisticated.'

Marianne laughed. 'It'll be our secret.' As if they were discussing lovable, provincial scamps instead of men from one of the deadliest armies in the world.

Busch leaned forward and patted the side of her face affectionately and Marianne flinched. For just a moment, Gilbert saw something flash in her eyes, her face turn to stone, but before he could blink she was smiling again and he wondered if he'd imagined it.

'So sorry, sir, I got a fright.'

Busch didn't seem offended. His eyes had flared with interest.

Gilbert's fists clenched. 'I'll give the restaurant floor a mop now,' he said, making his way to the broom cupboard.

'Sounds good, afterwards you can help me peel potatoes,' suggested Marianne.

Busch stepped backward with a smile. 'You're busy, I'll leave you both to it. Just came by to give my congratulations,' he said, leaving a copy of the newspaper on the counter. He tapped a finger on it. 'I'll get this framed for your wall – your first review!'

'I'm honoured,' said Marianne. 'Thank you, General. See you tonight?'

'Ah, regretfully, no – but tomorrow – yes, if you could set aside your biggest table, I'd be obliged. We have some important people newly arrived to the city.'

'Certainly.'

In the third week that Luberon was open, they were finally paid a visit by locals. These were Gilbert's mother and his brother, Henri, and their neighbour, Fleur Lambert, and her daughter, Lotte. Only they hadn't precisely come on their own initiative. They'd been bullied into coming by Busch himself.

It was bad enough that Gilbert had to see the man at the restaurant most days, with his moon face, staring sloppily at Marianne, but Busch had come to Gilbert's home to visit his mother after he'd helped to arrange a doctor's visit.

'It's ironic,' said Gilbert's mother, Berthe, on the day they waited for the doctor to arrive, 'I might have a heart attack due to the stress of having him visit before he even comes to check my heart. Feel it,' she'd added, pressing Gilbert's hand to the centre of her chest, which was racing.

'Mum,' he said, wincing, taking his hand back.

His little brother, Henri, twelve with bright red hair and deep green eyes, was adding to the bald patches in the hall rug with his constant pacing. His small, freckled hands balled into fists. 'He shouldn't be coming *here*. It's too much to have them come here. Isn't it enough that they've taken over the whole city – will they take our homes next?'

Berthe looked at her younger son, and snorted. 'You don't think they already have?'

Henri blinked. 'I thought they were staying in hotels.'

She shook her head. 'Not all of them. Some families are sharing their apartments. How did you not know that?'

'Mum, enough,' snapped Gilbert. Henri was tightly wound up as it was. He took a deep breath and tried to defuse the situation. 'And don't worry, that's not what is going to happen. It's just a doctor's visit. That's all.'

'You don't know that,' said Berthe.

'Yes, how can you know that?' echoed Henri.

'I just do.'

When the doctor had arrived, promptly at eleven in the morning, they were all bickering and his mother was clutching her heart in an alarming way.

The man Gilbert showed into the living room wasn't who they had imagined. Someone with horns, perhaps. He was a tall, thin man, with a tired face and kind hazel eyes. While most Germans seemed to do everything fast – walk, talk, eat – he seemed to move slowly, like he was taking his time, with his words, his thoughts. It was calming.

'Good morning,' he greeted, in a gentle, soft voice, doffing his hat, respectfully, as Gilbert led him inside their flat where his mother was waiting in the living room. 'I am Doctor Cordeau.' He made his way to Berthe's side.

He spoke good French, with an Alsatian accent.

His mother, of course, jumped on that straightaway. She sat up in her pink armchair, her green eyes turning to skewers. While he took out his stethoscope and prepared to do his examination, she did the same.

'You're from Alsace?' she asked, brow raised.

'Yes,' he nodded, 'I grew up there, just on the border. This might be a little cold,' he said, indicating the metal part of the stethoscope. 'If you could open the top of your blouse just slightly I will have a listen. Do you have trouble breathing?'

'Sometimes. Which town was it?'

'Colmar. When do you find it hard to breathe – first thing in the morning, or perhaps at night?'

'Oh, beautiful, with the half-timbered houses and the canals,' she sighed wistfully. 'German now, I believe?' she said, then answered his question. 'And whenever I'm lying down.'

'Yes,' he said, and his face was sad too.

His mother let out a sigh of relief. He was, like them, just an unfortunate man caught up in an unfortunate war.

He continued. 'It makes sense that it's hard to breathe whenever you are lying down. I believe it is because there is some fluid build-up in your lungs. If you come to the hospital we can have these drained and then treat you with medication.'

'My lungs! But I thought it was my heart.'

'It is both, I'm afraid. But I think the procedure will help both organs function better. It is not a pleasant experience, though,' he warned.

Berthe sighed. 'Is it ever?'

But ever since the procedure, which Doctor Cordeau had performed himself, she had been making a remarkable recovery.

Every week her tablets were delivered by the doctor himself, who had become a friend, and she was putting on some weight from the extra food Gilbert brought home from the restaurant, which he shared with their neighbour, Madame Lambert. She had been shocked when she heard how affordable the new restaurant was due to the extra rations and the tokens Marianne was able to provide.

But if Gilbert's family had come around to the doctor, the same couldn't have been said for Busch when he decided to check on Berthe's recovery for himself. But it was soon clear he had another agenda as well.

He arrived at the exact moment Fleur Lambert had come to

visit too and after making his enquiries about Berthe's health he got to the point very quickly – he required their presence at the restaurant.

'I cannot believe you haven't yet come, Madame Géroux. Are you not feeling better? Do you not want to come see the restaurant in which your son is working so hard?'

Berthe blinked. 'Y-yes.'

'Good. That settles it. Spread the word that us Germans are not quite as fearsome as people believe…' he said with a smile.

Berthe produced a thin smile in response, but her hands fluttered to her chest. 'Oh yes, of course, General.'

'You will be my guests,' he said, and his genial expression wavered for moment, before they all nodded enthusiastically. He clapped his hands together and the sound, like a bullet, made them startle.

'I will see you all there tomorrow evening, then?' His eyes took in the Géroux family, then settled onto Madame Lambert. He raised a brow at her, and she nodded quickly.

After he'd left there was much grumbling, of course. Fleur was nearly purple in the face. But there was never any question of disobeying him. Even so, they found, when they were there, having dinner, that it wasn't as bad as they imagined. 'Much like the doctor's visit,' Berthe had remarked when Gilbert walked them home afterwards.

'I'm sure Marianne will take that as a compliment,' Gilbert said.

'She should be grateful for even that,' hissed quiet Madame Lambert in a rare display of pique. She had barely said a word, just sat and chewed, her face like stone. She was like a pot that had simmered all night and now was starting to boil.

'Well, quite,' agreed Berthe.

'Did you see her simpering after them with those cherry lips of hers, running around serving them as if they were kings? It was shameful!' spat Madame Lambert.

'I wouldn't say she simpered,' said Gilbert, ever loyal.

Madame Lambert and Berthe shared a look. 'Well, no man would,' said his mother.

'I liked her,' said five-year-old Lotte, rubbing a fist into a sleepy eye, her long blonde hair slightly mussed from where she'd rested it on the table while the grown-ups were talking. 'She brought a strawberry tart, just for me.'

Madame Lambert touched her daughter's head. 'Yes, that was nice of her,' she admitted.

Gilbert hid a grin. He knew it wasn't over: as soon as he left and returned to the restaurant to help with the clean-up, they would no doubt be up for a while gossiping. It didn't matter, Busch was no fool, now that Madame Lambert and Madame Géroux had visited the restaurant it would soon show the other locals that it was safe to do so too.

And he was right, the fact that quiet, reserved, and highly respectable Madame Lambert had attended Luberon was able to do what the *Pariser Zeitung* had not – spread the word – and by the first week of their second month other locals began to drift in.

Marianne made sure to make an effort with them, showing kindness and patience when they were short with her, even when their conversations were barbed, and designed to hurt. Like the hairdresser, plump, dark-haired, beautiful Madame Duchanelle with her cat-like green eyes, who wore her best dress, and complimented Marianne after Gilbert was sent to fetch her so that, as she said, 'she could give her compliments to the chef.'

When Marianne arrived smiling with her red lips, shining blonde curls, Madame Duchanelle was the picture of charm.

'Well, Madame Blanchet, I must say, I can see that you have been working hard. This place is a delight.'

'Thank you, madame,' Marianne had smiled, evidently delighted.

'Ah *oui*, it could not have been easy to achieve,' she said, waving a hand towards the back where Busch and his men were seated, dining and drinking, and generally giving off an air of great merriment.

'Oh... well,' said Marianne, giving a shrug.

'Don't be so modest, madame,' said Madame Duchanelle, a gleam in her green eyes as she smiled sweetly. 'It must have been hard work spending so much time on your back.'

Gilbert gasped. 'How dare you! She did no such thing!'

There was a sudden hush as all the diners turned to stare. There was a scrape of a chair as Busch turned towards them. His face, going from merry to wary in an instant, like a finger primed on a trigger.

Marianne, however, threw back her head and laughed. She touched Madame Duchanelle's arm like they were the very best of friends. 'Oh, you naughty thing. The only thing that hurt was my knees in scrubbing these floors. Don't mind her, Gilbert, she is only teasing.'

Gilbert turned red, and Marianne flashed him a warning look, her face turning to marble.

He was reminded once again of that time he'd seen something else come over her face, when Busch had touched her and she'd flinched. Like a mask had slipped.

She bent to whisper something in the hairdresser's ear, and then to Gilbert's surprise the hairdresser laughed uproariously. There was another scrape of chair, as Busch settled back in his seat, and soon the officers had returned to their drinking and carousing. It was like nothing had happened. Except for the beacons of red that were the tips of Madame Duchanelle's ears.

9

GILBERT

When the restaurant had been open for six months, Gilbert joined his local Resistance chapter, held in the Batignolles library under the guise of a student art group. He'd been a natural choice for recruitment, so their leader, a young Jewish woman named Sara, had said, as he was so well-placed in the shadows of the most popular restaurant in the area, barely acknowledged by the officers who attended the restaurant, dismissed as too young and inexperienced.

It was this more than anything that spurred Gilbert on to join the fight against them. He hated how powerless he felt. It wasn't even so much how the soldiers ordered him around, and treated him as if he was nothing more than a general dogsbody, it was the fact that they treated him as if he had no feelings at all. Particularly Busch, who felt that it was his right each night to come inside their kitchen to ogle Marianne, and casually touch her arm or her hair uninvited, while he watched, helplessly. Busch seemed to know it made him uncomfortable; in fact, he seemed to enjoy that just as much as he enjoyed casually assaulting Marianne.

Marianne, of course, made light of it. 'He's just an affectionate type, that's all.'

But he wasn't, not that Gilbert noticed. Busch didn't seem to make casual moves, only calculated ones.

'Just be careful, madame. Try not to be around him alone if you can help it.'

'Gilbert, you worry too much. But I promise to be careful.'

For the time being that was all he could hope for. That and doing something with the restless, angsty feeling that gnawed at his insides, which had led him to join the Resistance when Sara invited him to.

He hadn't told Henri, his little brother, who was far too keen to join. Henri said worrying things like that he wanted to knock German officers off their bicycles, or throw stones at them, which his mother and Gilbert had warned him within an inch of his life not to go through with.

Still, even Gilbert wasn't satisfied with just delivering pamphlets, which had been his main role for a while now. It was something the other members agreed upon, thinking that the more senior Resistance organisation would be very interested in him – considering he had a direct line to some of the biggest officers in the city, many of whom were visiting Luberon a few times a week. Every so often he was able to glean important information that might be useful. Unfortunately, as most of it was in German and he couldn't yet speak it, one of his first tasks was to begin studying the language.

'We've got to be careful, Gilbert,' Sara said. 'The place is crawling with Nazis, take it slow – they can't suspect you or it will all be over.'

Sara was Jewish and it wasn't easy for her; Gilbert could see the frustration on her face at being treated like a second-class citizen. It was scary too, as the rules for her kept changing, and her freedoms kept dwindling – this was the main reason she had started this particular Resistance chapter. But her cautious approach, which often ensured their safety, was a source of frustration for another of her early recruits, a young, sharp-faced woman with dark hair, named Louisa.

'So what, he's just supposed to sit on information if he finds it? He's right there, gift-wrapped and you want to do nothing. None of us can get that close to them without suspicion and yet here you want probably your best asset to continue delivering pamphlets. It's bloody ridiculous.'

'No it's not. Gilbert is young, and untrained – these are deadly soldiers from one of the most ruthless armies in the world. Tell me, are you just impulsive or eye-wateringly stupid, because right now I genuinely can't tell.'

The two started arguing, and the others shifted uncomfortably waiting for the blow-up. No one liked to go toe to toe with Sara, who was razor smart and methodical. But with Louisa, it was a regular occurrence. It wasn't just a clash of wills. It was a question of trust too. Sara didn't trust Louisa. Not since she'd seen her out one night with a Nazi. Sara told the others that she'd spied Louisa walking past curfew with a handsome officer, her hand on his arm, saying that it looked like she was getting romantic with him. But Louisa vehemently denied it, stating that she'd run out of time while she was playing lookout for a mission in which the Resistance was preparing to bomb a power line, but had to withdraw and scatter when a group of Nazis appeared quite suddenly. She'd used her wits to talk herself out of being caught out past curfew.

Most of the others just thought Sara had had enough of Louisa's undermining. Louisa, however, wasn't easily pushed around and she made no move to leave.

When the other members left, Sara was standing next to an older student named Guillaume, who Gilbert liked. She pulled Gilbert aside and told him that she was worried there was an informant, and to be cautious. 'It's one of the reasons I don't want you to do anything just yet, alright? I have my suspicions about Louisa. I think she's pushing you in order to expose us. Last night I was almost caught. I swear it was like they there waiting for me. I heard one of them say "the Jewish girl", but luckily I managed to slip away.' In the paraffin light she showed them her arms, which were covered in deep scratches from where – in order to escape being seen – she'd slipped down an embankment, and had to lie quietly in the mud for hours, till they'd moved on.

Gilbert didn't know what to say. Privately he just thought that Sara and Louisa's fight was a struggle for power. He didn't really think Louisa was actually going against them, it didn't make sense.

But he nodded anyway, because Sara was in charge.

Guillaume looked at Gilbert and said, 'Louisa's right about one thing, though, Gilbert. You are an asset, but trust Sara on this, take it very carefully, don't draw any attention to yourself, all right?'

Sara nodded.

Guillaume fixed a cigarette between his teeth, which he didn't light, just in case any of the officers were walking past and decided to investigate. They had put black card on the windows to block out the light, but scents would be hard to miss. 'How's your German coming along?' he asked him.

'Better,' lied Gilbert. It was a damnably hard language to learn, especially when you couldn't really advertise what you were doing and he was relying on teaching himself from stolen library phrasebooks which he kept beneath a loose floorboard in his bedroom. A bedroom he shared with his little brother.

'Good.'

.   .   .

The next morning, in the restaurant, Marianne was run off her feet. There were purple patches beneath her blue eyes and her quick smile was slower than usual. They had been getting busier as word spread about the restaurant, despite the fact that they only served two options a day – one for the lunch and another for the evening crowds. Still, they both didn't stop from eight in the morning till well past midnight.

'I think it's time we think about hiring another person,' said Marianne.

'Really? Can you afford it?'

'I think so. Someone local, though – I was thinking, what about your brother, Henri?'

Gilbert frowned. 'I don't know, Marianne. He's a bit... wild. My mother and I worry about him saying something stupid, risking his silly neck.'

'Mmm, why don't you ask him for a trial? We can keep him in the kitchen while you serve. The thing with people who run hot like that is that you need to make sure you don't give them too much time to burn. Work helps letting off steam.'

Gilbert looked at her in surprise. Perhaps she had guessed that it was one of his biggest concerns.

'That might help actually.'

She grinned. 'What's with the tone of surprise? When am I ever wrong?'

He grinned. 'Well, actually, when it comes to coriander...'

'Ah, well on that we will agree to disagree. Do you think he'd be interested?'

'Sure, I can ask. I'll speak to him tonight.'

Berthe, Gilbert's mother, was dead set against it.

She sat in her pink armchair in the living room, across from Madame Lambert, who was knitting in the blue one by the window. Lotte was making herself a cat out of yellow yarn, while Gilbert made it a pair of googly eyes out of card and Henri fashioned a walking lead out of discarded coloured wool. They were, as ever, the child's loyal subjects.

'I don't think Henri is up to the task,' said Berthe, taking a sip of the cheap chicory stuff that was used to replace coffee, then wincing. It was horrible.

'What do you mean by that!' shouted Henri, standing up.

She raised a brow. 'Well, that— just look at your response, you can't control your temper at all.'

'Yes, I can!'

Even Madame Lambert had to purse her lips so as not to smile. Henri appeared to get the hint, saying in calmer tones. 'I can, Maman.'

Berthe looked unconvinced. 'Can you? Can you stop yourself from telling the Germans what you really think, or resist holding out a leg to trip one of them as you did just the other week when we went to the market?'

He breathed in a deep sigh. 'That was two months ago, when I was twelve.'

Berthe snorted. 'So you're saying you're all grown up now?'

'No, but I'm not stupid enough to try that in a room full of senior officers.'

No one said anything.

His eyes bulged. 'You think I'm really that stupid?' he said, sounding affronted.

'You did threaten to knock them off their bicycles,' pointed out Madame Lambert.

'And you did want to put soap on the steps so they fell down,' said Lotte, helpfully.

Henri sighed. 'Again, all things I said, but didn't do, see? Besides, Maman, we could do with the extra wages. Your medicine alone isn't exactly cheap.' Busch and his men might have helped to get them the doctor but the treatment wasn't free.

'He has a point there,' said Gilbert, who felt privately that perhaps Henri was growing up, albeit slightly.

Berthe was unmoved. She looked at Henri and shook her head. 'You're too young, it would be too much to ask of you – to be around the Germans all day and not say anything, I just don't think you'd be up to it.'

Gilbert looked at his mother and then saw something else. Calculation. Ah, so this was psychology, he thought, and pursed his lips so as not to smile. Later she would whisper to Gilbert that it would only work if Henri thought it was his own idea.

Henri appeared insulted. 'I would!'

'Mmh,' she said. 'I will think about it.'

Marianne was right: keeping busy was good for Henri, who had managed to wear down Berthe until she reluctantly agreed to let him work at the restaurant so long as he behaved himself. It had been ages since Gilbert had seen his little brother laugh, and within hours of his first day working with Marianne, he'd come into the kitchen to find him chortling. The pair of them already seemed to have some private joke that involved singing along to Edith Piaf with a bad German accent. Soon he couldn't help but join in, the three of them howling with laughter.

When Busch entered, Gilbert and Marianne stopped laughing immediately. Henri carried on with his impression, and then laughed when he noticed Busch.

'Are you mocking my singing?' he said. His tone was genial but the room grew quiet and Gilbert's stomach flipped.

'Not yours, sir,' said Henri, beckoning Busch over, like he was including him in the joke. He led the officer to the hatch where they could just see one of the others, with a red face, deep in his cups and holding on to a bottle of wine while he sang rather out of key along to 'La Vie en Rose' on the gramophone that they had set up in the restaurant.

For a long moment, Busch stared and they all held their breath. Then he began ever so slowly to laugh, uproariously. 'Oh, you are a *dummkopf*, but your accent is impeccable. I think we have done well to have you here. Well done, Madame.' He raised a finger and smiled. 'This is exactly what we need – more fun, yes,' and he placed a gentle hand on Henri's shoulders, and winked at him. Gilbert thought for a moment that his knees might buckle in relief.

Henri, however, didn't seem to realise just how much of a close shave he'd had.

Busch looked at Gilbert in amazement. 'Like night and day, you two.'

'Yes sir,' he said.

'Mhm,' he responded, before leaving, and singing '*La Vie en Rose*' beneath his breath and chuckling.

After that night, Henri was a firm favourite of Busch's. He was christened Dummkopf and invited to do regular impressions of the officers, which Henri was only too delighted to do, having, as Busch had discovered, a natural knack for accents and mannerisms. Busch roared with laughter, falling to his knees and gasping for breath when, emboldened, Henri impersonated him, mimicking his frequent hand movements, open face and the smile that showed most of his teeth.

Gilbert thought he was playing with fire.

At first, he'd worried that Henri would let his temper fly, but he didn't. It seemed, for now at least, he did seem to know where to draw the line, and perhaps being allowed to openly mock the officers offset some of his emotions.

Soon it was clear that he would be better suited as a waiter at the front of the restaurant than at the back, and they switched roles, which worked better for Gilbert, who had never enjoyed serving. At least in the kitchen he didn't need to work so hard to school his expressions, which often looked worried, thanks to the sound of Henri's loud voice carrying and the moment of silence before the Germans laughed, when relief finally followed.

As time went by, Henri was often invited on slower evenings to join them in playing cards. This proved quite useful to Gilbert, who could hear them as they discussed their plans, while Henri kept them entertained.

On one afternoon, he was standing just behind the kitchen hatch, where Henri would leave the order slips – mostly for wine and other beverages, as there remained just one food option. Though there had been the rare occasion that a senior official had requested something else, like a steak, and Marianne had obliged. Usually, Busch would give her fair warning before he brought an important guest to visit, and she was given time to acquire any ingredients beforehand. There had been one or two occasions, however, when she had had to make a plan – involving Gilbert scurrying out, with a wad of cash, to bribe a butcher – the money supplied by the General in order to meet the requirement. In these instances, a bottle of wine or a few entrees usually filled the necessary delay.

If Marianne was ever annoyed that sometimes the Germans forgot to play by the rules, she never showed it.

On this occasion, however, the visiting officer, a man by the name of Harald Vlig, who had dark brilliantined hair and inscrutable button eyes, appeared satisfied to nurse a beer and discuss what sounded like important plans. Gilbert listened from the hatch, tensing when he heard the man ask after Henri. 'You sure he can't speak German?'

'Definitely not. He's a hot-head, and I'm quite sure if he knew my nickname for him meant half-wit he wouldn't be all that happy.'

At the word '*dummkopf*' Henri raised a brow and said, 'Sir?'

Vlig and the others stifled their laughter behind their cards and he replied, 'Very well.'

Gilbert closed his eyes as he continued washing a beer mug. There was no way he'd tell Henri that. He also thought it was slightly alarming that Busch had picked up on Henri's quick temper. He wondered when his brother had given that away.

But soon his thoughts were taken up by Busch and Vlig, who began discussing plans for what sounded like a covert operation. He looked up when he heard something about a map. Standing on tiptoe, Gilbert watched as Vlig and Busch bent their heads together. He saw the map, and heard the word 'kinder' which he knew to mean 'children' and then something that sounded like 'eradication'.

He forgot to breathe. He heard something about a school.

He took one of the order slips and started to write it down.

It happened so fast, he almost yelped. Marianne snatched the slip out of his hand and then set fire to it on the gas stove. It faded to ash.

'What the hell are you doing?' he hissed, whispering.

'Saving your life, don't be an idiot,' she said, smacking him on the side of his head.

Her face looked completely different from its usual sunny disposition. Her face like cut glass. Her eyes cold fire.

'Marianne – you don't understand. They're planning something – something to do with children. It could be Jewish kids.'

Jewish people in France, like the rest of Nazi-occupied Europe, had suffered dreadfully. From being listed as 'undesirables' to being declared third-class citizens, forced to identify themselves and live under curfews to now – the steady deportations to concentration camps.

Sara was now living in Guillaume's basement in fear of her life. Her aunts and uncles had already been taken. She'd only managed to escape because she had fallen asleep at the library the night before and got home too late. When Gilbert had heard, his stomach had twisted into knots. He'd been sworn to secrecy not to tell anyone, especially Louisa, which he'd agreed to, not because he really believed that Louisa was a threat to Sara but because of his loyalty to Sara. There was a plan in place to sneak her out of the country through the mountains. Not that she wanted to go, she still wanted to fight. She was talking of ramping up their operations, and going military, even purchasing ammunitions.

Gilbert had been stealing food to take to them whenever he could, and telling her not to do anything stupid. It was his turn to warn her to be cautious, it seemed.

Marianne pulled him aside now. 'Listen to me. It is unforgivable what they are doing – *monstrous*.' Her face flashed with such hatred that he actually recoiled. 'But you will get yourself killed,' she said, snapping her fingers, 'if you deliver that information to the Resistance.'

He blinked. 'You know I am working for them?'

She went to turn up the radio. Then said in a fake, cheery voice. 'Oh, I love this one.' It was Maurice Chevalier's *'Paris sera toujours Paris.'* She swayed her hips. 'You're right, I think a nice summer stew with courgettes would be lovely.'

He frowned, and was about to ask her if she'd lost her mind, when he saw out of the corner of his eye one of the Nazi officers glance inside, before grunting and going back to his table.

Marianne waited, and then seeing that the coast was clear, motioned for him to join her.

'What you heard earlier – this is the only place they would have discussed it. Which means we'd be the prime suspects if the information came out. Especially you as he saw you standing by the hatch.'

'I'm sure he didn't.'

'He did. Don't be *stupid*. As much as Otto Busch and the rest of the boots play at being gentlemen, they are deadly soldiers, first and foremost – and the first thing they would do is watch out for listeners.'

'They don't know I can speak German.'

'They don't know you don't. Promise me this stays here.'

He frowned. It seemed so wrong. He had a chance to do something, finally. But then he thought about that officer, ears pricked like a cat's.

He nodded.

As the summer wore on, there was awful news of a mass deportation of Jews – thousands of women, children and men, all corralled in the heart of Paris and sent to concentration camps.

Guillaume managed to get Sara out of the country through Spain.

Gilbert never heard anything about that school afterwards. Although he did hear that the brilliantined senior officer Harald Vlig – the one who Busch had locked heads with discussing the school, and had laughed at calling his little brother *Dummkopf* – had had a heart attack two days after he'd been to their restaurant. He remembered feeling gratified.

10

SABINE

Monsieur Géroux looked at Sabine now, his eyes solemn. 'What might have happened with that school haunted me for years. Then, in the Seventies, I watched a news story on the television about a school just outside Paris, very near the one I'd seen marked out on that map, that was thought to be housing Jewish children. It burned down, during the war, and the officials believed that all the students perished in the fire. However, forensic scientists examined the remains and were shocked to find that the bones were over three hundred years old. They also discovered that there was a secret passageway beneath the school, a set of tunnels, and within them were artefacts from the war period – discarded shoes and clothing. It appeared that someone had fooled the Germans with bones from the old cemetery, as there were signs that the graves had been dug up during the war. They speculated that the school and its many Jewish children received a tip-off somehow, started the fire and used the bones as a decoy for the Germans, managing to escape the country via a network of priests out of Italy.'

He didn't tell her that afterwards, he'd cried like a baby.

Sabine was sitting forward, eyes wide, as she listened in a mixture of horror and awe.

'You think it was the same school?'

It was after eleven and Sabine and Monsieur Géroux were still at Pistachios, their meals only half eaten. They were still caught in the arms of the past.

'Yes, I do. I never forgot the area they pointed to on that map, even though it was just a glimpse. And after that documentary came out, I looked up the school they mentioned – up until then I'd been too afraid to do so, afraid of what I would find, I think I half believed that because Harald Vlig had had a heart attack, perhaps their evil plan was stopped somehow. But I always knew in my heart that was likely wishful thinking. The documentary made me realise that I needed to know either way. What I found was that none of the other schools near the one I overheard the Germans mention had any Jewish children, hidden in secret or otherwise, on record, but it's not just that that convinced me it was the same one.'

Sabine blinked. 'What did, then?'

'The fact that there was no other record of a deportation of Jewish children anywhere near there.'

'Could they not have just covered it up – I mean, it is an awful thing, it would be understandable that a certain amount of shame would be involved.'

'Perhaps, but this was a lot of children; it would be hard to hide when people go digging afterwards, as other records of schools who deported children proved, so it's not likely. I really think it had to be that school, and somehow they escaped.'

Sabine gasped. 'You're right.' Then she looked up at him. 'Do you think she was involved in that somehow?'

'Marianne?'

Sabine nodded. 'Like she said to you – you were the only ones who knew of that plan.'

He sighed. 'I don't know. We might not have been. It would be nice to think that, but she was the one who stopped me from relaying what I'd overheard about the planned attack on that school to the Resistance and with everything that happened afterwards it makes me think otherwise.'

Sabine sighed. 'You're right. I guess it's just hard to imagine her doing what she did, after what you've told me so far.'

'I know,' he sighed deeply, rubbing his face. 'Trust me. I've lived with that for so many years and I still don't know why she poisoned all those people. Including Henri.'

Sabine stared at him in horror.

'Henri?' she said, gasping softly. She felt horror-struck. 'Oh, Monsieur Géroux, I didn't know.'

He nodded, looking away as tears filmed his eyes. 'He was one of the unlucky ones that night.'

Sabine reached over and squeezed his hand, not knowing what to say.

He nodded, then bit his lip. 'We haven't even got to that night yet,' he said, swallowing. 'When she—'

She knew of course the night he meant. The night Marianne decided to kill all those people.

She blew out her cheeks. 'Monsieur Géroux, we don't have to if it's too hard. I realise now what I was asking... it's a lot.'

He shook his head, and squeezed her hand in return. 'A week ago that's what I thought, but now I realise how much I've needed to speak about it. I've held it inside for so long, this part of me buried in darkness – it feels good, somehow, to finally let it see the light. To speak of my brother, to remember him, not just as a victim, but as a person.' He gave her a wobbly smile.

'He was a wonderful, funny person,' she agreed, looking away, and needing to dab her eyes. They both did.

When their eyes met again, she said, 'I'm honoured truly that you would tell me your story.'

He squeezed her hand in response.

It was getting late, so he suggested she come past the shop the following week, after work, so that he could carry on, and she agreed, realising he was likely wrung-out emotionally. She hadn't experienced it first hand but she felt that way herself, just listening to him recount this time in his life.

Before they bid each other farewell, Sabine hesitated for a moment, then said, 'I found this at the restaurant.' She gave him the small slip of order paper with the note that she'd found wedged behind the drawer, written in what she assumed was Marianne's handwriting.

'I mean, it's just a scrap. I didn't know if it would mean anything to you?'

He took out his glasses from his jacket pocket and tried to read it in the weak light. He couldn't even make out the first line, even as he squinted. All he saw was a splodge.

'I don't recommend getting old,' he joked and she laughed, as he tried to read the piece of paper with his arm outstretched, but it blurred in the light and the chicken scrawl handwriting didn't help.

'It says, the days are short, but the hours seem long and something about her needing to spend time with her boys,' said Sabine. 'I thought perhaps it was when your mother was ill.'

Monsieur Géroux's eyebrows shot up. 'Perhaps. Marianne often left us messages of advice, or reminders on slips of paper. I'd forgotten about that.' He looked sad, and she wished she'd never brought it up.

After that they said their goodbyes and went their separate ways, and it was only when she was home, snuggling into Antoine as he snored, and she went over everything that had happened in her brain, that she realised he'd kept the note from Marianne. Even now, perhaps, a part of him still could not reconcile the Marianne from his memories with the one who had later done what she did.

. . .

The next morning, far too early for Sabine, Antoine brought her a coffee in bed, and then proceeded to stare at her meaningfully. 'And?'

Antoine had clearly been dying to hear how her evening with Monsieur Géroux had gone, and crucially, hear about that night when Marianne had poisoned her customers.

Sabine frowned. 'We haven't got there yet.'

He raised his brow. 'What?'

'You don't understand, there's just so much history – they were real people, Antoine, and I think he feels that if he shares this story with me, I need to know that.'

'But?'

'I didn't realise how hard it would be to hear.'

'I can imagine.'

'No, you really can't,' she said, her face solemn, haunted, and then she told him everything.

His eyes widened in horror. Especially when she got to the part about the school. They discussed that for a long time. Antoine, however, had a theory of his own and seemed to think that Marianne had had something to do with the school – that she had somehow used what they'd overheard and that's how they knew to escape through the tunnels. 'I think maybe she tipped someone off.'

Sabine sighed. 'I think you're an optimist.'

'But it makes sense,' he argued. 'How many others really knew about that school – those officers chose that restaurant for a reason. The Batignolles – while charming – isn't in the centre of Paris, it's out of the way, and could be thought of as a discreet place to meet in order to have conversations you might not be able to have anywhere else... it stands to reason she used that information somehow. Or how else would it have happened?'

'We're speculating – who knows who else knew the plan in reality?' argued Sabine. 'Besides, how do you go from saving a school of children to killing your customers on purpose? The idea that she just sat back and prevented Monsieur Géroux from telling his friends in the Resistance fits more with what we know of her, I think, sadly.'

Antoine took a sip of his own coffee. 'Maybe.' Then he looked up at her, a thought seeming to light in his dark eyes. 'You said he thinks you look like her. Want to find out for sure?'

She blinked. 'What do you mean?'

'Well, that German propaganda paper you mentioned earlier – the one that did the article on Marianne, about her cooking and her grandmother, maybe we can find it?'

'How?'

He grinned. 'You're the librarian, you tell me? I just work at the post office, remember?'

She laughed, then thought about it for a while. 'It'll probably be at the BHVP – the historical library. If there's a record of it anywhere, it'll be there.'

'See? That's what I was thinking – that you'd think of something like that,' he said, and she laughed. 'Want to go on Saturday?'

She nodded.

That evening, Antoine was making dinner when he accidentally bumped the cat poster that had been up on the counter. There was an almighty crash and the sound of glass breaking.

Sabine raced to the kitchen. 'Are you all right?' she cried.

'Fine,' he called. 'I'm sorry, I turned to get the pan and my elbow knocked it over.'

They both winced at the mess. The poster was lying face down in a pool of glass.

Antoine set about picking up the pieces of glass, cupping them into his hand, then going to fetch the small broom and pan that always hung on the back of the kitchen door.

As he swept around it, Sabine lifted up the frame, noticing that the brown paper on the back was beginning to tear. It also looked oddly bulky, as if something had shifted in the fall. She felt the back and frowned. 'Weird. There's something here.'

Antoine was busy sweeping and didn't look up.

She sat on her haunches, and felt along the back. It felt like something had been placed beneath the paper. Curious. She opened up the slight tear in the paper more.

'What the—' she said.

'What?' asked Antoine, looking up.

She shook her head. 'I don't know, but it's something. She tore a strip and opened the paper wider. Inside she could make out something hard, which she prised out. To her surprise, it was a thick brown envelope. It fell onto the ground with an audible clunk.

'What the hell is that?' she whispered.

'Holy crap,' breathed Antoine.

They stared at it for a long time.

'Are you going to open it?'

She bit her lip. Yes, was, of course, the answer, but she hesitated. 'I just – if it came out of that poster – from that place,' she breathed, meaning the restaurant, 'it's probably nothing good.'

'You don't *know* that.'

She nodded. The only way to know was to open it. She tore the top of the envelope off, and then jiggled the contents out onto the floor. Several things began to fall out. She picked up the first one. It was a small notebook, bound in red and white. Then she opened it and blinked in surprise.

'It's a recipe book,' she breathed.

'What? Really?'

'Yes,' she said, flicking through. The first page had a small inscription. *'For Ma Petite, all my love, Grand-mère.'*

As she flipped through the pages, the handwriting, which looked quite childish and round at first, began to change, becoming elegant as the pages and perhaps the writer herself, grew.

Sabine blinked as she looked at it. 'This looks like it was from when she was a little girl.'

Antoine frowned. 'So it was true, then – that part about Marianne learning to cook from her grandmother?' he asked.

'It must have been,' she said in awe.

The other item was something that caused her to gasp.

'Is that – a passport?'

It was.

'What?' breathed Antoine.

She opened it up to the identity page then frowned.

It was Marianne. Or at least who she assumed it had to be, as Monsieur Géroux was right, she looked a lot like Sabine.

Except that it wasn't Marianne at all.

She stared at the name in confusion. 'Elodie Clairmont?'

'Who the hell was Elodie Clairmont?' echoed Antoine.

Sabine hadn't told Monsieur Géroux about the passport. She knew she would, but she couldn't find the words just yet.

On Saturday morning, Antoine was surprised that she still wanted to go to the BHVP historical library. 'This just feels like a bit of a puzzle, and if I could find the other pieces, I don't know, maybe there will be something there.'

'Something like a clue or something she might have given away in the article?' he asked.

She sighed. 'I'm reaching, aren't I? There's probably nothing there.'

'Not necessarily. Besides, she's real for you now, that's enough reason to go – I mean, even I want to read that article the Germans wrote about her.'

She nodded. 'Me too.'

They took the metro to Saint-Paul and walked towards the

beautiful Hôtel de Lamoignon, where the historical library was located. Housing more than a million documents on the history of Paris, dating back from antiquity to modern day, it included maps, photographs and countless donations over the years.

As a librarian, a part of her always got a thrill to visit, to be surrounded by such old books, but today it felt different. More momentous in a way.

The library was enormous, and beautiful. Sabine felt like she was walking inside living history. The staff were helpful, and suggested that they could use the reading room if they required. After a bit of digging, ten minutes later they found where they needed to start, in a large bound volume that was full of the German daily newspapers from that time, and another that held the weekly French editions. Sabine and Antoine brought the volumes to a large desk and sat down beneath the green lamps.

'I'll take the German ones,' offered Antoine. 'I did German in school.'

She nodded.

They got to work, at first exclaiming at almost every article, which seemed bent on showing a favourable slant on the Occupation – seeming to imply that the Nazis were single-handedly responsible for saving French culture.

'They sure went out of their way to praise the French,' said Sabine as Antoine read her an article in praise of French food production.

'Haven't you heard? Flattery will get you everywhere.'

'Except with the French.'

They laughed.

There were articles on plays, concerts, nightclubs. 'It's like they were desperate to make it look as if everything was normal.'

'Yep, as if the French hadn't noticed they were in fact invaded by aliens.'

Sabine snorted.

. . .

An hour later, Antoine found the article they were looking for from 1942.

'I think this is it!' he cried.

Sabine leaned over and scanned the page, gasping aloud as she read the section Antoine's index finger was pointing at.

'*Food like my grandmother used to make.*'

'Oh my God, it does look like you,' he said, eyes wide.

Sabine gasped. He was right. The photograph was in full colour; it had been worth it just to come here and see that, she thought, as it showed a woman with shoulder-length blonde hair and painted lips parted in a soft smile. She was holding a whisk in one hand and a bowl in the other. It looked like she'd just been surprised.

Beneath the photograph the caption said, '*Marianne Blanchet der Besitzer des neuen Restaurants in Batignolles, genannt Luberon.*'

'What does this say?' she asked.

'It says, she is the owner of the new restaurant in Paris, called Luberon.'

The resemblance was there for sure, but the chin and nose were a little different. Sabine frowned as she stared at her, wondering why she had done what she had. What made a woman – who up until then had seemed kind and brave enough to open a restaurant with the aid of the Germans in order to feed the locals cheaply – change overnight?

Antoine translated the rest of the article, and transcribed it for her into her notebook.

Sabine read over his shoulder, but when he got to the part about Marianne's grandmother she read aloud as he wrote.

'*Blanchet's attitude is refreshing – she is bringing the countryside to Paris, she says, by cooking the kind of food her grandmother used to make in Provence.*

'"When I was little, she ran a small farmer's café restaurant in her village, and she served just one meal a day: lunch. As a customer, you almost never knew what you were going to get, it was part of the charm. People came because they enjoyed the surprise and the good food. No one was ever disappointed – not so that I ever knew anyway."

'One couldn't for a moment imagine other nations, like the one across the pond with their "toad in the hole," ever being so adventurous. It is a quintessentially French trait, this bold and brave approach to their love of good food. And now, just like her grandmother's café in Luberon, there is no menu, just a long line of people who come to Madame Blanchet's restaurant knowing that whatever she decides to make that day is likely to be wonderful.'

'So her grandmother was a cook too. In Provence. Which means that perhaps she came from there,' he said.

Sabine nodded. 'It was on my mother's birth certificate. La-something, she was born at an Abbey.'

'So that explains the name, Luberon, at least,' said Antoine.

'Yes. So, we know at least that part is true – that she lived in Provence, and perhaps her grandmother really did have a restaurant, which explains the recipe book.'

She nodded.

Then he frowned. 'You know what I do think is surprising is that she was called madame, even then. Was she married?'

Sabine blinked. 'Actually, I asked Monsieur Géroux this myself. He said that it's just tradition to call a cook madame, for some reason. Or at least that's what Marianne had told him.'

'What was your grandfather's name? Wasn't it on the birth certificate?'

Sabine stared at him. 'Yes, actually.' There had been a name there, but she hadn't paused to commit it to memory. She did remember feeling relieved that it was a French name, and that her mother was conceived before the war. But she hadn't thought about her grandfather in all of this, she'd been so consumed by Marianne, if she were honest.

'What happened to her husband?'

'I have no idea.'

Sabine could hear the phone ringing as she opened the door. She raced towards it only for it to cut out. She frowned, then put the phone back, only for it to ring again. What on earth? she thought, worried. She picked it up again, suddenly nervous.

She could hear heavy breathing down the line.

'Hello?' she asked, eyes wide.

'Madame Dupris! Oh, Madame Dupris, at last.'

Sabine's eyes widened in shock. 'Monsieur Géroux?'

'Yes. Oh yes. I am so glad you're home, I have been calling – and calling.'

Sabine blinked. It wasn't like him to be so... well, pushy.

'Are you all right?'

'No! Well, yes, oh yes, maybe for the first time in years.'

'What, why – what's happened?'

'That note – the one you gave me. First, though, please tell me as I have to double check, to be sure – you found it there, at the restaurant?'

'Yes – it was wedged right at the back of a drawer.'

There was a whining sound, like he was keening.

She flinched. 'Oh, monsieur, I'm sorry.'

'No, no, don't be sorry. Oh, madame – it is proof, you see. Proof she never meant to kill my brother.'

11

GILBERT

NINE HOURS BEFORE – PARIS, 1987

Monsieur Géroux watched as the sun rose outside his bedroom window. Time to get up, he thought with relief. He hauled himself up, and everything in his body began to ache. He groaned, then took a sip of water from the glass on his nightstand.

He'd spent most of the night thinking about the past. When he'd left Sabine at the restaurant, he'd been pleasantly numbed by the cheap wine. But by the time he'd got in his bed, his thoughts had begun to race; when he did fall asleep his dreams were all of the same thing. He was back in the kitchen at Luberon, and he kept seeing the order slips above the waiter station. At first there were dozens. He went to reach for them, and they melted into nothing, until only one was present. He stretched on his tiptoes, but the slip started to float up and up, towards the ceiling, growing smaller and smaller and further and further away.

He woke up with a start, then turned over, only to be back at the beginning in the same dream. This time the kitchen was covered in slips. Everywhere. On the counter, in the bubbling pot. When he turned to look at the pot, which was hissing and spitting, he opened the lid, and inside was a ticking bomb.

He yelped, then dropped the lid. One of the slips flew up into his face, and he picked it up, and saw that it said, *Danger!*

The others said the same thing. Everywhere he looked it said the same thing.

He rushed to the pot, but it was too late – before it exploded he woke up in a cold sweat, his heart thundering in his ears.

He lay in bed panting for ages. It took forever for his breathing to calm down. Eventually he switched on the light, and started working on a crossword puzzle to steady his nerves.

Early on, he'd found that crosswords were one of the few things that helped to distract his thoughts. His brain was still foggy from the wine and lack of sleep, but when he was finished an hour later, he was able to fall into a dreamless sleep – for an hour or two, only to be awakened just before dawn by Tapis's bladder; the dog insisted on being put out right then. When they returned from the street corner, he huddled in bed for warmth and the vague but hopeful wish that he might still get some more sleep but it was hopeless.

Coffee, he thought, then padded his way into the kitchen, feeling like he'd aged in the night.

He felt calmer now, though, but still puzzled by those dreams. Was it just the shock of seeing that order slip? he wondered. This tiny little reminder of life before everything changed.

He didn't know.

While the coffee simmered on the stove, he found his glasses on the small table in the kitchen where he'd left them the day before. He got up then went to search his jacket pocket for the little slip, coming back into the kitchen with its fluorescent light. He poured his coffee, then sat down and stared at the order slip.

He saw what looked like a smudge on the first line. He rubbed it, but it didn't budge, so he got up to fetch a cotton bud from the bathroom – one of the tricks of his trade to remove stains and other such material from old books – and he lightly dabbed at the first line until very faintly he could make out the pen beneath. It was a date.

4th January 1943

The days are short, but hours can seem long, H. She needs to spend these last ones with her boys. That's an order.

M.

His heart started to pound. The fourth of January 1943. It was the day before the murders. The day before his beloved, naughty little brother was poisoned.

12

GILBERT

His mother had taken a turn in the first week of the New Year. She'd battled a cold all through December, and hadn't seemed to make much of a recovery. It appeared that her medication was no longer working the way it had the year before, and the fluid build-up on her lungs had got increasingly worse.

Doctor Cordeau had seemed sad when he delivered the news, looking up to Gilbert and Henri from where he knelt by her side. He shook his head, just once. 'I think you will both need to prepare yourselves.'

Berthe closed her eyes, but not before they saw the track of tears fall into her pillow.

Gilbert knew she cried for them only, not for herself.

Henri got up to leave. His face was ashen.

'Where are you going?' cried Gilbert, shocked. 'You can't leave Maman now.'

Henri looked past him to the ceiling, his lip trembling and tears spooling from his eyes. 'I'm sorry, I have to go, Gilbert.'

Gilbert's heart ached. 'Just a moment, then,' he agreed. 'We must be strong now, later we can...' He meant fall apart, but he couldn't finish the words, as he was choking on them. He knelt by the side of the bed, and wedged his fist into his mouth, and the sound that came out of him was wild.

There was a gasping sound from Henri, who barrelled past him and was out of the door in seconds, into the cold January night.

Doctor Cordeau's eyes were full of pity. He came forward and clasped Gilbert's shoulder. 'Is there someone I can call – your neighbour, Madame Lambert, perhaps? Marianne?'

Gilbert struggled to speak. 'No. Just... just Henri, see if you can find him.'

The doctor nodded. 'I'll bring him back.'

After he left, Gilbert went to pour himself a glass of whisky, which he downed neat. It was the first time he'd ever drunk hard liquor and it burned as it went down, but it helped, slightly. He blew his nose and went back to his mother's bedside.

Now that the doctor had confirmed it, he could see it – what he'd pretended not to see – how close she was to the end. His mother's beloved face was thin and pale, her lips bloodless. Every breath a wheeze. It was agony watching her struggle for breath. With his father gone, he and Henri would be orphans, they would be all the other had in the world.

He took a seat on her bed and reached for her hand. It was cold and he began to rub it gently in his.

'That's nice,' she said. 'Tell me about the roses,' she added, closing her eyes. 'In the Tuileries.'

He smiled through a veil of tears. It was a game that they'd started to play over the winter, as she got weaker, and it was getting harder for her to get out. They struggled to make their flat warm with the coal shortage too. At first, he used to read to her but then later he'd started to remind her of things she loved. Beautiful, summery things.

She closed her eyes, and he dashed away a tear, and began to describe her favourite part of the gardens. 'The blush roses are as big as your hand, the smell is intoxicating, and when the wind blows, petals scatter all along the path.'

'Where am I?'

'You're sitting on that little stone bench you love under the canopy of roses, you have a coffee in your hands from the café.'

'Wine... it's afternoon,' she corrected, a slight grin on her face.

'Oh, *d'accord*, it is the afternoon,' he agreed. 'The summer sun is warm, but not overbearing. Dozing by your feet is a cat.'

'I... like... cats.' She was slowing down slightly, each word a bit harder for her to get out, her breath wheezing a bit more.

He knew. Of course he knew.

'Black... and... white,' she said.

'Don't talk,' he said, biting his lip to stop himself from howling again. She sighed and he continued. 'It's slightly fat. Yet distinguished, a gentleman of means,' he added.

Her lips twitched in a smile. She liked that.

'Its belly is full from the saucer of milk you brought it.'

She frowned slightly, a question on her face, and he grinned.

'You got the milk from your love affair with the man at the cheese shop down the road.'

She raised just a finger to tap him in reprimand but it was a momentous undertaking. She sat back exhausted, and gave a slight wheezing laugh. When she'd settled down, he carried on with his story, keeping anything that would over-excite her from his imaginary tale.

She fell asleep, as he described reading her favourite childhood book, *Le Petit Prince*, in the sunshine.

He stayed with his mother for a long time watching as she slept. She looked peaceful.

There was a soft tap on the door, and it was Doctor Cordeau. 'I found Henri – he said he would be back shortly.'

Gilbert nodded, relieved. 'Thank you.'

The doctor nodded. 'I think if you don't mind I will stay here with you, just outside.'

He placed a chair outside Berthe's room.

Gilbert's lips wobbled, he nodded, not having the words to convey how grateful he was for that.

The hours passed and Henri did not return.

Doctor Cordeau offered to go find him again.

But Gilbert was angry now. 'No,' he said, flatly. 'He's been told twice now.' He closed his eyes. 'He obviously does not want to be here when it happens.'

Doctor Cordeau nodded, but he offered no condemnation for the boy. 'Try not to hold it against him, soon you will be all the other has.'

Gilbert's lips shook as tears began to fall once more. 'I can't promise that, doctor.'

It was two in the morning when Berthe Géroux slipped away. Gilbert had been staring at her and still didn't see the moment it happened, but Doctor Cordeau did. When he pronounced it, it still came as a shock, and Gilbert slid onto his haunches and cried, burying his face in his knees.

The doctor stayed with him as he sobbed, bringing water and more whisky for the shock.

He must have fallen asleep sometime before dawn, because he woke up to the sound of knocking. When he went to open the door, he found Madame Lambert in her pink frilly robe, her thin face twisted in pity. 'Oh Gilbert, oh my dear—'

Doctor Cordeau must have told her, he thought.

Gilbert's face crumbled. 'Thank you, madame. I am grateful that you have come but I—' he swallowed, 'I can't be around anyone right now.'

'Someone told you already?' she breathed, clutching her chest with a slim hand.

He frowned. 'Told me? I was there—'

'What!' she cried. 'You saw it? But how then are you... still... here?'

He stared at her incredulously. She wasn't making sense. 'She was my mother, madame, I was not going to leave her to die alone, where else would I be? I don't understand.'

Dawning comprehension was lighting on Fleur Lambert's face. 'Berthe!' she cried, sinking against the doorway. 'She – she's gone too?'

He frowned. 'Too? Isn't that why you are here?'

She shook her head, and clapped a hand over her mouth in horror. Behind her there was the sound of rushing feet. It was Doctor Cordeau. His face appeared stricken. 'Oh, Gilbert, I have terrible news.'

Gilbert looked from him to Madame Lambert in confusion. An anxious knot was beginning to form in the pit of his stomach. The word 'too' was sitting there like something about to explode.

'Oh, my dear, boy,' said Madame Lambert. 'I don't know how to tell you this, especially now, hearing about dear Berthe...'

He blinked. 'What is it?'

But Madame Lambert seemed to freeze, unable to say it aloud.

The doctor's hazel eyes were full of pity. 'I have some awful news, son. It seems there was an incident at the restaurant last night.'

'An incident,' breathed Gilbert, his heart beginning to pound.

His first thought was for his brother.

'Henri – he wasn't – he—' He didn't seem to have the words.

'He was found there, along with the others. It seems he was poisoned last night, along with five others.'

Gilbert looked at him in shock, finding his words in his anxiety somehow. 'Poisoned? But that can't be right, he wasn't working last night.'

Doctor Cordeau shook his head. 'Nevertheless, he was there.'

The world felt like it was falling away from Gilbert's feet.

'Is he – is he all right?'

Doctor Cordeau closed his eyes for just a second, like he didn't want to face him. Then he shook his head. 'I'm sorry, he passed away.'

Gilbert's knees gave out. On the fall down, he heard, like through a tunnel, Doctor Cordeau say, 'No one survived.'

Gilbert's lips began to wobble, he saw stars. This was all just some horrid nightmare. He looked up though a haze of tears, the words 'no one survived' echoing in his skull.

'And... Marianne?'

'She's disappeared.'

It took a moment for Gilbert – in the midst of all the horror and grief – to comprehend.

'She fled after she poisoned them all,' spat Fleur Lambert, finally able to speak. Her hands balled at her sides, her eyes glassy, her face twisted with loathing.

13

GILBERT

Monsieur Géroux stared at the order slip.

Marianne had never meant for Henri to be there that night. He was sure of that now. It was there, in black and white.

Perhaps Henri hadn't got the note somehow?

Even so, it wasn't as Monsieur Géroux had believed for years – that Marianne had somehow asked him to work there that night. Henri's last words, 'I have to go,' had over time come to mean something else to Gilbert, not a plea to get away from the pain and heartache that lay in store for him in witnessing his mother's passing but something else, an obligation, perhaps?

Gilbert had tortured himself with those words for decades, and now – now he at least knew she hadn't actually wanted Henri there.

Henri's death was the thing that had confused the authorities the most. It was what had made them believe that Marianne had somehow snapped or was some kind of sociopath.

Six people were poisoned that night: four were Nazi officers; two were French; one was from the Resistance, Louisa, the woman that Sara had disliked so intensely, as they had a power play for leadership of their chapter; the other was Henri.

Louisa – it was thought by the authorities – was a collaborator, which would have served as motivation for Marianne, along with the Nazis, but Henri?

She had adored the boy, right from the start. The two were always laughing and she was quick to give him an affectionate hug. Gilbert had seen it often enough, and was usually included in her big bear hugs. He remembered telling the authorities that the following day.

It was like he was living a nightmare, after losing his mother, to discover what had happened to his brother. None of it had seemed real. When one of them asked if they thought it was possible that Henri was a covert collaborator, he remembered actually bursting out laughing. 'They called him *Dummkopf* and they thought he didn't know what it meant. But he wasn't an idiot. He might have come to tolerate them, but he despised them really, that's why he mocked them to their faces.'

14

SABINE

Antoine poured another glass of wine. They were on to their second bottle already.

They had taken their discovery to Monsieur Géroux's apartment in the Batignolles. The passport she had found hidden in the poster with the odd name Elodie Clairmont, the recipe book, as well as the box where she was keeping the other documents, like her mother's birth and adoption certificates.

When Monsieur Géroux had phoned Sabine to tell her about his own discovery, the fact that Marianne had left a note for Henri telling him implicitly not to go to the restaurant the night she poisoned those people, changed things.

Everything they thought they knew seemed turned around; it was exciting. It might mean that there was a lot more to this story than they'd realised. A version where Marianne Blanchet or Elodie Clairmont or whoever she was hadn't actually intended to kill her young friend.

It still didn't answer the question of what had happened or

why she'd wanted to kill those people though. But they had a good idea. Thanks to Monsieur Géroux.

Shortly after they'd arrived, and Sabine had introduced Antoine, the older man had led them into his living room, where a folder was open on the dark wood coffee table. He took out something to show them.

'This is a press clipping from that night. It's the only one I kept. It came out a few years ago when a journalist ran a piece on it for the local newspaper. I don't know why I kept it, really, perhaps it was because it had photographs of the people who died. It felt wrong to throw it away... but I didn't read it, I couldn't,' he admitted.

Sabine's eyes widened. 'May I?' she asked.

He nodded, and she knelt down before it.

PUTTING A FACE ON THE VICTIMS OF MURDER RESTAURANT

More than thirty years ago, at the restaurant Luberon, known to most of us in the village now as 'Murder Restaurant,' which opened during the Occupation of Paris in 1942, the owner, Marianne Blanchet, poisoned and killed six people. She was later executed for her crimes. It's a story that most people in the Batignolles village know even if they don't know all the details, like who were killed. They were French locals, Henri Géroux, aged twelve, and Louisa Tellier, aged twenty-two, German officers, Otto Busch, thirty, the Nazi cultural liaison officer for Paris, Karl Lange, senior Nazi public relations officer for Paris, Hans Winkler, his junior officer, and Frederik Latz, Busch's secretary.

To this day it was never understood why Marianne Blanchet did what she did. We asked some of the locals their thoughts.

'I think she was just evil,' said Eva Moulin, aged forty-nine. 'We all try to make sense of things like this, but there often isn't a reason for it other than that.'

Likewise, Paul Dupont, local baker, seventy-three, notes that she was probably just disturbed in her head, or womb. 'Hysteria – plain and simple, a disturbance in the womb most likely, what sane person would kill a child?'

While modern scientists no longer believe in the diagnosis of hysteria, or conditions affecting the mind from the womb, the idea that Madame Blanchet was clinically insane is one that persists. Doctor Samuel Allard, who lives in the village, agrees. 'The signs really do seem to point to something like schizophrenia – this was a woman who it seems served most of these same clients for over a year, without incident, until something went wrong, perhaps in her mind. You have to remember that back then treatment for such conditions wasn't well understood...

Sabine stopped reading. 'They clearly all think the same thing.'

'That she was mentally ill,' said Antoine, reading it over her shoulder.

'Yes,' said Monsieur Géroux. 'I don't think I ever did, though.'

She frowned. 'Why not?'

'I was with her every day, and if that was true there would have been signs, particularly in the days before it happened. My wife's brother, Giles, suffered from that illness, and you could tell whenever he was off his medication or needed to have it adjusted. He would start to say strange things, often showing signs of paranoia or acting like he was suffering some delusion. I mean, I'm no expert, but there was nothing like that. I think that's why it was harder for me – if I could have just believed that she had had an episode like Giles used to have, I could have forgiven her. I would have known she wasn't herself, that she would never ordinarily have done what she had. But I never felt that to be the case here. It was so... cold. And even the fact that she knew to run away: I mean, had she been ill I'm not sure she would have had the self-preservation to run away... Giles would not have been able to, not that everyone is the same of course, but even so it just never rang true for me.'

Sabine nodded. 'I agree. I mean, personally, if that was the case – that she was just ill – I could feel better about it in a way. Things are changing with mental health nowadays. Slowly, sure, I mean,' she rolled her eyes as she muttered, 'hysteria, a disturbance in the womb, for goodness' sake. But the passport definitely makes me think it was something else, not mental illness.'

Antoine nodded. 'Me too.'

Sabine looked at the photograph of the victims. 'I can't believe I'm seeing them,' she said. Busch was blond, with pale eyes. His features were symmetrical and some might consider him good-looking. He wasn't her type, but there was a manly, farm boy sort of wholesome look about him that would appeal to many. The other men had brown hair. Latz had sharp features and dark eyes. Lange looked older, and had a moustache and light eyes. Winkler's hair was wavy and he had small sunken eyes that looked slightly menacing.

Louisa Tellier was a brunette, with a sharp, intelligent-looking face. She had a small painted mouth and wide eyes studded by black mascara.

Seeing Henri, though, was the worst. He had eyes that crinkled in the corners and freckles, he was laughing. She touched the image and bit her lip. It was a nice face, she thought. She could see Monsieur Géroux in it.

Monsieur Géroux came to stand next to her. His eyes grew sad as he looked at his brother's face.

'I have been thinking about something else too, that might have been motivation. Not for Henri, but in terms of this woman,' he said, pointing at the Frenchwoman, Louisa. 'She was in the Resistance with me – except that for a long time the leader of our chapter, Sara, believed that she was an informant.'

They all gasped.

'You see, someone informed on my friend, Sara. Thankfully, she got away in time, to someone she could trust: Guillaume, a friend of ours. But she told me when I went to bring them food that she feared that there was an informant. She implied it might be Louisa but Guillaume and I just dismissed it as girlish rivalry. They had never got along, and there wasn't a meeting in which the two didn't disagree or get into some kind of squabble. Despite the fact that Sara was the leader, and we trusted her, on this one point we didn't take her seriously. She had no real proof apart from witnessing Louisa speaking to a Nazi one day in a flirtatious way, which Louisa had vehemently denied, saying she'd only asked one for a light for her cigarette. Louisa might not have been our favourite member but we never had any real cause to believe she was an informant. But what if she was?'

'It's possible,' said Sabine. 'And perhaps, somehow, Marianne knew that.'

'It doesn't explain Henri, though.'

'No,' agreed Sabine. 'But maybe that was just collateral damage somehow.'

'Maybe,' agreed Monsieur Géroux, though the idea caused him pain, and he frowned.

Sabine took out the things she'd brought. 'Maybe these will give us some clues?'

She took out the English passport first, and showed it to Monsieur Géroux. Then Sabine took a sip of wine, while pacing the floor in the sitting room.

'So which name was the real one?' she asked. 'The passport

with Elodie Clairmont – or the one on my grandmother's birth certificate, Marianne Blanchet, the name you knew her by?'

'Can I see the birth certificate?' Monsieur Géroux asked.

She nodded, and took out the document from the box she'd brought with her, which included the passport and recipe book – it had seemed natural to bring them all, she was glad now that she had thought of it.

He put his glasses on and stared at it for some time. Antoine leaned in for a closer look.

But of course the name Marianne Blanchet was still there, and didn't quite tell them anything, apart from confirming their confusion.

Monsieur Géroux made a 'hmm' sound.

'What is it?' asked Sabine.

'It says your mother was born in the Abbey de Saint-Michel in Lamarin. Well, I was thinking, if the abbey is still in operation today, perhaps someone there might be able to shed some light. Marianne told me that she grew up in Provence, perhaps that part was true – perhaps it wasn't far from this abbey?'

'It's possible,' said Antoine. 'Did the abbey handle the adoption?'

She went through the box until she found the adoption certificate, and then nodded. 'Yes, they're listed here too.'

Antoine took it from her, and then looked at the birth certificate.

'That's interesting,' he said.

'What?' asked Sabine.

'The dates from the birth certificate to the adoption are quite far apart. Your mother was born in 1938, but she was only adopted in 1944. Do you think Marianne raised her until then?'

'Not while she had the restaurant – that was from '42 to '43,' answered Monsieur Géroux with a frown.

'Maybe the abbey will know something about that. Hopefully they are still in operation. I'll see if they are listed in the directory tomorrow morning and try to give them a call.'

'Fingers crossed,' Monsieur Géroux agreed. 'You will let me know as soon as you find out?'

'I will, definitely. You deserve to know the truth, Monsieur Géroux. It is your story to discover as much as it is mine.'

PART TWO

15

PROVENCE, 1926

The cream Rolls-Royce sped through the Provençal countryside towards an old farmhouse in the distance, bordered by vineyards on one side and tall cypress trees on the other. The light that filtered through the car window was lemon bright as it reached the young girl who sat mute at the back, face turned away from the view, golden hair a mess of knots, like a weaver's nest.

The driver glanced back at her with a look of concern, as he had every half hour or so.

She couldn't be that much older than his own daughter, around nine or ten, he thought, wondering what she was thinking, as he'd wondered for most of their long journey. She hadn't said a word.

Not even when he'd arrived – a complete stranger – to fetch and take her to a new home after the death of her mother.

Mute, apparently.

A neighbour who'd looked after her until arrangements could be made had explained, after he'd turned up at her door in Montmartre, the fashionable area of Paris that reminded him of a village, with beautiful buildings, cobbled streets, bistros and a basilica. A world away from his home in Hertfordshire. He'd knocked on the apartment door in a building that was rendered a faded salmon colour, and a thin, kindly-faced Frenchwoman with dark hair and eyes and a faded elegance – marred ever so slightly by stained, smoker's teeth – had answered.

He'd introduced himself as the chauffeur, doffing his cap. 'I'm Jacob Bell. I'm here for the young miss?'

'Madame Gour,' she said, shaking his hand. 'I'll call her.'

He'd released a sigh of relief that she'd spoken English. His French was terrible, and what little he knew he'd been happy to forget after the war.

'Elodie, *viens vite, l'homme est la!*'

The child had come quickly, like she was expecting him. She was small, with pale blonde hair and intense blue eyes. They completely took him aback.

They were Clairmont eyes, that was for sure.

'Hello,' he'd tried.

But the child only continued to stare.

Madame Gour had waved her hand, as if to scrub the air in dismissal. 'She won't answer – it's not personal.'

Then just as quickly as she'd arrived, the girl disappeared.

'Gone to fetch her things,' Madame Gour explained when he'd looked startled, thinking for a moment that she had run away. He got a glimpse of the interior of the apartment: herringbone floors, a faded Persian rug, and a gilt table where a painted vase housed exquisite blooms, in a rich blowsy pink that he didn't have the name for.

'You know,' she said, lighting a thin cigarette then taking a deep drag; when she exhaled, she blew the smoke away from his face, 'she hasn't said a *word* since it happened. Not one,' she emphasised, holding her index finger up. 'We found her there –

with her mother's body,' she said, pointing with her cigarette upstairs to a flat on the left.

'Oh no,' said Jacob, wincing. He hadn't known the details.

Madame Gour nodded, pursing her lips. '*Oui*. She didn't want to leave her, kept prodding her as if she thought she would wake up.' She made a prodding motion and he cringed.

'That's... well, that's horrible.'

'*Oui, très horrible.* I've been trying to do my best with her, but she screams blue murder when I try to comb her hair. Maybe I'm rougher than her maman. I had only boys myself, you see. Poor thing.'

He'd started to feel nervous then, now that he was here, and his task was before him. It seemed so strange to him that Lord Clairmont hadn't wanted to come along to see his daughter here himself. The housekeeper back home, Mrs Harris, had said the last time he'd seen her she'd been just a babe.

It wasn't his job to question his employers, though. Jacob's mother had reminded him of that enough times when he took the post. She'd had a lifetime in service, so she knew better than most what was expected.

Still, it seemed *cruel* that he'd left this task to a servant, especially given that the girl's mother had just died. Jacob wasn't even taking the child to Lord Clairmont, he was sending her away to her grandmother in the countryside for the summer. Likely didn't want to mess up his own vacations plans with an illegitimate child from an affair he had during the war, which had caused enough trouble in his marriage already. At least that what's Mrs Harris speculated upon hearing the arrangement. Jacob was inclined to agree.

He'd never understand them, his supposed 'betters,' and that was the truth. His father, who had never learned to read or write and never had much more than a farthing to his name, had more honour and true gentility in his finger than the whole lot of them combined as far as he was concerned. Especially now when he thought of that poor child and everything she'd been through.

It wasn't like they hadn't been aware that the girl's mother wasn't well. She'd written letters apparently, most likely to avoid that very situation. Even so, Lord Clairmont had, as usual, taken his own time. Not that he would ever say any of *that* to Madame Gour. He wanted to, though. He felt like he ought to apologise, but of course, he wouldn't.

'So – she doesn't speak – at all?'

'Not a bean. But don't worry, she won't give you much trouble.'

That would make a first, he couldn't help thinking, for one of the Clairmonts.

Elodie returned with a small, battered suitcase and a knitted doll under her arm. The neighbour squeezed her shoulders briefly then gently steered her towards the front door. 'Let me know how you are doing, all right?'

The child simply frowned.

'I'll pass the message on – ask her grandmother to write, I have your details,' Jacob offered.

'Thank you,' said Madame Gour.

'My name is Jacob,' he said, turning towards the child. 'I'll be taking you to your grandmother in the countryside. You'll like it there, I'm sure.'

She stared at him, a look of confusion on her face.

'Your father sent me,' he explained, looking from Elodie to Madame Gour in hesitation.

Elodie still looked perplexed.

'Can't understand you,' said the neighbour, finally putting out her cigarette in an ashtray on the marble table. 'Hasn't learned English yet,' and she proceeded to translate for the child, who nodded when the word 'father' was mentioned.

The child held out her hand in a question. Madame Gour seemed to guess somehow what she wanted to know. '*Ton*

Papa?' she guessed. The child nodded and Madame Gour asked, 'Will her father be there – wherever you are taking her?'

Jacob made his excuses.

'Ah well,' tutted the neighbour, imparting the news to the child. 'I'm sure it can't be helped,' she said generously to Jacob. Then she turned to the child. 'I didn't know you had a grand-mother still living.' First in French, then English for his benefit.

The child shrugged; it appeared it was news to her as well. 'Where is she living?'

'Provence,' he answered.

'Ah, *bon*,' she said. 'It is a lovely part of the world.'

Jacob swallowed, feeling uncomfortable. Reminding himself that he was simply doing his job, and that meant not ques-tioning the way his employer chose to fill his time.

'Well, follow him, *cherie*,' she said, giving the child a last squeeze. 'To a new life, I hope it is happier.'

Jacob picked up the little girl's suitcase and steered her down the stairs.

The child seemed to hesitate, giving one last look at the stairs, her eyes drifting up past Madame Gour, perhaps to her old home. She bit her lip, sighed, then followed.

The child looked surprised when he directed her to the car parked on the street, opposite a florist. A group of well-heeled Parisian ladies, with mid-length dresses and fashionable bobs, was lingering nearby, perhaps to see who owned the flashy motor car.

The child however, seemed a little afraid. He guessed she'd never been in one before.

'It's perfectly safe,' he said as he opened the door and gestured for her to get inside.

She hesitated to get in, the knuckles on her small hands turning white as she clutched her suitcase to her chest.

He tried to take it from her but she shook her head. He

shrugged, opened the door and after a pause, she climbed in and sat down. He shut the door behind her.

The first part of their journey passed in relative silence. Broken only by Jacob, every so often forgetting that she couldn't understand him when he spoke.

They spent the night at a small establishment on the route, where the inn-keeper's wife came to his rescue, and took Elodie under her wing, helping to get her settled for the evening, while he retired to a cold room near the stable yard.

They started early the next morning; Elodie took her familiar seat and rested her head against the window while Jacob drove on.

As the countryside began to change, the sun intensified, and Jacob had to roll up his shirtsleeves and loosen his collar. He kept pointing out how beautiful it was as they passed rolling vineyards and fields full of wild pink and white flowers, villages perched on hilltops made of honey-coloured stone, full of sheep and other animals. But of course she didn't understand him at all, and she barely looked outside the window.

At last they arrived and he idled before pulling into the long sandy driveway. The house had blue shutters, like lidded eyes, and the crumbling stone walls appeared to be held together by the roots of lavender and roses which rambled all along the perimeter.

'It's nothing like Clairmont Manor,' he breathed, as she couldn't understand him and would not repeat it. 'But I'll tell you a secret, I think if I were in your shoes, I'd prefer this – it's charming.' He broke into a wide grin. *Charming* wasn't a description one could say about the manor house. Words used to describe that would include 'grand,' 'austere' and 'imposing'. And, admittedly, handsome.

'You will be all right here. I'm sure.' Perhaps he was trying to convince himself.

The child hugged her knitted doll to her chest and didn't

meet his eyes. She showed no curiosity about where they were. Jacob could guess that for her, without her mother, it didn't matter where she was. She closed her eyes, and leaned her head against the interior.

Jacob felt his heart go out to her; he'd never seen a child look so forlorn before. He wished he spoke her language, that he could give her some hope... but even then he wasn't sure how much it would help.

Jacob parked on the long gravel driveway, and the pair climbed out of the car. Shortly afterwards, a small, thin woman hurried out of the farmhouse, dressed in a blue house dress. She had silvery hair, cut into a bob and had on a frilly apron that was speckled with flour.

Jacob straightened his appearance, and doffed his cap. For a moment, he was afraid that she wasn't expecting him, until she rushed forward with a smile on her tanned face when she saw Elodie.

'*Ma petite*,' she exclaimed, enfolding the child in a hug. 'I finally get to meet you.'

At first Elodie stood like a statue. But then, as the older woman continued to hold her, she relaxed, breathing in the scent of flour and lilacs.

The woman looked up at Jacob, and smiled, then held out her hand, adorned with several silver rings.

'I am Marguerite Renaux,' she said in a pleasantly accented voice. 'Thank you so much for bringing my granddaughter to me.' Her brown eyes were warm, and he was grateful to see the kindness in them.

'It is my pleasure,' said Jacob, who meant it. Feeling, for the first time in two days, that he was doing the right thing. He handed Madame Renaux the child's suitcase, which she took in both of hers.

'You want to come in – have something to drink?' she invited. 'Or eat – I have *cassoulet*.'

He shook his head. 'Can't, I'm afraid, I'm expected.' He was due to take the car down to Cannes where his employers were spending the summer.

He hesitated, though, remembering just in time his promise to the child's neighbour, Madame Gour. He opened a small notebook he used to record the fuel mileage, turned over to a fresh page and wrote down the neighbour's name and address and then tore it off and handed it to Madame Renaux. Then he explained what the neighbour had said about the child being mute. Leaving out the part about the child holding on to her mother's body – no one wanted to have *that* image burned into their brain.

'She doesn't speak?'

He shook his head. 'Not a word, even in the two days we took to get here. I just thought you should know. The neighbour – Madame Gour – asked if you wouldn't mind letting her know how the child fares.'

'I will do that,' promised Marguerite.

Marguerite looked at the child as she watched the driver go with a lost expression on her face.

'He was a nice man?' she asked the child.

Elodie nodded.

'I thought so too.'

Elodie looked at her curiously, perhaps because she had spent so little time with him in comparison, and the old woman shrugged. 'The older you get the more you get a sense for these things.'

The girl just stared with those intense blue eyes of hers.

'So you are how old – nine?'

She shook her head, then waved a finger to indicate more.

'Ten?' guessed Marguerite.

She nodded.

'You can read, write?'

The child nodded again.

Marguerite had to bite her lip to suppress her emotion; of course, Brigitte, her late daughter, would have taught her herself.

Marguerite was glad to see that at least the child was responsive. She seemed just as curious about Marguerite as she was about her, as she reached towards Marguerite's face. If Jacob was still there he would have remarked upon it in wonder, considering how guarded she'd been for most of their time together.

Instinctively, Marguerite bent down and the child's fingers fluttered against her cheeks, like a butterfly, or a person reading a map.

'We look alike?' guessed Marguerite. 'Your maman and me?'

The child nodded, with a look of wonder in her eyes. Eyes that seemed to be on the verge of brimming over with tears.

Marguerite had to look away for a second, to surreptitiously wipe a corner of the apron beneath her eyes. When she looked back at the child, her face had cleared and she put on her bravest smile, then clapped her hands together. 'Do you like cake?'

The child frowned, then nodded.

'Well, come in, come in – I just started making it – we can finish it together.' Then Marguerite caught the child staring at her. 'What is it?'

The child shook her head. Even if she could, she wouldn't have known how to explain the feeling that had come over her, like getting into a bath after a long day, or like spotting familiar terrain after you had been stranded in a seemingly endless desert.

It was relief.

16

PROVENCE, 1926

Marguerite wasn't like the neighbour who had taken her to live
with her after her mother died. Madame Gour had poked and
prodded and tried to get her to talk – even once coming up
behind her to scare her into it.

Her grandmother just let her be sad. Perhaps because she
was sad too. But it was a different kind of sad.

Years later, Elodie would realise that it was because for
Marguerite the loss of her daughter had occurred many years
before – when Brigitte had run away from home, with a man
Marguerite knew was never going to marry her. He'd set her up
in a house in Paris after Elodie was born. It gave Marguerite no
satisfaction to know she'd been right.

That first night, she steered Elodie into the kitchen. A large
room with shiny copper pots hanging from hooks, a massive
blue range in the corner, and a large wooden table, covered in
plenty of scratches from years of use. Herbs on the windowsills
and sweeping views out across the vineyards. It was a cheerful,
welcoming place.

She put Elodie's suitcase by the door. 'We'll deal with that later,' she said with a wink, and then invited her to come wash her hands, so that together they could finish making the cake.

After Elodie had washed her hands, Marguerite measured out the ingredients, and then passed them to Elodie to add to a mixing bowl, showing her how to crack an egg on the side and distribute its contents without getting any shell inside. When Elodie tried, though, it slipped out of her fingers and fell onto the floor.

Marguerite laughed when she saw Elodie's wide, shocked eyes. She said, 'Don't you worry, *ma petite*. It's all part of being a cook – it's not a job for someone who doesn't like mess,' and she quickly scooped it up and away. 'Now the magic starts,' she said. 'While we wait for the cake to rise.'

Elodie found herself starting to smile, only to quickly frown. She shook her head violently, and went to sit at the long wooden table, her head in her hands.

'What's wrong – are you not feeling well?' Marguerite asked.

Elodie, of course, said nothing. It felt wrong for her to feel like this, she thought. Like she was betraying Maman. How could she feel, even for a moment, that everything was going to be all right when Maman was dead? She wiped her eyes.

Marguerite put a hand on her shoulder and then guessed what might be the problem, cursing herself. She had wanted to make her first night here special, she was clearly trying too hard. 'You miss your maman?'

Elodie nodded.

'You think maybe it's wrong to have fun when she's not here?'

Elodie bit her lip, then closed her eyes and nodded.

'Did she like it when you had fun?'

Elodie looked up with a frown, but didn't answer.

'I think she liked it, no?'

Elodie nodded, slightly.

'I think she'd want that for you, *ma petite*. You know, my daughter and I didn't have the easiest relationship, but there was one thing I could never say about her.'

Elodie looked at her in anticipation.

Marguerite pulled a chair out and came to sit next to Elodie. 'Brigitte would never want anyone to feel bad. If you're sad, you're sad, that's OK. But it's OK if sometimes you feel a little better – it's like...' She paused for thought, then pointed outside. 'See that cloud there?'

Elodie looked, her brows knitted.

'Well, today it was a beautiful sunny day, right? But when that passes over the house it'll be a bit shady for a while. It will move on and the rest of the evening will still be sunny until nightfall. It's the same with your feelings. You feel sad she's gone, right? But you don't have to be sad all the day – for you, it will be the opposite maybe, a bit of sun coming to take the place of those clouds. That's why I thought we could do some baking. So you can feel a bit of sunshine while you remember her at the same time.'

Elodie nodded. She hadn't thought of it like that. To be honest, her life lately had been nothing but cloud. But she understood what Marguerite meant. Maman wouldn't want her to fight being happy, she'd always tried to kiss her tears away.

'Did you know that she used to love baking when she was a child?'

Elodie looked up at her in surprise. Then shook her head.

'Oh yes. Loved it. I think it would make her very happy that you're learning to bake.'

Elodie hadn't considered that. It made her feel a bit better, to think that.

The honey cake was light and airy, and Marguerite cut her a thick slice. Elodie managed a few bites. She listened as her grandmother told her what they'd be doing over the next few months, and how it wasn't quite decided what was happening with her father – if he was going to come collect her or not this year. The thought that she might still move on, yet again, and have her future unsettled, caused the anxiety to rush up and choke her, and she thought she might be sick. She put her piece of cake down, swallowing heavily. Everything was so uncertain. It was all too much. Her head started to swarm.

Marguerite watched helplessly as the child sprang from her chair and brought the cake up in the sink. She came forward to stroke her hair, moving it away from her face. She felt the child's forehead, and rubbed her back.

'Have you been feeling ill – should I call the doctor?'

Elodie shook her head.

'I think I should – you must be coming down with something.'

Elodie shook her head again, then waved her hands shakily.

'I don't understand,' said Marguerite.

Elodie sighed and tried to explain without words, patting her heart, and her head, which just seemed to make Marguerite panic more.

'You have a condition – your heart?'

Elodie sighed once more, she was feeling tired and she wished her stupid mouth would just work. She opened her lips, but only a puff of air came through. Then she held her fists together in front of her face and squeezed like she was stressed.

'I don't understand. You're angry?'

She shook her head, flapped her hands wildly, tapped her heart twice, then clenched her fists in front of her face again.

'You... stressed?' guessed Marguerite.

She nodded.

It took a moment for Marguerite to understand and she felt awful. 'It happens when you are anxious,' she realised. Feeling worse – it was no doubt from her prattling on nervously about the girl's father and her living arrangements. She wanted to be honest, but now she realised that it wasn't the best time.

She'd wanted to raise Elodie as her own, but he hadn't quite agreed. He'd made promises to her daughter, Brigitte, to look out for the child, and it seemed he was reluctant to dishonour that memory. He'd loved Brigitte in his own way, it seemed. If he hadn't been married already, he may well have married her. Which only made things harder for him at home. The fact that he'd betrayed his marriage by having an affair with a French nurse, which had resulted in an illegitimate child conceived during the war, was a contentious issue between them.

He'd made it clear to Marguerite that he desired to have the child brought up English and this was his eventual intention; however, for the time being, he was willing to let her recuperate with Marguerite until arrangements could be made – legally, because he had claimed and provided for the child while Brigitte was alive, he was her guardian. Marguerite had no rights, something that caused her pain. She wished, as she had wished so many times over the years, that her stubborn, beautiful and headstrong daughter would have just come home to her. But the last fight they'd had, when Marguerite had warned her that he would never leave his wife, had opened a rift that the younger woman was unwilling to mend, even, or especially, when her mother was proved right. It hurt Marguerite so much that she hadn't come around when she fell ill. But Brigitte was like that: stubborn, and unforgiving right to the end.

'I think it is bed for you. Too much information too soon – I'm afraid that is always my way, but let's take it slowly from now on, *d'accord*? Nothing is decided, and tomorrow we can have an uneventful day.'

Elodie nodded. Slow sounded good, as did uneventful. She just wanted to sleep, to dream a dreamless sleep.

Marguerite poured her a glass of water, picked up the suit-case she'd left by the door and then guided Elodie to a room down the corridor that overlooked the vineyard. Outside the late-summer sun was finally beginning to set, in shades of cerise and apricot.

There was a single bed with a pale linen duvet cover and beneath the window a large jug full of dried lavender made the air fresh and clean. It was only moments after Elodie sank beneath the sheets, tired from travel and the emotional toll of so much change, she fell into a heavy slumber and got her wish, as no nightmares disturbed her rest.

17

In the morning, Marguerite woke Elodie up with a cup of tea and asked, 'You know how to swim?'

The sun was golden, even at this time of day, so much brighter than in Paris. It fell across her bed, making her feel languid and drowsy, which made a pleasant change from the anxiety that had been her constant companion since Maman had died. That and the nightmares.

Elodie rubbed her eyes, sat up and then slowly shook her head. Her hair was even knottier now, listing to the side, a weaver's nest that has been deemed unsatisfactory and half demolished now.

'Would you like to?'

Elodie considered for a moment, then scrunched her face and shoulders as if to say, *I'm not sure.*

'Well, if you do, it will have to be in your underthings today, but tonight I could make you a bathing costume.'

Silently the older woman vowed that part of the day's activities would include tackling the child's hair. With hedge-clippers, if necessary.

Still, Elodie looked undecided.

Marguerite shrugged. 'Up to you – I did say we could take it slow. But I figured a little paddle in the river, perhaps with a nice *pain au chocolat* after, wouldn't be fast... Or would you prefer to stay in your bedroom all day?'

Elodie shook her head, quickly. She had a weakness for chocolate.

'A little fresh air and gentle exercise will be good for you. You'll see.'

Elodie shrugged. It did sound nice. The trouble was that despite what Marguerite said, it still felt wrong to her to be doing anything that might make her forget Maman. But Maman, she knew, would tell her to go swim, so that's what she would do.

She swung her legs out of the bed, and still sitting, had a sip of tea. She pulled a face and set it down.

'Would you prefer water?'

She shook her head: what she'd prefer was coffee. But she knew that some people disapproved – Maman had thought it was amusing so she'd allowed it, but some of her friends had been shocked. Elodie knew that it was perhaps best not to test those waters just yet, but even if she did, she didn't have the words. She'd tried over the past few weeks, but nothing would come, her throat felt tight and sore, perhaps from the constant scream that had lodged there, unreleased, since her maman had died.

'Now I know you don't talk, just yet,' said Marguerite. 'And that's fine. In your own time, *d'accord*? But when you do I would like for you to call me Grand-mère, all right?'

Elodie nodded.

They walked down to the little river that flowed through the bottom of the garden. Elodie dipped a toe in, then immediately brought it out again.

It was cold!

Grand-mère took off her house dress and waded into the water in a red bathing costume that came up to her knees. She was thin, with strong arms, and tanned skin. 'Come on, don't be a chicken,' she said to Elodie.

Elodie hesitated then followed, putting both feet into the shallow water, wincing at the temperature again.

'Hold out your hands,' said Grand-mère, and Elodie did as instructed, while Grand-mère took them instantly, helping her to wade a little deeper, while her legs trembled with fright and cold. Grand-mère waited, making sure she could stand easily.

'The best thing to do,' said Grand-mère, 'is get completely wet, fast,' and she let go of Elodie's hands for a moment, before she ducked below the surface. She came up gasping, but said, 'Ooh, it's lovely!'

Elodie looked doubtful and Grand-mère laughed. 'You do the same.'

Elodie shook her head violently.

'Come on, I'll keep hold of your hand, just bend your knees, yes, like that, and fold yourself down. We'll do it together.'

Elodie did as instructed, sinking down onto her haunches until her neck was submerged. 'Now push up with your feet and lie back.'

There was another violent shake of her head.

'Look, I'll keep hold of you,' said Grand-mère, coming behind her and resting her hand on her back. Elodie swallowed, then lifted her feet, and automatically her body started to rise. She panicked, lost her footing, but Grand-mère caught her, before she could fall forward, helping to steady her onto her feet.

'Let's try again. You almost had it.'

Elodie looked at her doubtfully but did as instructed. This time, as her feet lifted up and she leaned backwards, she felt Grand-mère's hands on her back, supporting her.

'Just lean back, relax. Just float.'

Elodie felt her strong arms beneath her and she felt her body relaxing. It was quiet with her ears beneath the water. Above her head the summer sun dappled through the willows, they waved their long fingers along the banks, and as she stared at the blue sky above, her hands skated the water and she felt again that sense of peace.

Afterwards, when they had gathered their things, Elodie wrapped up in a large fluffy towel that had been washed and rewashed often, she found herself feeling hungry, ravenously so.

'Works up an appetite, right?' said Grand-mère, laughing as she heard the audible noises coming from Elodie's belly. 'Come on. Let's go make an omelette.'

Elodie's eyes widened and she nodded, offering a small grin, like a peep of blue sky.

'You like them?' said Grand-mère.

Elodie nodded.

'Good, let's do that, then. Then after breakfast we are going to tackle this,' she said, laying a hand on Elodie's hair.

Elodie pulled a face.

'Don't worry, I have a trick to get out the tangles,' said Grand-mère, as they entered the farmhouse kitchen and she began to gather the ingredients together.

'Crack the eggs into the bowl for me,' said Grand-mère and Elodie began, gently cracking the shell against the side, and then opening it in two like she'd been shown the day before. A tiny piece of shell fell into the mixture, and Grand-mère showed her how to remove it with the shell, by scooping it out. 'It acts almost like a magnet, it's odd,' she said. 'Tomorrow when I open the restaurant you will get to see a real kitchen.'

Elodie looked confused. She opened her palms as if to say, *Isn't this real?*

'Oh, of course, but this is much smaller.' She took the whisk and pointed. Elodie's eyes followed where she indicated out of the window, where she could see in the distance a barn-shaped building made out of stone.

'That's my restaurant,' said Grand-mère. 'It's a simple place, really, serving the locals around here. I only open for lunch in the week. When the old owner passed away, I decided to take over. I am not a trained cook, but I figured, well, I am not dead yet, my husband is gone, so I don't exactly have to ask anyone's permission, the vineyards are managed by Monsieur Blanchet, and so what must I do with my time... knit?'

Elodie grinned.

After their breakfast, Grand-mère combed out all the tangles in Elodie's hair by the warmth of the range in the kitchen. There was something soothing about her hands on her head. It reminded Elodie of Maman, she even smelled similar.

In the evening, Grand-mère cut up some old material and began to create a swimming costume for her, in shades of dark navy and red. The sewing machine whirred as the summer rain beat a tattoo against the glass, and when Elodie went to bed, she dreamed of the river, where she floated, the gentle current carrying her beneath the willow trees where she could see the sun and the sky and the birds. She stayed that way for ages, until her fingers began to grow soft and webs began to grow and slowly ever so slowly she began to turn into a fish and swim all the way to the sea, where her mother was waiting for her and pointing to what looked like oysters but were in fact small cakes.

Early the next morning, Grand-mère took her to the village. It was called Lamarin, perched on a hilltop, where honey-coloured stone houses spooled around it with shutters in shades of pale blue and cherry red. It was surrounded by a lavender ocean, with fields as far as the eye could see of purple flowers. It was breathtaking. She was shocked that she hadn't seen it the day she'd arrived. She'd been so focused on not looking out the car window.

They were there to visit the local market, a bustling place in the village full of stalls, from cheesemongers to people selling rag rugs and even chickens. Grand-mère was only interested in the fresh food. Fresh tomatoes, melons so ripe they made your mouth water, crisp salad speckled with water, and just-caught mackerel from Marseille. She ordered several things, which she asked to be delivered to the restaurant.

'The first lesson in good cooking,' she said, 'is to use what is in season. It is the base layer. Use only what is of the best quality – you cannot fix bad quality with a sauce. It is like a woman trying to disguise who she is with make-up, instead of using it to enhance what she already has.'

Elodie's eyes widened.

Later, Grand-mère took her to her restaurant.

It was small; a converted brick building that once held pigs, so Grand-mère said when they walked back, their hands laden with string bags full of produce.

'It's not fancy. But I like it.'

Elodie liked it too. As the morning wore on, she helped by staying out of the way, watching with fascination as her grandmother's hands danced as they chopped and whisked and created mouth-watering dishes.

By mid-morning the customers had started to queue outside and Elodie watched as her grandmother wrote down the specials on a chalkboard outside. She explained that because she was only one person and didn't have staff, she only served one option for lunch, which she wrote outside on a board – that way if somebody didn't want it they could go somewhere else.

She raised an eyebrow. 'But, of course, no one dares.'

It was true, Elodie saw, as most people walked straight past the sign, not bothering to check what was on offer. She realised then that here in rural France, food was taken just as seriously as within Paris. What's more, they liked to be surprised. And over the course of that first week she witnessed as her grand-mother fed many of the local farmers, shop-keepers and wives from the village and its surrounds. There were a lot of people who seemed curious about the little girl who had come to live with Marguerite Renaux. Some remembered her mother, Brigitte, some, especially the older ones, came forward to squeeze her cheeks and to tell her how much she looked like her.

Elodie learned fast when to disappear when one of them started towards her with a look in their eye, their fingers like a set of lobster pincers. When Marguerite asked her what she was doing one day, watching as she began slowly to back away, Elodie pinched her thumb and forefinger together and then subtly indicated an older woman advancing towards them, fingers snapping.

In realisation, Marguerite had to stop herself from breaking out into giggles.

Soon life in Lamarin took on a rhythm; they got up early, and went swimming in the river before they headed out for the day. By the end of that first week, Elodie was able to do a pretty decent doggy-paddle, and they would lie on their backs, treading water, watching the light filter from the vast willow trees.

Afterwards they often ate their breakfast as a picnic, while they warmed themselves on the riverbank, lying on towels on top of a large green blanket. The food was simple but delicious. The pastries weren't as fancy as the ones from Paris, or as deli-cate, but they tasted just as good and it was amazing how wonderful a hardboiled egg could taste after a vigorous swim. Or how good a simple fresh baguette was on their way home from the bakery. Elodie found it was customary to break off the tip and eat it on the way home.

She found, too, that life in Provence was very different to Paris. It was slower here, and things were savoured more. Here everyone greeted you with a smile.

As the weeks passed, Elodie learned how to cut an onion, how to boil potatoes, how to cook an omelette herself. And soon, being in a kitchen with her grand-mère, with the wireless on, swaying along as the older woman sang, she realised that at some point she'd stopped reprimanding herself for enjoying herself, and the pain of losing Maman, while still hard, was no longer quite as raw.

18

Elodie found her voice on a Saturday afternoon, while Grand-mère was having a coffee with her friend at a stone café in the village with white roses rambling along the walls. Elodie had wandered outside, around the corner towards the village green, bored, and found a group of men playing a game of *pétanque* in the warm summer sun, their shirt sleeves rolled up as they threw the little ball into the dust.

Along the perimeter of this court were other men, farmers and shopkeepers, some with large bellies, most with moustaches and berets, all standing around and watching. Elodie got the scent of aniseed, as she watched them sip small thimblefuls of cloudy liquid. She stared at their tiny glasses curiously.

'It's *pastis*,' said a boy of around ten or eleven. He had nut brown skin with light brown hair and eyes, and a smile that tilted a little to one side, like he was letting her in on a secret. On his shoulder sat a crow who cocked its head at her curiously. She stared at the crow, then back at the boy.

'Tastes a bit like liquorice—'

'Liquorice?' she said, only to realise with slight shock that she had said it out loud.

He nodded. 'From the aniseed. You want to try some?'

Her eyes widened and he grinned. 'Just a sip. I'll ask Papa, just wait.'

He went off to speak with an older man with dark hair and a very wide moustache, and soon he came back with a small glass full of the pale liquid and handed it to her. The crow travelled down his arm, as if to have a better look at her.

'This is Huginn,' he said, introducing the bird.

'Huginn?'

'I named him after Odin's ravens.'

Elodie didn't know who Odin was. But she knew this wasn't a raven. 'But it's a crow.'

'I know. I had two roost in my garden so I named them. Muninn was his mate but she's left to roost somewhere else, she found another partner. Was a bit of a drama, actually, poor Huginn was quite upset.'

Elodie looked at the bird in sympathy.

'Go on, take a sip,' encouraged the strange boy.

She took a tiny sip, then coughed. 'It's strong, but sweet.' Odd, she thought.

'Do you like it?'

'Do you only get to play that if you do?' she asked, seeing all the men playing and sipping their thimblefuls of *pastis*.

The boy laughed. 'Maybe. Can you play?'

She shook her head. 'I do like this, though,' she said.

'Well, that settles it. Huginn and I will teach you how to play *pétanque*, if you like.'

'That's what it's called – the game?'

He nodded. 'Come on,' he said, then picked up a spare *pétanque* ball from near his father.

She followed after him and the bird, who had settled back on his shoulder for a moment, before deciding to fly off and investigate some interesting food on the other side of the verge.

'He'll be back,' said the boy, pointing out a small patch of grass that was away from the others. Then he went over the rules of the game, which was pretty much just trying to get the ball to go as far as it could and then marking that distance from the player who'd gone before.

Elodie could see why they could drink liquor and play now.

Later, when Marguerite came to find her – accompanied by the boy's father, Monsieur Blanchet, who it turned out managed Grand-mère's vineyard – they found the pair of them playing and laughing and for the first time she heard Elodie's voice as she accused the boy of cheating, but there was a smile on her face.

'No, see, I'll use my left arm – as it is the weaker one,' he said.

'How can I tell if that's true?' she asked and he lifted his shirt sleeve to show her his arm and hand which was slightly smaller and looked stiff. 'I had polio when I was little,' he explained. 'It works fine but it's not as strong as the other.'

Elodie, who didn't know what polio was, touched it, softly, then nodded. 'D'accord, that seems fair,' then she stopped, 'unless it will hurt?'

'No, it's fine.'

Marguerite swallowed.

The boy's father looked at her curiously, and she ran a quick finger beneath her tearing-up eyes. 'Forgive me, monsieur, just this is the first time she's spoken since she came to live with me. I think your son, Jacques, might be sent from the fairies.'

His face softened and his lips twitched. 'We always say the birds, as he is always with them.'

They watched as a crow came to settle on his shoulder. The boy encouraged the crow to hop from his shoulder to hers. Elodie's smile when the crow landed on her made Marguerite catch her breath.

'I was afraid she wouldn't make any friends this summer.'

'Ah well, Jacques will make friends wherever he goes, don't

you worry. It'll be nice for one of them to be human for a change though,' he admitted.

As the long summer days wore on, Elodie's limbs turned tanned and strong from the gentle river swims and she began to put on some weight from the rich wholesome fare. Colour had returned to her cheeks and her long blonde hair was glossy.

Marguerite found that once Elodie started speaking she didn't stop, rambling off a mile a minute about all the things that she had been dying to know about.

She would enter the restaurant kitchen like a whirlwind, carrying bunches of herbs, picked from the *potager*, Marguerite's vegetable garden, and demand the names for everything, a large smile on her face.

'This one, Grand-mère,' she said, brandishing a twig, which she parried beneath the older woman's nose like a knight with a sword, only to sniff it herself. 'Isn't it heavenly? What is it?'

Grand-mère, becoming used to these flights of fancy, smiled. But before she could answer a crow tapped on the window and Elodie looked up to see Huginn, and behind him, the boy. 'Jacques!' she said.

'It's lemon thyme,' said Grand-mère. 'It works really well with lentil stews.'

But the child was already out the door, and running after the crow and the boy who was waiting for her.

Marguerite rolled her eyes but she was smiling.

'Elodie!' cried Grand-mère. 'Be back here at noon, to serve.'

'*D'accord!*' she called, and Marguerite laughed as she watched the two head off. The old cat, Pattou, who used to belong to the former owner of the restaurant, padded inside and Marguerite said, 'We've been abandoned. I don't suppose you want to help peel the potatoes?'

In answer, Pattou went to go sleep on the windowsill.

. . .

Jacques brandished the butterfly net as he explained. 'So we're going to catch them and put them in a jar with holes,' he said, as Huginn hopped from his shoulder and walked down his arm to get a better look. His look was so human and curious that it seemed he was thinking the same thing she was... and was just as taken aback.

'You're going to *kill* them?'

She couldn't disguise the shock in her voice.

'No,' he said, giving her a *what do you take me for* sort of look, his mouth in his familiar half smile. 'I'm going to *draw* them,' he said, taking out a sketchbook from his satchel, along with a canvas roll that had slots for his pencils. 'But sometimes that does require catching them so I can get it right. After I've done a quick sketch and made a note of the colouring, I release them. Sometimes they linger and you don't have to catch them at all... but mostly they fly off just as soon as you look at them.'

'Oh,' she said, breathing out in relief. It wasn't so much that she was uncomfortable at the thought of killing insects, she could do it if she had to... thinking of a wasp she'd killed instinctively when it launched itself at Pattou a few days earlier. It had been the idea that Jacques, who appeared to love nature so fiercely, would hurt something so innocent, that made her feel that way.

It was hard catching butterflies, she found, especially if you didn't want to kill them. You had to be careful not to damage them.

'Whatever you do – don't touch their wings,' he warned. 'They're so delicate, they can tear easily.'

On her first attempt down by the river, when they spotted a small pale blue specimen, which Jacques said was called a Provence Chalk-hill Blue, he muttered something else in a different language. '*Polyommatus hispanus.*'

'Pollytomato hiccup? What does that mean?'

He laughed, then said it slowly, '*Polyommatus hispanus* – it's the Latin name. That's the scientific name – they always use the Latin name for the natural world.'

'Why do they use Latin for scientific names?' she asked, and he explained.

'It's to simplify things – which sounds odd, because no one speaks Latin anymore – but that's sort of why it works. So many plants and animals have lots of different names, but if we have a common name for things it's understood all around the world. For instance, in German – butterfly is *Schmetterling*.'

'It is? How do you know that?'

'My mother was from Lorraine, it's on the border – her family spoke both German and French at home. She taught me the language when I was little.'

Elodie spotted the butterfly then, just off a patch of wild-flowers. She chased it, falling over onto the side of the riverbank, and the butterfly went flying off.

When she stood up at last, the mud was covering her all the way to her waist.

Jacques helped her out, but couldn't help giggling, especially when she narrowed her eyes at him, only to have her shoe get stuck in the mud and for her to fall onto her backside, and she joined in.

They laughed even louder when one of the villagers walked past and gave them both a second look.

When she finally got free and they were sitting beneath one of the large willows, Jacques opened up his sketchbook and did a rough sketch of the butterfly from memory, making a note of its hue. She saw him write in pencil that it was paler than the typical ones he'd seen. When he was finished, she rubbed her hands on the grass to get rid of any mud, and asked if she could have a look. He passed it over.

'These are wonderful,' she exclaimed. The sketchbook was

full of nature drawings, illustrations and observations; it was dominated by birds.

'So many birds,' she exclaimed, then laughed aloud when she saw that many of the birds didn't have fancy Latin names at all!

'Geoff?' she asked, grinning widely. 'Aimee? Those can't be their scientific names, can they?'

He grinned in response. 'No, but they are all friends, you see,' and he explained about how his mother had taught him how to make friends with birds by creating a welcoming place in their garden and home.

It was the second time he'd mentioned her, but Elodie was sure that she had never seen her back at the house.

'Is she—?'

'She died,' he said, nodding. A shadow passed over his eyes. 'It was a year and a half ago.'

He took the sketchbook from her, and then flipped the pages until he came across a coloured illustration of a woman with long brown hair like his. She was sitting in their cottage garden, and all around her were birds. A blue tit was sitting on her lap. Next to the picture, he had recorded a poem.

'It was my mother's favourite. By the German-Jewish poet, Heinrich Heine.'

He said the words in German, then translated it for her into French:

'There lies the heat of summer
On your cheek's lovely art:
There lies the cold of winter
Within your little heart.
That will change, beloved,
The end not as the start!
Winter on your cheek then,
Summer in your heart.'

Elodie touched it. 'It's beautiful. I didn't know she died, Jacques, I'm sorry.'

He nodded. 'When I heard that you'd lost your mother too, I came to find you that day outside the café in the village.'

'What, why?' she breathed.

'Because, I thought, I don't know... maybe I could help, somehow.'

She swallowed, touched more than she could say. 'You have,' she said.

'I'm glad.'

There were still times that she woke up in tears because in her dreams she was still with Maman, but because of Grandmère and Jacques, it felt like she could live with the pain, which was always there; the small winter that was always in her heart.

'When did it become better for you – does it get better?' she asked.

He picked up a pebble and played with it. Huginn called out to Jacques, then went to scratch in the ground. They saw him happily unearth a worm and gobble it up, and watched him for a moment.

'It took a long time. Papi helped, but he was grieving too. I found being busy was good, I created a garden for her full of her favourite flowers, with areas for the birds. I spent most of my time watching them, spending time getting to know them; I didn't really want to be around humans, apart from Papi. Well, until I met you,' he said, almost shyly.

She looked away, blushing slightly. Glad that she could at least help him too.

19

A few days later, Jacques showed her the garden he'd created for his mother. It was to the side of the farmhouse he shared with his father. There was a meadow full of pink and purple wildflowers, interspersed with white and cerise roses, and everywhere there were pillars and posts with bird baths and nesting boxes. Off to the side was a bench, which they sat down on.

'Papi helped me make the boxes, to help the birds roost,' he said.

Huginn flew from his shoulder to go and investigate one of the bird feeders.

'I've never known anyone who loves birds the way you do,' she replied. 'To be honest until I met you I never thought of them having personalities like Huginn.'

'They're all so different. I'm going to study them professionally one day. I want to be like Heinrich Gätke, he wrote my favourite book, *Heligoland, an Ornithological Observatory.* He was a painter who went to go live on the North Sea island, Heligoland, in 1841 and while he was there he became fascinated with birds, realising it was an important area for bird migration. I'd like to go there and study at the Institute of Avian Research when I'm older.'

She touched a poppy, felt its soft folds, and said, 'You won't look after the vines like your father?'

He shook his head, then pulled a face. 'No. I'm not looking forward to breaking that news to him.'

Her eyes widened. 'He doesn't know that's what you want?'

He shook his head. 'He *does*. But he also thinks it's a phase I'm going to grow out of,' he sighed. 'He's always talking about "one day when you're older and you run the farm..." I've tried to make him see that this might not happen but,' he shrugged, 'it's like he doesn't want to hear.'

Elodie didn't know what to say except, 'He'll want you to be happy, though.'

Jacques sighed. 'I don't know. One day I'll have to confront him on that, but not today.' Then he looked at her, raised a brow and said, '*Pétanque?*'

She nodded. *Pétanque* was always a good idea as far as she was concerned.

As the summer moved to autumn, they spent most of their afternoons together, going for long rambling walks often accompanied by Huginn, though sometimes other birds visited too, ones that Jacques had helped over the years, like a great tit named Charlie, and Sofia, a starling, whose wing he'd once helped set.

Elodie told him about Paris, and how the city never slept and what it was like living with her maman, who had many friends and used to visit cafés and attend parties and was so much fun. 'I see Grand-mère in her – that fun side.'

Though her mother's fun side, she would realise later, was much wilder, a streak of rebellion that bordered on recklessness. But ten-year-old Elodie just remembered the fun, the parties, the late nights, the fashionable, beautiful people. Grand-mère was fun in a more earthly way.

One winter's morning, as the Mistral, the famous north-westerly wind that blew in from the south, made its presence known, Elodie was snuggling in the farmhouse kitchen next to the warm range with Pattou the cat on her lap. His whiskers twitched in his sleep, and she was trying to resist the urge to feel the soft pads beneath his paws.

'I have something for you,' said Grand-mère, coming in from the living room with something behind her back and her lips curling up at one side, like she was imparting a secret.

'What?' asked Elodie.

'This,' said Grand-mère, showing her a small book that was covered in red-and-white check fabric. It was bound with a red ribbon.

'What is it?' asked Elodie in surprise.

'Open it.'

Elodie opened it and saw that on the first page it said, 'Recipes'. Below this was an inscription from Grand-mère:

For Ma Petite, with love. Here's to a life filled with good food and company, for you will be richer than a king with these to dine on.

When she flicked through the book, though, it was full of blank pages.

She looked up in surprise. 'But – it's empty?'

Grand-mère grinned. 'Yes, for now. Well, I have had some news – it's not official yet – so let's not get carried away but it does seem likely that you will be getting to stay with me for a while longer.'

Elodie's smile widened. She wanted nothing more. While

the idea of her father was intriguing – she'd heard stories of him when she was little, stories of a handsome, dashing soldier – even in her mother's colourful prose she couldn't quite disguise the image of someone who was aloof, and slightly cold; an image that had regrettably only strengthened after he'd failed to come collect her after her mother's death...

She wanted to meet him, but the truth was, she loved it here.

'I thought that since you'll be staying longer, perhaps I could start teaching you, officially. So that perhaps when you're older, well, who knows? You could take over or—'

'Work with you?'

Grand-mère grinned. 'Yes.'

'I'd like that,' said Elodie, eyes shining.

Grand-mère was serious about teaching her to cook.

'So when I was young, I learned the way a lot of young women learn – from my mother who learned from hers and so on. But what I'm going to do differently with you is start you off the way I learned when I went to work for the old owner of the restaurant, chef Du Val.'

Elodie did a double-take. 'You went to work for the former owner?'

'Oh yes. He was getting older, you see, and needed more help and I knew about home cooking but nothing... professional. He gave me an education in the process. What I discovered, though, was that a lot of what I knew – sort of by instinct and years of cooking – had a reason, an explanation. Like knowing instinctively when a dish needed something acidic, or salty or more aromatic to round out a flavour, you see?'

Elodie did not, but she nodded anyway.

'So the first thing to being a good chef is what – do you think?'

'An imagination?' Elodie guessed, thinking of what she'd just said, and also about how her grandmother could turn simple everyday produce into dozens of tasty dishes.

'Yes, I suppose,' she said with a laugh. 'But what I was going to say is that the first thing to know is a little boring, but necessary – it's called *mise en place* – everything in place. This is about ensuring you have everything you need before you begin. Gathering your ingredients and your tools. So today we're going to make a simple country stew, something to warm the bones. Follow me.'

Elodie followed Grand-mère into the pantry where she gathered vegetables from her store, choosing onion, carrots, sweet potato and tinned tomatoes, and from the shelves, dried lentils, and herbs that she'd dried in the summer from her *potager* – thyme, basil and oregano – and laid them all out on the large wooden table. When Elodie got to work dicing an onion, Grand-mère exclaimed in awe as she tucked her thumb away and chose the biggest knife on display to chop faster and more efficiently. 'How did you know to do that?' she asked, rushing forward to still her small hand.

'I watch you do it every day, Grand-mère,' said Elodie.

Grand-mère grinned. 'Touché. But watching is not the same as doing.' She raised an index finger, and showed Elodie a patch of scar tissue. 'I got this from going too fast – so go slow so that you can go fast.' This was one of Grand-mère's life mottos, she was to find.

'What does that mean?'

'It means slow and steady wins the race – whereas if you go too fast and say, slice a finger off, well, you'll end up taking twice as long, you see?'

Elodie grinned. 'But I could just be fast and careful.'

'I'd appreciate just careful, first.'

Elodie shrugged, though she vowed one day she'd chop even faster than Grand-mère.

By the time the rich lentil stew was perfuming the air, rousing Pattou from his slumber, Grand-mère was making plans for them to make the five basic sauces, and telling Elodie about the famous French chef, Escoffier, who had created them all. She ruffled her blonde hair and said, '*Ma petite*, you'll be the best chef in Provence, in no time.'

20

Couchon, the large spotted pig that was the prize truffle hunter of Monsieur Blanchet, shot off like a bloodhound, with a squeal of such infinite excitement and interest it was almost indecent to witness. Jacques and Elodie laughed as they followed through the forest. It was barely dawn, and the only light that guided them came from the lingering moon.

Spring was on its way, but it was still cold, and billows of steam blew out of their mouths when they breathed.

Beneath the vast oaks, Elodie's booted feet trod on thick rotting leaves, slick and wet, as the water and mud oozed beneath them.

Mirabeau, the smaller black pig, raced to join Couchon at the base of an enormous tree. The animals pressed their snouts into the leaves and shivered with glee. Monsieur Blanchet yelped, then shoved Couchon out of the way, scooping up a truffle the size of Elodie's fist and placing it into the waiting basket.

There was a cheer from Jacques and Huginn, who made a shrill cawing sound above as he flew.

Monsieur Blanchet broke off a piece of sausage for the pig

as a reward, then gave it a tantalising sniff of the truffle, and a lusty smack on its rear so that it tore off towards a new likely spot.

It was an honour to be here, Elodie knew. The truffle hunters were a closeted tribe, keeping their secret places full of the black gold to themselves. To be safe, Jacques had kept his hands over her eyes when they came to fetch her in their van. Only once they'd driven for several miles and had arrived in a dense forest did Monsieur Blanchet give his son the signal to release her to look.

She had no idea where they were, but it did still look like they were within the Luberon, an area that contained her village amongst others, as well as areas of natural beauty like forests and mountainous regions, though she couldn't say for certain.

Soon she was helping Couchon and the others, pushing away the great pigs to get at the truffles which were placed into Monsieur Blanchet's basket.

By the time the sun had risen, they all had smiles that stretched for miles. Jacques' hands once more were covering her eyes on the return journey, and Elodie could smell the scent of the truffle on his fingers.

She shifted in her seat and Jacques momentarily removed his hands. 'Ah-tut-tut, keep them on, I can't have your Grand-mère out here stealing my truffles for her restaurant.'

Elodie grinned.

'Aha! Because she would, wouldn't she?' said Monsieur Blanchet, seeing her grin from the rear-view mirror.

Elodie shrugged. It was likely. Grand-mère was very nice, but she was a bit of a bloodhound when it came to good produce.

In her pocket, for her trouble, Monsieur Blanchet had given her a small truffle the size of two buttons; it shocked her to discover that this could fetch well over ten francs. She had no intention, though, of selling it.

'So what are you going to do with that truffle?' asked Monsieur Blanchet when he at last said it was OK for Jacques to release his fingers as they were nearing Grand-mère's house.

'I am going to surprise Grand-mère with breakfast in bed. I'm going to make an omelette.'

He kissed his fingers to his lips. 'Perfect,' he said.

When they pulled up outside, Elodie saw that the front door was open, and she could see Grand-mère was already awake. She rushed up the drive, as Monsieur Blanchet and Jacques trundled away in their van with the prize pigs who had earned their breakfast.

Elodie waved, then raced inside, her smile wide, as she fetched the truffle from her pocket, speaking a mile a minute in French. 'Grand-mère!' she hollered. 'Truffle hunting is the best. I promised on my life not to reveal Monsieur Blanchet's secret locations so he could let me follow his prize pigs, Couchon and Mirabeau, around – oh, it was so wonderful. I have a truffle, my very own one, can you believe it? I thought I'd make us an omelette for breakfast, what do you think?'

'I think *not*,' exclaimed a shocked, masculine voice in heavily accented French.

Elodie blanched, turning around slowly. Just off the hall, in the living room to her right, stood a tall man with dark blond hair and very blue eyes. Next to him was an elegantly dressed woman in a beautiful yellow gown. Her hair was like something out of a magazine, coiled around her ear in perfect waves. She put a cautionary arm on his hand and said something to him in another language. He shook his head, and turned to glare at Marguerite.

'Is this what she has been up to – screaming like a banshee

in the house, chasing after some farmer's pigs – and *cooking* like some, some common servant?' His eyes were bulging out of his head.

'Yes,' said Grand-mère simply. 'I make no apologies for our life here. This is how things are. You knew that when you met Brigitte.'

He looked utterly furious.

The other woman looked at Elodie. She didn't smile; what she saw seemed to cause her pain. 'Clairmont eyes,' she whispered.

She had, however, said it in another language, so Elodie did not understand.

The man looked suddenly bashful as he glanced at the other woman, and he spoke to her again in another language. His tone was soothing, conciliatory, gone was the display of anger. The other woman did not look soothed. Far from it. Her face seemed like it had been cut from marble.

Elodie looked from her to the man and then to her grand-mother. It was beginning to dawn on her who this was, and the realisation – far from bringing her excitement – was filling her with dread.

Marguerite stepped forward. 'Elodie, this is your father,' she said in French, confirming the worst.

He was looking at her like she was a kind of nasty insect, one he didn't particularly want to deal with.

She flinched, and crept closer to Grand-mère.

The woman said something in English, addressing Elodie, who did not understand a word. She stared. 'Pardon?'

The woman's eyes widened. 'Did you not understand me?' she asked in French.

'No, I'm sorry – I do not know English.'

'This is your father's wife, Lady Clairmont,' said Grand-mère, introducing her.

This shocked the woman, who said scathingly, 'She can't

speak English? Why, she's been raised as a perfect heathen, though why I am surprised is beyond me.'

Her father frowned at Lady Clairmont. 'Well, it could have been avoided if you had only allowed—'

'Charles,' said Lady Clairmont in a chilling voice. 'Not now.'

He looked away and swore under his breath. Then he looked at Elodie and started to make things worse. 'The mind boggles at the lack of sense your mother displayed – why was she so insistent that I take you in if she couldn't even be bothered to ensure that you would have a chance of thriving. Same old Brigitte, eh? About as much sense as a pea...'

Elodie's eyes flashed. 'Do *not* speak like that about my mother,' she warned.

'He can say whatever he pleases about some common—' began Lady Clairmont, who was cut off by Marguerite, whose cheerful brown eyes had turned to stone.

'Careful, madame, that is my daughter you're talking about and this is my house. Can I ask you to keep a civil tongue?'

Lord Clairmont's eyes flashed. 'We should keep a civil tongue. By God, that's rich – when she came in here squawking like some fishwife.'

'That's different – she was not rude.'

'Rude? How dare you?'

But this was too much for Elodie. She'd been looking forward to meeting her father for years... and this was him? This small, pompous person who had come to Grand-mère's home and shouted at her. Whose first glance at his own daughter wasn't one full of kindness or love... but disappointment? How dare Grand-mère? How dare he! She didn't care who he was or what title he had – it meant nothing whatsoever to her, she felt spitting mad, and all she saw was red, as everything she'd been through over the past months bubbled up inside and she flew at him in a rage, and kicked his shin.

They all turned towards her in shock.

'Elodie,' breathed Grand-mère in surprise.

Lord Clairmont puffed himself up like a bear and looked ready to throttle her.

Ducking below his outstretched arms, she tore off out of the house. Blood rushing in her ears, as she ran as far and as fast as her legs allowed.

Inside Marguerite was trying and failing to calm down the Clairmonts.

'Let's just take a breath.'

'Are you quite insane?' snapped Lady Clairmont. 'Those manners of hers are shocking – the eyes might be Clairmont, but that is French blood – she's wild.'

Marguerite gritted her teeth, praying for strength.

'She will cool down, don't worry.'

But she didn't.

By ten that evening, even Lord Clairmont was starting to look a little worried. Marguerite had called on her neighbours, including Monsieur Blanchet and Jacques, beginning to truly worry when he said she wasn't there.

'You're sure you don't know where she is?' she asked the boy. 'I know she's your friend, but this is serious.'

'I am,' he said, his dark eyes anxious. 'I *wish* I was hiding her.'

'Jacques,' snapped his father.

'No,' he said, wincing, 'I just mean then I'd know she was safe.'

Marguerite touched the boy's head, and nodded. She could well understand that.

They combed the fields, and the buildings all around Marguerite's farm, until they found her hiding, unbeknownst to anyone, with the pigs in Jacques' father's barn. She was lying fast asleep next to Couchon.

Her father was mortified.

'Like I said, a perfect heathen.'

Lady Clairmont didn't say a word, she just nodded, brows raised.

Marguerite looked at them both. 'Look, perhaps it's best then if she stays with me.'

'So that you can continue to raise her like this?' he snapped.

'I quite agree,' said Lady Clairmont. 'Something has to be done.' Then she looked at Marguerite and said coldly, 'We will collect her in the morning. Please ensure she is ready.'

'But—' cried Marguerite, looking at Lord Clairmont askance. 'No, please, Charles, you promised – you said next year perhaps.'

'It is Lord Clairmont, Madame Renaux, and I promised you that I would let her stay with you while she recovered. When I arrived I did not see a grief-stricken child. What I have found is one who cannot speak English, who has the manners of a gutter-rat. So unless you want to guarantee that she never comes to see you again I suggest that you ensure that she is dressed and ready and in a more amenable temper when we leave tomorrow morning.'

21

FARRENDALE LADIES' COLLEGE, OXFORD, 1927

The building was made of grey stone and looked like a tomb, rising up from the ground into the pewter sky.

Elodie felt a shiver pass through her that had little to do with the cold, rainy weather. She rubbed one bare calf against the other, as they turned goosepimply from the cold. She was dressed in the uniform. It too was grey.

She wondered, if so much of England was this grey then why did they choose to wear it as well? But that thought was dashed out of her mind as she watched a sturdy woman come out of the twin oak entrance doors, then march across to meet her.

Jacob Bell, the chauffeur who had once again come to take her to a new life, turned to Elodie. 'You'll be all right, miss, just hang in there,' he said, though of course it wasn't his place to say so. She didn't really understand him, but she got the sentiment at least.

She didn't have it in her to nod.

Leaving Lamarin and her life in Provence had been almost

too much to bear. When her grand-mère had broken the news to her that she was to leave, she'd sobbed all night. Her father didn't seem to like her at all, so why did he want her to come in the first place? 'Can't I just stay here – I'll be no trouble, I promise,' she begged.

Marguerite's eyes had spilled and she had placed her head on top of her granddaughter's. 'Oh, I know that, *ma petite,* I wish you could stay, too, but unfortunately your father is your legal guardian. He promised your mother that he would look out for you. So for him that means he will raise you as a proper English lady, something he is convinced is now necessary after the events yesterday.'

Elodie frowned.

'However – it is not all bad news, *ma petite,* he has promised me that you will be allowed to come visit in the summer.'

Elodie broke away from her embrace. 'I can come back?'

'Yes, he has promised – however—'

'What?' she breathed.

Marguerite sighed. 'He said that if you give them any trouble, he will not let you come back here.'

Elodie swallowed.

'So you must try, *ma petite,* to rein in your temper.' Marguerite's eyes softened. 'I didn't even know you had one until I saw you kick him like that,' she said with a half smile.

Elodie bit her lip and sighed. She did know. It had been a long time since she'd been that angry, not since Maman, who sometimes used to leave her alone when she went off with one of her boyfriends... but she didn't tell Grand-mère that, it would only pain her.

Her father had come to collect her early the next morning, so she didn't even get a chance to say goodbye to Jacques, which was like a double betrayal. Grand-mère had promised, as she gave her one last, teary hug, that she would let him know.

After the ferry crossing in Dover, she'd spent only two

nights at her father's house, a vast sprawling estate with neo-colonial columns and gardens that looked so geometrically precise they could have been measured with rulers.

It was there that she got to meet her older half-siblings, Freddie and Harriet. They both spoke French, and had been far more welcoming than their parents.

Freddie was seventeen and was going to be attending Oxford in September. He looked like a version of Lord Clairmont, albeit one with more than a dash of empathy.

'Beastly business this whole thing,' he'd said, when they were all left alone in a beautiful old room filled with books, velvet sofas and a roaring fire. 'Must have been ghastly leaving France; such a wrench, I should imagine.'

'I can't believe father,' agreed Harriet, taking a sip of wine. She had pale hair, and a face that looked more like her mother's. 'Ripping you away from all that.'

Elodie didn't know what to say. Until they'd been introduced she hadn't even been aware that she had siblings. 'I asked mother if we couldn't just hire you a governess, but she's adamant about Farrendale – it's run by her old governess, you see,' said Freddie.

This was how she discovered that she wasn't even going to be staying there, but attending a boarding school for girls.

'It's near my college, so I could drop in on you, if you'd like?' offered Freddie.

'I'd like that,' she'd said, meaning it. In this new world, she couldn't be sure of a friendly face.

The following morning her bags were packed for her and she was instructed to get dressed in her new uniform. Then, she was taken to her new school. As Lady Clairmont hadn't come out to see her off, she realised that this was probably an arrangement that would suit them all.

She still couldn't fathom why she was here if they didn't

even want her around. Surely, she could have just learned English in a school near Lamarin?

Now as she stood before the grim school entrance, the sturdy, officious-looking woman who had made her way over to them introduced herself as Mrs Knight. She had flaxen hair, and sharp features. She consulted a wristwatch that she'd pinned to her tunic. It was similar to Elodie's uniform. 'I'll take that,' she said, reaching for Elodie's suitcase. It was full of new clothes, none of which she'd had any choice in choosing.

'Come along,' she chided as Elodie turned to bid the driver goodbye, with a small, sad wave.

'I understand you don't speak English yet,' she said in a plummy, accented French as she began to march back inside. Elodie raced to keep up. 'You will bunk next to one of our top girls – she is fluent in French, she will show you the ropes—'

'Oh, there's another French girl like me?' asked Elodie, perking up slightly at the thought.

'Certainly not, her father is a Lord.'

'So is mine,' said Elodie, who didn't know what that had to do with anything.

'Except that she is a lady, and you are not,' said Mrs Knight, who pursed her lips, her words designed to cause offence.

Elodie didn't really care. Her mother had explained that she wouldn't inherit a title because they had never been married. It didn't bother her.

'That's all right, no one has titles in France anyway. No one alive, that is – the Revolution, you know?' and she made a slashing motion across her neck in explanation.

Mrs Knight's eyes widened in horror. She changed the subject fast. Every other sentence though was designed to barb. After a while Elodie started counting them to stop them from hurting.

'For the first few months you will be tutored in English only – you're a bit old to be learning it now.' *Barb.*

'But Mrs Hammond has promised she can work miracles, which you will need, but no doubt with your lack of education you will be quite far behind.' *Barb, barb, barb.* 'However, you will be expected to work hard.'

By the time she was shown the dorm room, Elodie was quite wishing that Mrs Knight didn't know French quite as well as she did.

She had to still her tongue quite a few times and remind herself of Grand-mère's words to keep her temper with the rude, odious woman.

The dormitory overlooked a large field, and housed six other beds. She'd been informed that breakfast was at seven, 'sharp,' luncheon was at twelve thirty, and supper at six. 'Lights out at nine. I realise it will be quite different from your experience; I gather you were allowed to run wild.' *Barb.*

'Only a bit,' admitted Elodie. It sounded so regimented. So very different to Lamarin. She felt a pang so bad she had to hug her stomach.

She raised a brow. 'You're not going to be sick, are you? You don't want to let your family down, buck up.' *Barb.*

Elodie felt the familiar rush of panic, but swallowed it down.

'What?' Mrs Knight asked, finally looking at her, sensing her stare. She seemed uncomfortable.

Elodie said nothing. She was just marvelling at how quickly it was that she'd come to hate her.

After she put her suitcase down and unpacked, she was taken down to meet her tutor.

It was a pleasant classroom with several wooden desks and chairs in neat rows. Huge arched windows overlooked the grounds, and at the front of the classroom was a woman, dressed in forest green. Her medium brown hair had a wave and was bobbed. Her eyes lit up at they entered.

'Ah, the French girl,' she said, holding out a hand to shake Elodie's. Her green eyes were warm.

'Yes,' said the house mistress, as if she were handing over an item of some distaste, 'This is Elodie Clairmont – and she does not speak a word of English, you will have your hands full, Olivia. The look I was given when I told her the way things were... well!' she said primly. 'Defiant, that's what, can see that right away.'

'Thank you, Mrs Knight, I'm aware she doesn't speak English just yet, I'm sure we can handle it from here.'

As soon as she'd left, Mrs Hammond's lips twitched, 'So you gave her a look, did you? Well, I wouldn't encourage it but she could tempt a *saint* to violence.'

Elodie snorted.

Mrs Hammond brushed off her clothes. 'But I'll deny ever having said that, it's our secret, all right?'

Elodie nodded.

'So English, how much do you know?'

Elodie pulled a face.

'That little, hmm?'

She nodded.

'That's all right. Look, it's going to be a bit of a slog but we will get through it.' Then she invited Elodie to sit, and brought over textbooks and workbooks.

By the end of her first day, Elodie was bone tired. She'd never spent that long at a school before. Her mother had taught her herself when she was little – how to read and write, simple mathematics and lessons in history and geography, but that was all, and they usually only lasted a few hours a day.

This was different – focused learning on one subject. Mrs Hammond was firm, but kind.

She had met the other girls at luncheon. There were six of them, who boarded like her, and they seemed a firm group. Unfortunately, the one who could speak French best seemed the least interested in her. She was tall with thick black brows and gimlet eyes. She wasn't quite rude, but she made it clear that she did not appreciate that she'd been told to make her feel welcome. It appeared that her main objection to Elodie was her being an illegitimate child. She explained things with reluctance, like the nightly routine, and where to put their laundry and how to fold her clothes.

One of the others, a plump, kind-faced girl named Kitty, tried to make her feel welcome. It turned out that she too was considered a bit of an outsider, because unlike the other girls, her father wasn't a gentleman. He was a banker.

'Why does it matter?' Elodie asked, when the other girl confided this to her in a whisper the next morning at breakfast.

Kitty helped herself to a slice of toast, and began to butter it. 'It shouldn't, but here, well, it just does.'

'It doesn't in France,' said Elodie and she told her a little about her life in Provence. But it was soon clear that Kitty couldn't understand too much of what she was saying.

'I'm sorry,' she apologised, 'I get my tenses mixed up, I'm hopeless, I will try to get better now that you're here, though,' she said warmly, incentivised to learn now that there was a real chance of a friend.

Elodie was touched. 'Don't worry, it's me that needs to learn English.'

The girls around her were speaking English and giving her covert glances. It was clear that they were speaking of her. It riled her that she couldn't understand.

'It would help. I'm a dunce with languages. They all think you'll never be particularly good.'

Elodie frowned. 'One of the others said that unless you learn a language when you're really young you'll never be fluent

– so you'll probably always come across as a bit of foreigner.'
The girl who said that actually said that she would likely always
have an accent but Kitty didn't know how to say that in French.
Her words though caused a small seed of determination to grow
in Elodie's heart. She would show them, she vowed.

22

1927

'This is ridiculous – it makes no sense,' cried Elodie. In front of her was a full chalkboard of verbs and tenses. She had no problem with those, but it was the words – the hundreds of seemingly identical words that were the same, but meant different things.

'How can you have so many words that are so like each other – through, thorough, tough – why didn't anyone think of these things?'

Mrs Hammond sighed. 'I know. It's maddening. It's time for a break, anyway, but buck up. You might not see it, but your English is improving.'

Elodie blew out her cheeks. It was improving – because they were working on it around the clock. She didn't have lessons on anything else. It was why she had started now rather than in September, she'd discovered, so that she could learn the language before she joined the others in the new school year. She wasn't even going to get to go to Provence for the whole summer, as a result. She would be going in August only, and continuing her private lessons with Mrs Hammond until then. When she'd found that out it had been like a blow to her chest. But she focused on the shimmering mirage that was August, like a precious jewel.

After three months, Elodie was able to communicate well enough to have a good sense of what everyone was saying. After six she could hold her own in most conversations. Being young and treated to daily exposure had helped, as well as the resolute will to fit in and not be made to feel like so much of an outsider. The other girls had come around a lot more, and now Elodie counted Kitty and two other girls as friends.

A month before she was due to leave for Provence, her half-brother, Freddie, came by to visit, to see how she was getting along. She found that she liked her older brother. He was handsome, and caused quite a stir when the other girls saw him from the windows making his way across the grounds.

Freddie suggested they go for a walk, perhaps to get away from the many pairs of eyes that had suddenly been turned on him as soon as he'd entered the school. Kitty and the other girls had peered at him from the stairwell as soon as he'd been shown into the visitors' lounge just off the stairwell.

They walked in the school gardens and he seemed impressed by her grasp of English. 'Remarkable, Elodie, you sound almost English – I had to pause for a moment when I remembered it was you. You've come on swimmingly.'

When August came at last, Elodie found that she was so excited to go back to Provence she barely slept – and it was the most excited she'd ever been to see Jacob Bell, the chauffeur, who was amazed to find the young girl he'd met over a year ago now so changed.

When at last they arrived outside the old farmhouse, bordered by vineyards on one side and tall cypress trees on the other, Elodie jumped out of the car, thanking the driver profusely, and then ran towards Grand-mère who stood waiting for her in the late-summer sun.

As the old woman held her close, Elodie breathed in the scent of flour and lilacs, and closed her eyes in relief.

She was home.

23

Elodie was plaiting dough for an apricot *tarte tatin* when she heard a rap at the door. She turned to see Jacques, taller now than the last time she'd seen him, and thinner, with his brown tousled hair lightened from the sun, and his dark eyes crinkling at the corners in delight.

'So it's true.'

'Jacques!' she cried, stepping forward, then stopping awkwardly as she had been about to embrace him.

He seemed to be in the same predicament, though he was staring at her, the way someone did a sunrise, in awe. 'You're here! Papi said, but I raced here, to see for myself.'

She noticed then the colour on his cheeks, the dust on his clothes and his shoes.

'It's true,' she declared, grinning so widely it felt like her face might stretch in two. 'I am.'

He leaned against the door jamb, and sighed happily. There was a caw overhead and Huginn came in to land on his shoulder. He did a small hop as if he too couldn't believe that she was here. Elodie reached over and stroked his glossy feathers.

She felt a fizz of joy bubble up inside. She didn't have the words to express just how much she had missed her friend. What a joy it was to speak her own language and be understood. To not have to have constant reprimands to 'stand up straight', to 'speak slower', to 'slow down'... here she could just be herself.

'We have so much to catch up on,' he said, smiling wide. 'Like Luc, he's a blue jay who is such a character, you definitely need to meet him, although he's a big thief, I must warn you. I helped fix his wing a few months ago and he repaid us all by stealing the buttons off all my shirts. Also, Couchon has had babies.'

'Wait – what? Couchon is a girl?'

He snorted. 'Such a city girl, didn't you notice her teats?'

She frowned. Perhaps she had, now she thought of it.

'Also, Papi says there is a new area,' he waggled his nose, 'top secret, for truffles, he said you could come with.'

Elodie felt a pang, before her world had come crashing down again, she'd been excited to make her first truffle omelette.

Forgetting about propriety, she reached over and clasped his hand tightly. 'I missed you!' she said, overcome.

He grinned, revealing his dimples. 'Are you staying now – for good?'

'I'm only here for the month.'

'A month?' he cried.

She frowned sadly. 'I know, it's awful, but from next year they've promised I'll get the whole summer, every year.'

'Every year,' he repeated, like a benediction. 'It's better than nothing.'

She nodded.

'What are you making?'

'*Tarte tatin.* Do you want to help?'

He grinned. 'Sure.'

They got to work, making a lattice for the upside-down tart.

'So Madame Blanchet is still teaching you to cook?' he asked.

'Yes,' said Elodie, filling him in on their plans. 'I can't tell you how wonderful it is to be back here in this kitchen. The food in England... well, let's just say it's not like Provence,' she said, thinking of some of her dinners.

'What did you eat there?' he asked, curious.

She told him about bland, dry pork chops and boiled, unseasoned potatoes, reheated jacket potatoes with beans... food that had been edible, but not exactly fine dining.

Just then, Grand-mère came inside, wiping her hands on her apron, fresh from feeding the chickens.

'Jacques,' she said, 'I wondered how long it would be before you came around.'

He consulted a freckle on his wrist, 'Ah, about a second after Papi told me Elodie was here.'

They all grinned.

'It was the same with this one, I had to stop her from coming to wake you up at the crack of dawn this morning.'

'Really?' he asked; he looked utterly delighted.

Elodie nodded.

Marguerite couldn't help touching her heart at them.

'You know,' Jacques said, 'Elodie was just telling me about what the English eat – after I told her about our plan to go truffle hunting again – you know they have soldiers for breakfast?'

Elodie snorted as she put the tart into the oven to bake.

Marguerite's eyes had gone huge. 'They're *cannibals*?'

Elodie laughed. 'No, Grand-mère. Toast soldiers. They cut their toast into strips, called soldiers, and they dip these into soft-boiled eggs.'

'Eh, but the English are obsessed with war, no?' she observed.

'I mean, no more than the French, I think, from what I could tell. It's actually very nice, I'll make it for you,' said Elodie.

'All right,' said Grand-mère, who was always up for a culinary adventure.

'What else do they make?' asked Jacques, taking a seat at the table. Huginn, however, knew this was a step too far for him, and flew out the window at Grand-mère's raised brow – she was not about to have a crow at her dinner table.

'There's toad-in-the-hole,' she said, using the English words, which she translated for Jacques' benefit.

They both blanched and she had to laugh.

'A whole toad?' breathed Jacques.

'But why do they call us frogs, then?' asked Grand-mère.

'Toad in the hole,' corrected Elodie, laughing. 'It's not an actual whole toad.'

Grand-mère started laughing. 'Oh, well, that's a relief. Though you know they call us "Frogs" because we eat frogs' legs.'

Elodie pulled a face. So did Jacques.

'Children. Pah, you've both been spoilt – they're really nice.'

'You pull off frogs' legs?' asked Jacques, horrified.

'Not lately, too old to catch them, I'm afraid,' and they all giggled again.

'So what is it the English make, if it's not actual toads?' asked Marguerite.

'It's sausages cooked in a pudding with gravy.'

'Sounds disgusting.'

'No, I liked it.'

'Careful,' warned Jacques. 'They might just make an English girl of you yet.'

She flicked him with a dishtowel. 'Not likely.'

The days ran into each other, a blur of sun, swimming, exploring the countryside, observing the birds, cooking, and visiting the village with Jacques. On one sunny afternoon, they played *pétanque*, and stole a bottle of Monsieur Blanchet's *pastis*, growing tipsier as the day wore on. They fell asleep in his mother's wildflower garden, Jacques dozing lazily at her side.

When Marguerite and Monsieur Blanchet found out there was hell to pay. Elodie woke up to them arguing, only for the world to start spinning, and she had to throw up.

Their punishment was merciless. The next morning, they were made to rise at dawn and do manual chores, all day. By the time the afternoon arrived, she was like a zombie. When Jacques arrived he looked just as bad. 'Papi made me work in the hot sun in the vines all morning,' he said, looking green.

'I swear I will never drink again so long as I live,' she told Jacques.

Overhearing this Marguerite couldn't help but laugh. She and Monsieur Blanchet had agreed on their punishment together, and there was nothing that turned someone off drinking too much like a hangover in the hot sun.

But all too soon their month was over.

Elodie cried just as much as she had on that first night when she found out she had to go. 'When will it get easier to leave?' she asked Grand-mère, who patted her back and tried to swallow her own tears.

'I think that will only happen when you start seeing your school and your life there as home.'

'So never,' she said, with a watery smile.

Before she left the next morning, she snuck off to Jacques' house, tapping on his window. He was already awake, along with the birds.

He opened his bedroom window with a smile, and she climbed in.

'I'm like one of your birds,' she said, watching in awe as a blue tit flew out the window, disturbed by her arrival. Huginn, however, hopped over to greet her, and she stroked his soft feathers. He put up with it for a moment, then followed the blue tit outside in pursuit of breakfast, and perhaps to go and torment his former mate, Muninn.

'A summer bird,' he agreed, then sighed. The thought made him sad.

She bit her lip, her eyes filling. 'I could just hide away with Couchon again.'

He laughed, then came over to give her a hug. 'Don't tempt me.'

She placed her hand on his shoulder. 'I'll write,' she said.

'You'd better.'

24

PROVENCE, 1930

The summer Elodie turned fifteen she had been looking forward, all year as usual, to coming home. To being with Grand-mère at last in Lamarin, with the Provençal sun on her shoulders, as she walked through the beautiful, cobbled streets and of course, perhaps most of all, she looked forward to spending time with Jacques.

Yet, on her first day back, when she wandered down to the village shop thinking that she might make a picnic for the two of them so that they could catch up, she saw him bagging produce for a girl she had never seen before who had long brown hair and long tanned limbs. She kept touching his arm. The two were laughing, their heads a whisper length away from the other.

Elodie stood rooted to the ground, then promptly turned on her heel and marched away before he saw her.

She was furious and she didn't know why. But as she pounded the street, her legs pumping furiously, she came up with a few reasons.

She felt betrayed.

But it wasn't, she told herself, firmly because she thought of Jacques as hers, though she did, of course. It was the betrayal of friendship. 'Friendship,' she said aloud, startling a pigeon who was basking in the sun a metre away.

'Yes, that's what is what it is – a betrayal of friendship,' she hissed, warming to her theme. All the letters he'd written over the years, all his long accounts of all his various animal friends and not once, not ever, had he mentioned *that girl* with those very long legs.

'What is a betrayal of friendship?' asked a curious voice.

She whipped around.

There was a nun standing behind her. She had a sweet, round face and her habit was long and white and blue. Bits of reddish hair were just visible at her temples.

Elodie realised that she had taken the path to the abbey without realising it. It was a beautiful old honey-coloured building with an old-fashioned garden full of roses that bordered the lavender fields; the sisters used the lavender to make all sorts of healing goods, from soaps to honey and perfume.

'Oh, I'm sorry, Sister,' said Elodie, who coloured further, her face turning blood red.

'Don't be,' said the sister. 'You look hot. I'm Sister Augustine. Would you care for some rose lemonade?' She had on gardening gloves and was holding shears, and had been, until Elodie's outburst, pruning the roses nearby.

Elodie found that she would. She didn't at all feel like she would like to go straight back to Lamarin. In fact, for the first time since she was ten, she didn't want to be in Provence at all.

The sister guided her towards a table beneath a wide umbrella, removed her gloves and placed the garden shears onto the top. It was peaceful here with a sweeping view of the lavender to the right and the abbey gardens to the left. The abbey itself was beautiful, with wonderful stonework and arches in the windows.

Elodie saw some of the other sisters walking in the gardens and into the building, but she and Sister Augustine were, for the moment, quite alone.

It was lovely, but she couldn't appreciate it, not with her emotions all over the place.

The nun poured her a tall glass of lemonade. Elodie took a sip, and it was sweet and delicious, but it may as well have been made of sand.

'So what was this about friendship and betrayal?' she asked.

Elodie sighed. 'It's nothing.'

'It didn't look like nothing. It looked like if you carried on that way you might get carted away.'

Elodie looked at her in shock and to her surprise she laughed.

The nun winked. 'Tell me about it?' she invited.

Elodie took a deep breath, and then she did. 'Well, see, my friend Jacques...'

'Is he your boyfriend?'

'No, he's my best friend.'

'Right, carry on.'

Elodie nodded. 'Well, see, we have been friends for years and we tell each other everything and now – well, it's like I don't know him at all!' Her nostrils flared. 'You know he is obsessed with birds – obsessed – he sends letters to me in England full of all his observations, with sketches and detailed migration patterns. I could tell you every little bit of bird gossip there was to know in Lamarin, but did he spare even one sentence to tell me about his new human friend? Since when does he have human friends?'

Sister Augustine took a sip of her lemonade. 'So until now he has never had any other friends, besides you?'

Elodie frowned. 'Well, no, there are some village boys he

gets on with, and there are his cousins.'

The nun's lips twitched. 'So this friend... it's a girl, then?'

'Well, yes, but that's not what's bothering me.'

'Right, it's because—?'

'Because he didn't tell me.'

'Oh yes, indeed. So, it's not because you are jealous?'

She blinked. 'I'm not jealous.' Which was when she realised she was. Wildly so.

The nun took another sip of lemonade 'I think if you have a good friendship, don't let this ruin it. But also, you're growing up, things are bound to change.'

Elodie frowned, she didn't want anything to change.

'How old is he?'

'Sixteen,' said Elodie.

Sister Augustine nodded.

Elodie felt the blood rush to her ears. 'You think – are you saying she might be his girlfriend?'

'I don't know. It's possible.'

Elodie's hands shook as she took a sip of lemonade. 'I thought speaking with a nun was meant to make you feel better.'

Sister Augustine laughed. 'I usually find that it's like medicine, sometimes you feel worse before you start to feel better. My advice: talk to him.'

Advice Elodie ignored.

It took Jacques three days to finally get Elodie alone.

She had made sure that she was never alone with him. She always had an excuse whenever he came around, such as saying she was busy helping Grand-mère in the restaurant or doing her chores.

On the third morning he took matters into his own hands and decided to visit her just before dawn. There was a tap on her window and when she went to open it, and let him in, it was with some reluctance. 'Aren't you too old to be climbing through my window?'

He grinned. 'I don't think so. Besides, you are the one who usually visits me.'

She stepped backwards, and wrapped her arms around herself. 'I think Grand-mère wouldn't like it.'

'Since when do you care?'

She frowned. 'I've always cared what she thinks,' she hissed.

He stared at her, then shook his head. 'What's wrong with you?'

'Nothing is wrong with me. I just don't think you should be here.'

'Something is wrong. You keep avoiding me and now you don't want me here.'

'I haven't been avoiding you.'

He gave her a look. 'I've known you for four years. Usually it's you waking me up at dawn the second you're back from school. What happened?'

'I've been busy, that's all.'

'Busy. OK. I didn't know we were too busy for each other.' He looked hurt.

Her lip wobbled. 'Neither did I – but clearly you're busy too.'

He looked confused. 'No, I'm not. Unless you mean the job at the village shop.'

'Yes, also with your new friends.'

He looked confused again. 'New friends?'

This was too much – now he was lying to her! 'Yes! I saw you,' she hissed, 'with your girlfriend, how could you not even tell me about her, I thought we told each other everything.'

'New girlfriend?' he mouthed in confusion. Then suddenly his face cleared and he said, 'You mean, Josianne.'

Josianne. The name slithered in her soul. She glared at him.

'How would I know what her name was? Like I said you never even told me about her.'

He stared at her, then blinked. Suddenly a smile of realisation and sheer delight broke across his face. 'She only works there on Mondays – so that's what happened, you saw her and thought – what?'

'I saw her and thought—' she blushed, her throat turned dry, 'that you were keeping a big part of your life from me, and I thought well, as we are best friends, and that I was surprised...'

'Oh, you were surprised?'

She frowned at him. 'Fine, I was hurt.'

'Hurt?'

'Can you stop repeating everything I say?' she hissed.

'So you were jealous?' he said, looking at her from the side.

'No! I mean, yes, no... Why are you looking at me like that?' she snapped.

'Like what?'

'I don't know... You look so – so – happy.'

'I'm thrilled,' he said, grinning so wide that his dimples showed. His brown eyes danced. She wondered when he'd become this handsome. It annoyed her too.

'You're thrilled?' she said in confusion. 'That I'm jealous?'

'Yes. Josianne is not my girlfriend, by the way.'

Then he darted forward and kissed her.

She blinked, touching her lips, speechless.

'I've been waiting for ages for you to catch up.'

'Catch up?'

He touched her face, and she found herself leaning towards his touch, like she was being pulled by a magnet.

'To realise you were in love with me.'

'But that's not – I don't – wait...' she fumbled. 'You've been waiting, why?'

'Because unlike you, I've known I was in love with you since the first day I met you.'

25

PROVENCE, 1932

'Read it to me again?'

Elodie and Jacques were lying in the wildflower meadow, which over the years had grown even larger. They were watching Huginn as he tried to teach his hatchlings how to hunt for peanuts. It mostly involved begging the humans.

Jacques smiled.

'*Dear Monsieur Blanchet,*' he began. '*It is with great pleasure that we would like to offer you the apprentice research position under Doctor Franz Goethe at the esteemed Heligoland Bird Observatory, one of the world's first ornithological observatories. We are thoroughly impressed with your self-study of the migration patterns of Mediterranean birds. Your role, should you choose to accept, will be to aid Doctor Goethe in his research on bird migration and contribute to the annual report.*'

Elodie smiled. 'You did it, Jacques. You've actually managed to make your dream come true.'

'One of them, anyway,' he said, reaching for her hand.

Kissing the inside of her palm, he closed her hand over it; a kiss for her to keep.

He hadn't asked her to marry him, but she knew he would. Once she was finally finished with school.

They had plenty of time.

'The only thing that makes me sad about it is that our summers will be cut short,' he said. 'I won't be able to spend more than two weeks with you – it's our busy season, apparently.'

She sat up on her elbows, then leaned forward and put her head on his shoulder. 'It won't be forever.' Then she sighed. 'Though it'll feel that way.'

He played with a strand of her hair, which Huginn decided to come investigate. 'Shoo,' he said, laughing.

'Have you told your father?' she asked.

He sat up, then put his head in his knees for a moment. 'No. I have to break it to him tonight.'

She patted his back. 'Good luck.'

Jacques had reason to be apprehensive. Monsieur Blanchet did not take the news at all well. Elodie heard them fighting in the vines near Grand-mère's house, and they were still going at it later that morning when she went down to help Grand-mère at the restaurant. The old man kept tearing at his thinning hair, and shouting words like 'duty' and 'my only son'.

'So it hasn't gone well, then?' asked Grand-mère, handing her an apron, and looking at her face.

Elodie shook her head, then got to work washing the vegetables the older woman had left near the sink.

'We're doing roast pheasant today with summer vegetables,' she said.

Elodie nodded, and began to chop the vegetables. She told Grand-mère what Monsieur Blanchet had shouted outside.

Grand-mère paused her preparations of the pheasants. 'Oh, George,' she whispered. 'I will talk to him – he doesn't want to make my mistake.'

Elodie looked at her curiously and her face turned grave. 'When your mother ran off with your father – I also used words like that. Well, we know how that turned out, she never came home. It's not worth it.'

Elodie nodded. 'I think Jacques is different.'

'What's different is he has you.'

Elodie brought fresh strawberries from Grand-mère's *potager* for the nuns at the Abbey de Saint-Michel. Sister Augustine was working in the garden when she saw her come in. 'Oh, I was hoping I'd get to see you,' she said, smiling in welcome.

The two had become firm friends. Ever since she had discovered for the first time that the feelings she had for her best friend might be more than she bargained for.

'I brought strawberries.'

'Wonderful. Do you feel up to helping an old woman with her gardening?'

Elodie smiled. The nun was barely a few years older than her.

'Of course.'

As they got to work on dead-heading roses, Sister Augustine looked at her. 'So, tell me about it.'

'About what?'

'The reason you're here?'

'I don't have a reason, I wanted to see you.'

The nun waited. 'You always come to me when you've got a problem. I don't mind, I like to be feel needed; think of it as my job.'

'But you're not a priest.'

'More's the pity.'

Elodie looked up at her shocked.

'What, you're the only one affected by sin? Hate to disappoint you.'

Elodie was amazed. 'So if you could you would have been a priest?'

'Absolutely. I don't want to be a man, but it would have been nice to have the same duties of a priest. I think I'd give a good sermon.'

'I know you would.'

The nun smiled. 'It's OK, though. I'm content here with my work, but I do like to help, so feel free to share what's bothering you.'

Elodie grinned. There was something about Sister Augustine, a sense that she truly wasn't being judged, that she was allowed to be human, that allowed her to be more honest with her than she was with most.

She told her about her worries for Jacques and his father and her own struggles. 'I've told him that I'm fine with only seeing him two weeks a year – but honestly, the idea makes me feel *ill*, we already have so little time together.'

'What did you tell him?'

'I told him I was happy for him and that we'd get through it. He has enough on his plate.'

She nodded. 'You will get through it.' Then she picked up an orange. 'Eat something,' she said.

Elodie quirked a brow. 'Priests forget about things like food.'

'Do they?'

'Oh yes.'

Elodie had a wedge of orange, and it did somehow make her feel slightly better.

26

PROVENCE, 1933

It was March when Marguerite awoke to the smell of baking. A shadow passed over her closed eyes, blocking the pale spring sunlight as it trickled through the half-lidded shutters.

She frowned as she opened her eyes to see Elodie staring at her with eyes that were violet blue in the early morning sun. She was dressed in a cream sundress and was wearing one of Marguerite's gardening cardigans. Her smile lit up the room.

'Elodie?' breathed Marguerite.

'Surprise!'

Marguerite got out of bed quickly, and enfolded her into a hug. '*Ma petite!* Oh, it is so wonderful to see you! But... how are you here now?'

Elodie hugged her back and she closed her eyes like she was breathing the older woman in. Marguerite caught a glimpse of the open door behind and the luggage in the hallway. 'That's a lot of luggage,' she said, pulling back slightly to stare at the younger woman.

Elodie nodded, then grinned as she put her hands on her grandmother's shoulders. 'I've made a decision.'

Marguerite raised a brow. 'Yes?'

'I have decided that I am done with school and I am moving here – I mean, obviously, if you'll have me, of course.'

Marguerite gasped. 'Elodie! What happened? Are you in trouble?'

Elodie shook her head. 'No, nothing like that, don't worry. Well, see it was like this. It was my birthday—'

'Yes, of course – last week? You got my gift?'

'I did,' said Elodie, her smile stretching wider, as she fished out the small silver necklace with two tiny charms, a spoon and a spatula. She hugged it to her chest. 'I adore it.'

Marguerite smiled. 'I'm glad.'

'But, see, it's what changed everything.'

'Oh? How's that?' she asked, taking a seat on the bed, and inviting Elodie to join her. Elodie sat cross-legged on the blue-and-pink patchwork quilt at the end.

'Well, see, it arrived on Saturday, while I was sitting in the school library with some of my school mates. It was raining, one of those weeks when it seems like it will never stop, and then suddenly the post arrived and there it was, this little ray of sunshine from you. Some of the girls crowded around to see what I'd been sent, abandoning their books and games, any excuse for some distraction. When I took the necklace out, I gasped in glee, and hugged it. Most of them were curious, though less so when they found out it wasn't from a boy.' She grinned.

Marguerite chuckled.

'Anyway,' continued Elodie, 'one girl kept laughing at it. The idea of it being a silver spoon and a *spatula*. She said maybe in France you're born with a silver spoon and a *spatula*, because you need to use it to cook for everyone else.'

Marguerite winced. 'Oh.'

'No, no, it's fine. It was sort of amusing, or it might have been if she'd delivered it a bit better. I suppose. That girl tries to get a rise out of everyone, I hardly take notice of it anymore. No, it was my friends that upset me really.'

'Oh no, I'm sorry, were they cruel?'

'No, nothing like that. They're pleasant enough. It was the polite look of confusion on their faces that did something to me. Not one of them understood why you had sent me that necklace. And as I watched them trying to find the words, trying not to laugh at that girl's joke, I realised that after all these years they still didn't know who I was, you see? I mean, they'd heard the stories, but this place wasn't real for them, and they just sort of assumed I'd grow up and be like them – go on to university, perhaps, find a job in an office, a husband and have children, and all under those dark grey skies. Which was *not* my plan at all. And I just thought, can I blame them for thinking that... when here I am doing exactly what everyone else wants for my life, apart from me? I thought... what am I doing here? Why am I still here, now? I mean, when I was ten, well, I had no choice... but now? Now I did. So, I stood up, smiled, and said, "Well, I think I'll be off now, actually," and I went to my room, packed my bags, said my goodbyes and walked the hell out.'

'What?' cried Marguerite.

Elodie bit the side of her fingernail, then grinned widely. 'I know! I just thought, life is short, Grand-mère,' her eyes were solemn, 'we should spend it doing what brings us meaning, with the people we love.'

Marguerite's eyes filled with tears, and she nodded once, said, 'You're right,' then kissed Elodie on both cheeks, clasping them in her hands. 'But... what about your father?'

Elodie sighed. 'Well, yes, he was predictably outraged...'

Grand-mère pulled a face. 'So you did speak to him?'

'Yes. I telephoned him. He threatened to cut me off, warned me that I was throwing away my chances at making a good match, et cetera. Honestly, I think it's better to break away now. That's not the life I want – that's a life other people planned for me, starting with my mother. So I got the train to London, to Freddie, my half-brother, you know?'

'Oh yes, I know.' Over the years she had heard about him, he was something of a character.

Elodie grinned. 'Freddy gave me some money so I could get here. I mean, he did,' she admitted, 'at first, try to talk me out of coming, to carry on and go to university and all that – but when he saw my mind was made up, well, he gave in.'

Freddie had become a real friend as well as a brother over the years. She laughed, remembering his face when she told him why she wanted, needed, to come here. After she'd described Lemarin, the restaurant, the village… and Jacques, after a while, he had stared at her over the pot of Earl Grey tea they'd ordered in a tiny teashop near Westminster, where he worked, as a junior secretary in the prime minister's office. 'Blimey, El, now I want to come too,' he'd muttered with a grin, his dark blue eyes so like hers, sparkling.

'You must!' she'd replied.

Now Elodie told her grandmother, 'Actually, he said he might come for a visit if that's all right?'

'Of course. It was good of him to help you.'

Elodie nodded. 'He said he'd try speak to father too, but I'm not holding my breath.'

Then she looked at Marguerite, realising she'd never exactly asked her permission. 'It is alright that I came? I mean to help you… not be a burden or anything.'

Marguerite picked up her hand and squeezed it. 'It is more than alright.' She grinned. 'So you've truly done it,' and then she couldn't help herself, she jumped up and squealed, and started to bounce on the balls of her feet. It was all she wanted if she was honest.

'I did!'

They did a kind of jig together on the flagstone floor.

'Shall we celebrate with a swim?' asked Marguerite.

'Yes! We can have croissants after, I just baked some.'

And together they raced to get changed and then with their arms around each other they made their way to the river, in the early spring sunshine.

The crow took to following her most days. He was there at dawn when she and Grand-mère went swimming, flying up into the willows on the riverbanks, and then coming out to join her at the restaurant in the afternoon, forever hopeful of some tiny morsel she had on offer.

Whenever she saw him, she smiled. It was like having Jacques with her. She wondered about him often on that small island.

She could picture him in the marshes, as he made his observations, sketching, a world far away from theirs. But it was spring there too and they both dreamed beneath the same moon, there was always comfort in that.

His letters helped, though the news that was coming out of Germany made her worry for him too, what with this new leader of the country stirring up all kinds of trouble, and spreading all kinds of hate, particularly towards Jewish people. She hoped he was being careful. In his letters he never mentioned the mainland, and when she asked, he was always quick to tell her how little the island played a part in those affairs, which was some comfort. She couldn't wait for him to come home, though.

Freddie visited in the first week of May, bringing the first taste of summer. He arrived, wearing linen shorts, his knees bony and pale, with a straw boater in one hand, his luggage in the other, and a look of wonder on his face as he stared at the roses and lavender hugging the farmhouse walls. 'Well, this is paradise. No bloody wonder you absconded.'

Elodie grinned, then stepped forward to embrace him. 'I don't think I've ever seen you out of a suit,' she observed.

He looked down at his knobbly knees. 'Yes, well... I was born with one on, you know?'

She laughed, and called out for Marguerite. 'Grand-mère, come quick, we have a visitor.'

Marguerite hurried outside, wiping her floury hands on her apron, then her warm amber eyes crinkled at the corners into a smile. 'Oh! This must be Freddie,' she said, warmly. 'Welcome.'

'Grand-mère!' he said, dropping his bag and giving her a very un-English bear hug.

Marguerite chuckled and embraced him too.

Within moments, they were old friends.

Elodie had never spent more than a few hours at a time with Freddie, but she'd always enjoyed them enormously. Their visits had mostly consisted of him dropping by her old school, while her school chums cricked their necks to get a look at the handsome, tall blond. Sometimes they used to have the occasional lunch in Oxford, followed by a walk along the canals, watching the narrowboats, which they both loved, until he graduated and moved to London and a life in politics. He'd got much busier, but he used to phone every week, no matter what.

Harriet, her older sister, hadn't reached out quite as much, but Elodie didn't mind. She and Freddie had just clicked, despite their differences.

But now they had a full two weeks. For someone who was used to a rather grander lifestyle with servants and a rambling estate, he took to the simpler life with aplomb, she thought. And Grand-mère found everything he said or did charming, which helped.

He quickly fell into their routine, rising to swim with them, in the little stream, then sunning themselves on the banks, Elodie picking wildflowers, Freddie dusting off his Wordsworth and Grand-mère tantalising them both with what she was thinking of making her customers for lunch, which made Freddie groan and say he may never fit into his dress trousers again.

One day, when they were visiting Lamarin, he sighed as he took in the beautiful vista.

'Perhaps I'll tell father that I'm defecting too,' he teased, as they sat drinking coffee in the village café, overlooking the green where a group of older men were playing *pétanque*. 'I could be like that fellow there.'

He had an impressively thick black moustache, a forest green beret, and a bulging belly, restrained by suspenders, into which he'd hooked one of his thumbs. The other hand was supporting a tiny glass full of pale liquor, which he downed in one. Then he set down the empty glass on the grass, and made himself comfortable by a plane tree, and was soon closing his eyes, the beret covering his face.

She grinned. 'The Provençals have mastered the art of work and rest, a fine balance. I think the *pastis* has something to do with it...' She smiled, then went to order them both a glass to get them into the mood.

In the days that followed, Freddie switched his straw boater for a beret and spoke more of giving his notice, and if he didn't love his job as much as she knew he did, Elodie was sure he would.

Part way through Freddie's holiday, Jacques surprised them with an early visit home.

It was Sunday morning and Elodie was baking a lemon cake in the farmhouse kitchen while Freddie helped Marguerite as she used his hands to wind yarn around while she made a new rag rug.

Elodie looked from the mixing bowl and saw that someone was approaching the house in the dusky light. Then she yelped, as she recognised his figure, setting her spoon down with a clatter, and the door crashed against the wall, as she raced outside, her cry of 'Jacques' answering the others' questioning looks.

Freddie and Jacques took to one another fast. It was an odd thing, thought Elodie, watching as these two men, so very different from one another, raised on separate continents, one acerbic and witty, the other withdrawn and deep, somehow found a mutual regard, One that centred, primarily, on *pétanque*.

The two played every afternoon after lunch. Elodie and Marguerite sat on a picnic blanket in the vines watching them, and laughing at the serious expressions on their faces.

One afternoon, Marguerite began to cough, then rubbed her chest.

'Still not over that cold?' asked Elodie.

Marguerite had developed a mild summer cold, and had seemed to recover pretty well, but her cough was still there.

She nodded. 'I'm sure it will clear up soon – it's good for me to take a little break, I think.'

She'd decided to take a few days' rest, closing the restaurant during Freddie's second week and Jacques' surprise visit so that they could make the most of the time. They had been doing a lot of swimming, sitting outside in the vines, playing *pétanque*, and having frequent picnics.

Freddie and Jacques took a break, their faces glistening with sweat from their game, and ready to sit in the relative shade.

They were speaking of Germany, and carried on their conversation as Jacques came to sit behind Elodie. She leaned against his knee, listening in.

'So you're not worried about what's happening on the mainland, then?'

'Not overly. I mean it's a concern, we're all keeping an ear out, so to speak. But the island where I'm stationed, Heligoland, while owned by Germany, yes, is in many ways a world apart.'

'That's good to hear,' said Freddie, reaching for a grape. 'Used to belong to us, back in the last century – it attracted a lot of the upper crust at one point, artists, writers, that sort of thing.'

Jacques nodded. 'Hard to picture that now. It's quieter, I suppose, just us researchers and the islanders, which is better for what we need to do.'

'Just so long as that madman doesn't begin spreading his ideas there too,' said Marguerite. 'He's doing enough damage where he is.'

The madman was, of course, Adolf Hitler, the leader of a fanatical group of patriotic German thugs, who had – to the surprise of everyone – been made chancellor of the country at the beginning of the year.

'He seems to have got where he is by stirring up hatred and working on people's fears,' agreed Elodie.

Freddie nodded. 'I always thought that they made a mistake there with Germany, after the war.'

'What do you mean?' asked Elodie.

'The crippling reparations, really. After the Great War everyone thought someone needed to pay, but I think they put too much pressure on Germany, really. It's such a proud country. It's one thing to defeat your enemy, there's honour in that... but it was a bit more brutal, if I'm honest, their punishment. And it's led to a generation fuelled by resentment. Hitler has used that to his advantage – preyed upon it really.' His words brought a chill to the afternoon. 'Forgive me,' he laughed, trying to make light of it, 'I could be accused of anti-patriotism with those thoughts.'

'You're right, though,' said Marguerite, who coughed again.

She patted her chest then took a sip of wine, and carried on. 'About how he is preying on people's fears, all this nastiness about the Jews.'

'Just awful,' agreed Elodie, who'd heard awful stories of his followers looting shops belonging to Jewish-owned businesses, his attempts at making them second-class citizens, with odd laws that wanted to force them out of their jobs. There had been some pushback from senior officials, thank goodness, but it did seem like it was not a good place to be of a different faith – or to have an opposing political view. Intellectuals, writers and artists were all having a hard time.

'Just be careful, Jacques,' said Elodie. 'You don't want to get involved in any of that.'

'Oh, he won't last,' said Jacques. 'Most people – most sane people, anyway – think he's awful – he'll soon get voted out. They'll see sense.'

'Will they?' said Freddie, sounding doubtful. 'I hope so.'

Elodie looked worried and Freddie waved his hands. 'Apologies, you're probably right, I do tend to think the worst sometimes.'

Jacques took her hand in his, and gave her palm a kiss. 'I promise to get very away from the island, the minute Herr Hitler comes anywhere it.'

'You promise?'

'The very minute.'

27

PROVENCE, 1933

As June arrived Elodie woke every morning to the sound of birdsong, the scent of lavender and her grandmother's calls to go swimming. They marched down with their arms linked, and towels draped around their necks.

One particularly fine day, when the light was so bright and luminous, bouncing off the water as they lay in its shallows, Elodie stared as it shone on Grand-mère's hair, which had fanned out around her, almost all white.

'What are you thinking of?' asked Grand-mère, as she caught her staring.

'Just you – just how much my life changed the day I was brought here, and how wonderful it is.'

Grand-mère's hand reached out for hers and she gave it a little squeeze. 'Mine too.'

They drifted in the water for a while longer, watching the sky filtering through the willow trees.

Afterwards they made breakfast, a fluffy truffle-studded omelette, and ate it straight from the pan.

The only small dark spot was Grand-mère's cough, which returned every evening. The doctor said that it was nothing to worry about, and that the summer sun would do her the world of good, and she should try to ensure that she took things a bit more slowly.

It made Elodie grateful that she had decided to move in when she did, so at least she could ensure Grand-mère did, in fact, take his good advice. Their days were often really busy, full of trips to the market then preparing food for the restaurant. The days of the chalkboard with the single offering written as a notice had long since gone as no one bothered to check it. They trusted Marguerite completely. And thankfully that trust fell on to Elodie as well, who soon was trying out her own experiments.

She convinced Grand-mère to hire an extra helper in the kitchen, one of Jacques' cousins, Timothee, who washed dishes and acted as a server. It made a big difference.

Every Saturday when the farm restaurant was closed, Elodie went to the abbey to visit Sister Augustine, the kind-faced nun. Her face always lit up when she saw the girl, and she often put her to work with a spare pair of pruning shears. 'Roses are like children, you have to keep a firm hand,' she often said.

Elodie didn't mind. It was cathartic. They would walk around the vast garden together, against the backdrop of the beautiful old honey-stone abbey, and work as they talked.

The roses were at their best this time of year, from pale pinks cascading over trellises, to large whites like bridal veils climbing over walls, and row upon row of pale yellow or cerise bushes, next to stone garden benches, statues and fountains.

But even as spectacular as the roses were, they played second fiddle to the lavender, which was soon to bloom in the fields below, turning the horizon purple.

The nuns could time its arrival to the week, like the phases of the moon. When the lavender season began, their quiet days turned busy, as they tended it, and prepared for harvest when they would draw from the blooms the essential oil which would be used in all manner of tinctures and salves. People had been coming to the nuns for home remedies for years, so it seemed, and they obliged with all manner of homeopathic helpmates.

Elodie slept every night on a pillow that was full of sachets of lavender from the abbey.

'When will the lavender be in bloom?'

'Another week we think.'

'How's your grandmother's cold?' asked Sister Augustine, while she deadheaded a yellow rose bush. 'Last week you mentioned that she's still got that cough?'

'It seems better now. She does cough a little at night but now that summer is here, the doctor seems to think it'll clear up.'

'That's good to hear. I made a tea mixture that might help as well. Dried herbs and flowers like lobelia, from the *potager*. Good for the chest,' said Sister Augustine. 'I'll get it for you before you go.'

'Thanks,' said Elodie. Then she grinned at the nun. 'I brought you some of those little honey cakes you like.'

Sister Augustine's eyes danced. 'Thank you, I was hoping you might say that. Shall I pour us some lemonade?'

'Sounds wonderful.'

A week later, when the lavender arrived, so did Jacques. She awoke to the sound of him tapping on the window, before sunrise. Elodie quickly went to open it but he held a finger to his lips then told her to follow him. She grinned.

They raced down the gravel drive into the cool morning air, stopping only so that Jacques could pick her up and hug her tight, where no one could hear.

'You're early!' she said, kissing him.

His brown eyes danced in the early light. 'Well, my last surprise went so well, I thought I'd try it again.'

His hair was longer, his face tanned. She touched it, committing all the changes to her heart. He appeared to be doing the same with her. 'Your hair seems lighter,' he marvelled, picking up a long blonde strand.

'All my time outside,' she said, and told him about her time in the gardens at the abbey as well as her daily swims with Grand-mère. He told her about everything that had been happening on his little island. So far it seemed like things in Germany had calmed down somewhat. 'For a while some of the senior researchers were thinking of packing up. But it all seems to have calmed down a bit. Freddie says that maybe it's just the usual political rally stuff – once they get elected things calm down a bit.'

'You speak to Freddie?' she said, surprised.

'Oh yes,' he said with a grin. 'Just a note every so often. He wanted to stay in touch.'

She smiled. 'I'm glad.'

For now, though, they had a whole month together, and they made the most of it. Elodie would slip away from the restaurant, so they could spend the warm evenings in each other's arms outside, just listening to the birds.

It was incredible how many still came to find him: the crows, blue tits and starlings. They were all old friends, who did not forget the kind boy who had befriended them.

Sometimes they would fall asleep in the meadow, their own private world, and they would study each other, counting the freckles and beauty spots until it felt to Elodie that she knew Jacques' body as well as her own. Their skin glowed from their love-making.

It was a drowsy afternoon, when even the birds were taking a break, when he asked her to be his wife. She was making herself a flower crown, and one of the crows, thinking this was a game, was trying to steal the daisies she assembled.

'Will you marry me?' he asked.

She looked up, and then saw to her surprise that he was holding up a blue leather ring box, and inside it was a gorgeous emerald ring surrounded by seed pearls.

'Jacques,' she breathed, her eyes brimming with emotion.

'It was my mother's,' he said, almost shyly. 'She would have wanted you to have it.'

She dashed away a tear, and then took his head in her hands and kissed him fiercely.

When he put it on her finger, she looked down at it and then back at him, and felt overcome with happiness.

And just for a moment she worried about that happiness, worried that something might come and take it away like it had when she was nine years old and her world turned upside down, but she shook the thought away, like a shiver.

28

PROVENCE, 1934–37

Grand-mère and Monsieur Blanchet were delighted that they planned to wed. Elodie's father was not quite as thrilled, but now that she was living in Provence, he didn't exert quite as much influence over her as he once had.

Freddie, on the other hand, was thrilled and vowed to move heaven and earth to make sure that he could be there when it happened.

They decided to have it soon, in the last week of Jacques' leave.

Marguerite woke Elodie a few days before the wedding, and told her to follow her. There was a smile on the older woman's lined face.

'Where are we going?' she asked, her bare feet sinking into the lawn outside the farmhouse.

'On a little walk. I had an idea,' she said, handing her a pair of summer slippers. The air was fresh and cool in the dawn.

They walked through the vines, and then veered off towards Monsieur Blanchet's property, turning right just before where his land and Grand-mère's met, separated by a small kissing gate where her vines stopped and his began. Somewhere between these two stood a small stone outbuilding. A place she had hardly paid much attention to as it was just a part of the farm.

Except, she was seeing now, it wasn't.

To her surprise, Grand-mère beckoned her toward this building.

It looked different from the last time she'd noticed it – years ago now. Back then, large old disused farm equipment had littered the ground, like tyres, and a few wine barrels. Now it was all cleared. The stonework had been cleaned and re-mortared. A flower bed had been created all around it, filled with lavender and roses, and blue shutters placed on the windows.

'We thought,' said Grand-mère with a smile, 'that this could be yours and Jacques', for the newlyweds,' she said, shyly, inviting Elodie inside.

Elodie gasped. 'Grand-mère! When did you do this?'

'It wasn't just me. Monsieur Blanchet helped,' she said. 'And Jacques of course,' and when she stepped over the threshold they were there beaming.

It was a tiny cottage with fresh flagstone floors, with a small blue kitchenette, next to a sofa, and a coal stove in the corner. There was a bedroom at the back, and on the twin beds that had been pushed together was a patchwork quilt.

'It's still a bit of a work in progress,' said Jacques, pointing out the windows that needed mending.

Elodie's eyes spilled over. 'No, it's beautiful,' she cried.

'Oh, *ma petite*,' cried Grand-mère, and soon they were all hugging one another. 'Oh no, now we're all off,' she said.

'No, no,' denied Monsieur Blanchet, who began to blub,

fishing out a red-and-white handkerchief from his trouser pocket, and blowing his nose hard. Then, hooking his thumbs behind his suspenders, he added, 'I *have* allergies.'

This made them laugh all the harder.

The wedding was held in the vines between both their family homes, not far from their new stone cottage.

Sister Augustine brought rose petals from the abbey and she helped to scatter these along the gravel pathway with Grand-mère.

Elodie wore a simple white silk gown with tiny roses embroidered along the bodice. Braided in the front of her hair were wildflowers from Jacques' mother's garden. The rest of it was left to curl naturally down her back.

Freddie wore his linen suit and straw boater and had been made Jacques' best man.

It was attended by all the local villagers and farmers, and when Elodie walked down the vines path towards them, carrying with her a bouquet of lavender and roses, they all cheered.

But she only had eyes for Jacques, who looked so wonderful in his suit, his dark eyes brimming with tears. Their vows were simple, traditional ones from the priest and when it was over they kissed for a long time in the late-summer sun while their friends and family cheered.

Married life, she found, was a happy one. In September he came home for several months and they would be together for the first time in years until the spring. They took one week to revel in being a newlywed couple, and then got down to the business of making a life together.

In the mornings while he watched the birds, she went swimming with Grand-mère, spent the afternoons in the restaurant, but their evenings, after dinner, usually in the company of Monsieur Blanchet and Grand-mère in the big farmhouse, were their own, and were filled with love.

In November, Elodie began to feel ill, and she found that almost anything could make her become sick. It wasn't until Grand-mère witnessed this one afternoon, just after she'd begun to fry up some truffles, and had to run outside to the privy, that she considered that she might in fact be with child. 'Have you had your monthlies?' she asked.

Elodie stared at her for some time, and then her eyes widened. 'I... haven't, actually. I'm late.'

Grand-mère smiled and she said, 'Well, that's how it starts.'

Elodie and Jacques were elated.

In February, though, Elodie woke up and she knew something wasn't right. There was blood on her sheets. She started to cry. Jacques called for the doctor, who tried to reassure her that a little blood wasn't anything to be concerned about.

'It doesn't necessarily mean anything, the important thing is to just keep calm.'

She tried to but it was hard.

Over the course of the next few days the spotting continued, and despite everyone's assurances she knew she was miscarrying, yet she thought that perhaps if she stayed still, very still, she could stop it from happening.

Jacques didn't know what to do, apart from hold her as she stared anxiously at the walls.

When the cramping began she started to howl, and that's when he fetched Grand-mère. She stayed with Elodie all throughout the night as her body began to prepare to give birth, the contractions ripping her apart, as she cried for the poor lost soul. It was a little girl. They named her Rose and buried her in the garden.

For weeks afterwards, Elodie found it hard to do anything, apart from cry, and remember to breathe in and out.

'When will it get better?' she asked Grand-mère one day as she lay with her head in the older woman's lap, while she stroked her hair as she cried.

'Little by little, *ma petite*, every day it will get a little bit easier, in the beginning the tears fall every hour, then every other hour, and then perhaps just once a day, and then perhaps just a few times a week... until you put yourself back together again, better, but not quite the same.'

Grand-mère had lost three babies and one grown daughter, so she knew better than most. She was right too. In time, Elodie got stronger and when Jacques returned to the island, she felt better. But what Grand-mère said was true: she was not quite the same.

Their lives became lived in the seasons, full of joy and love, yet sprinkled through with pain. Over the next three years, she had four more miscarriages, each one as devastating as the last. Grand-mère was there each time to help guide her back to life. Jacques said that perhaps they should stop trying, and she at last agreed.

Grand-mère's cough, which had never truly gone away despite all the best tinctures and remedies, had grown increasingly worse in recent months. When Jacques was away she stayed at the farmhouse and sometimes the noise woke her. It was a violent wet sound and she pushed her to see a specialist.

The older woman waved away her concerns. 'I'm just getting older, *ma petite*. It happens in the mornings and evenings, otherwise I'm fine. Right as rain.'

Elodie wasn't convinced, and together they went to go and see a different doctor to their usual one in the larger town of Gourdes. Doctor Christophe Bonnier was a tall man with grey hair and kind, hazel eyes. He performed an x-ray and when he came back with the slides, Elodie could see it on his face. They sat in his office while he spoke, but the only words she heard ricocheted around her skull.

Lung cancer.

When they got home, they walked to the river, and the two held hands. Every now and then tears leaked unbidden from Elodie's eyes. 'You're still young, not even seventy yet.'

Grand-mère shut her eyes, willing the tears away. Then she patted her hands. 'I have lived a good life, *ma petite*, a beautiful one, and thanks to you the last part of it has been the best.'

Elodie's lip quivered. 'Don't say it like that.'

'What?'

'Like it's the end.'

Grand-mère blew air out of her cheeks, then bit her lip. '*Ma petite,* I can't live forever.'

Elodie's face crumpled. Grand-mère gathered her up in her arms. 'I have no plans to die today or even tomorrow, *ma petite*, we will make the most of this time, *d'accord*? We will not be sad. We will make summer in our hearts – like Jacques' favourite poem, alright?'

Grand-mère was true to her word, and though she grew thinner, she made an effort to be just as lively as she had always been.

When it happened, in 1937, it was on a late-summer's day at the river. They'd gone down, slowly, and painstakingly, each step a trial. It was their usual morning ritual, except that it had become a different one, over the past few months, where they sat on the banks and watched the willows as they swayed in the breeze. Grand-mère leaned on her shoulder before she passed.

And afterwards it would be winter for a long time to come.

29

PROVENCE, 1937–38

Jacques stayed with her, looking after her and making sure she remembered to eat. Everything tasted like ashes, though.

Freddie arrived for the funeral and it was the first time in days that she was able to even partly smile at something. He wore a beret, out of respect, and his dark blue eyes shimmered with tears.

He bit his lip as hugged her a little awkwardly. 'I know she wasn't truly mine,' he said. 'But for a little while I did feel like I had a grandmother too.'

'Oh Freddie,' she whispered, eyes brimming over. 'She adored you and I think she would be so honoured by that.'

They buried Grand-mère in the abbey graveyard, and Elodie and Sister Augustine planted lavender and roses on her grave.

After the funeral, her many customers came to pay their respects, each one leaving behind a little something.

Through the filter of tears, and the grey haze of clouds that seemed to have descended over her, Elodie leaned against Jacques and whispered, 'What are they doing?'

It was Monsieur Blanchet who answered, mopping his eyes with his red-and-white handkerchief. 'They are leaving her tokens, little items to show what she meant to them.'

There were sprigs of herbs, spices and even the odd slice of cake.

'The priest is turning puce,' whispered Freddie. Elodie looked up and saw the priest who had conducted the ceremony looking appalled.

'He thinks it's blasphemous,' said Sister Augustine, putting a plate of strawberries on the graveside herself.

'Sister?' said Elodie in shock, watching her.

'I'll say my Hail Marys. Because lord knows, Marguerite enjoyed a good laugh.'

And to her shock Elodie found herself laughing even as she was crying on her grandmother's funeral, mostly because she would have absolutely loved that.

Afterwards Elodie climbed into her grandmother's bed, wearing one of her large cardigans. There were tissues in the pockets and tissues everywhere from Elodie's tears. Jacques came to cuddle her, and Freddie joined in lying at the foot of the bed and not saying a word.

Somehow it felt as if that was all Elodie needed.

Jacques didn't object when Elodie chose to stay in the farmhouse; he just took her cue and started to move some of their things out of their little cottage. Right then the only place she wanted to be was around Marguerite's things.

It was both joyful and painful.

She found her grief, though, was different to the loss of

her babies, which had been all pain. 'When you lose someone that you've known your whole life, pretty much, it's like you don't just mourn the person you lost at the end, you mourn everything that happened before. All those memories wash over you, like a tide, and it's so easy to get cast adrift,' she said.

'I can understand that,' said Jacques. 'But remember your memories will always be there, they won't get taken too.'

He was right, and in time, she began to take comfort in that.

Soon, there was something else to help distract her too. One day when she was undressing he gasped as he stared.

'Elodie!' he cried.

She looked down at her swollen naked stomach and then back at him, bit her lip and nodded, tears leaking down her cheeks, as he raced towards her and gently touched her belly. 'But you never said anything,' he whispered, in wonder. 'You're huge.'

She smiled at him through her tears.

'I know.'

She was further along than she'd ever been. 'I feel like maybe Grand-mère had a word with the man upstairs when she got there,' she murmured. 'Because,' and her lips wobbled, 'I'm starting to think maybe this one will get to stay.'

Jacques cried great sobbing tears, as he held on to them both. 'I think she must have,' he agreed.

By the time Jacques was ready to return to the island, they were ringing in the new year, 1938.

Since the Nuremberg Laws had passed, and Jews were no longer allowed to work, Jacques had been entering Heligoland via Denmark with false papers as opposed to straight from Germany, in the hope that it would mean he could get out easier, if they ever decided to check his documentation properly. Soon, though, they decided that false documentation would be safer all around and Freddie helped him with that.

It wasn't something he had shared with Elodie, however. But even as he'd assisted, Freddie had warned his brother-in-law, telephoning him before he left. 'I think whatever you're doing there, it's time to wrap it up, things aren't cooling down on that front.'

He meant Hitler's attitude towards the Jews.

In Germany, Jews had been stripped of their citizenship, and Jacques was careful not to travel that way just in case he was subjected to any unwanted attention. But how long would that route be open for him? Jacques agreed. 'I just have to finish up the season, and then I think you're right, it's time to think of other things, closer to home.'

'Good man. I believe they've turned a blind eye for some time to the island but that won't be forever.'

'I'll just be another few months, the government is beginning a bit of a reclamation project soon to restore the eroded land, so we want to finish up what we can.'

Overhearing this, Elodie nodded. 'The sooner the better.'

Jacques repeated to Freddie what she said and he agreed. 'Yes. And I believe you have someone new to think of too.'

Jacques looked up from the telephone and whispered, 'You told Freddie.'

She grinned and nodded. 'Yup.'

They shared a smile.

'Exactly, my friend,' said Jacques. 'I hope you're getting excited to meet your new nephew or niece.'

'Too excited. I'm already picking out a mini *pétanque* set and a beret.'

Jacques laughed. 'They're going to love you.'

· · ·

After Jacques packed up his bag, he sat on the end of the bed, next to the old cat, Pattou. 'I could just stay,' he offered.

Elodie squeezed his hand. 'Don't tempt me. You know I'll tell you to.'

He leaned against her shoulder and sighed, then touched the belly. 'Six weeks,' he promised. 'Then I'll be home.'

'Six weeks,' repeated Elodie.

But she couldn't stop the tears when he did finally leave. She watched him go down the gravel path, and in the distance a pair of crows seemed to call farewell.

To distract herself she re-opened the restaurant.

Everywhere there was Marguerite's presence, but it was a good thing, she found. Like her home, it was a place of familiarity, of memory and comfort. She put on her grandmother's apron and got to work.

She was in every pot and pan Elodie's fingers touched. The radio, when she switched it on, was playing some of her favourite music, and Elodie felt a sense of coming home.

On her first day back, it appeared like every villager was in attendance, Monsieur Blanchet amongst them.

When she and her new kitchen helper, Jean, a young boy of fourteen, another one of Jacques' cousins, brought out the plates of cassoulet, they stood up and applauded.

Elodie lifted up the corner of the apron and dabbed her eyes. 'Thank you all,' she whispered, touched.

With Jacques away, she cooked for Monsieur Blanchet, who came around often to keep her company, most likely on Jacques' instructions to ensure that she didn't wallow in Grand-mère's bed, wearing her old clothes, which was of course all she wanted to do.

They forged new ground, and unlocked their own friendship through chess. One evening, after dinner, he'd suggested a game, and when she admitted she'd never played it before, he was amazed. He set up a beautiful hand-carved set that unbeknownst to her had been kept in her grandmother's living room for decades.

While a cheery fire glowed, he rubbed his thick, bushy moustache, twisting the corners upwards, and then he smiled as he explained the rules. 'It is a two-person game. There are sixteen pieces of six types for each player and each one moves in its own unique way. Want you want to do is capture your opponent's king.'

'So that is the most powerful piece on the set?' she asked, looking at the black king, bigger than all the others, with a solemn expression, that he was pointing at.

He raised a brow. 'Oh no, m'dear,' he said, moving to another slightly smaller piece. 'While the king is important, of course, he can only move in one square in any direction, so long as a piece is not blocking its path. The queen, however,' he said with a smile, 'can move in any direction and in any number of squares. In terms of raw power – she's the one that holds all the cards.'

'Interesting,' said Elodie.

They played chess after that every night. It was a game of strategy, of being just a few steps ahead of your opponent.

Elodie found, to her surprise, that she was a natural at it.

30

1938

Every week, Jacques sent a letter.

She looked forward to these more than she could say. They would arrive, smelling faintly of the island, of water and salt, and something that was uniquely him, sandalwood and berg-amot, perhaps, from the home-made soaps prepared by the nuns at the abbey.

She would press each letter to her nose and breathe it in before she read his words. Over the years, he'd shared a glimpse of his studies with her: the patterns and changes he saw in the birds he observed, as well as the cold and wind he felt there along that northern point, so very different from their sunshine corner of the Mediterranean.

His letters though, recently, held new stories of the arrival of a group of Germans from the navy who were beginning work on a reclamation project. He wrote:

> *So far, they're staying on their side of the island, while we keep to ours. We were concerned that they might be a bit domineer-*

ing, and we should pack up and leave, but they've made an effort to not be too intrusive, which has surprised us – I think we were expecting them to be domineering and possessive... but the official message appears to be that their instructions are to be respectful. I am meeting with one of them this week to show them around our sites of interest. I must admit it's a relief. Though, if I'm honest, I'm beginning to count the weeks till I can come home to you. As polite as they are, it does make me a bit apprehensive having them here.

Love to you both (give the belly a kiss from me).

Jacques

Elodie and Monsieur Blanchet were relieved that for now the news out of the island was good. She read him her most recent letter one night after dinner. He was sipping pastis, and staring at the burning coals in the fireplace. Before them both was the chess set, ready for their regular evening game.

Monsieur Blanchet was to go first, but he'd yet to make his move. He sighed. 'I think I will rest easier when he's home,' he admitted, and she saw the dark circles beneath his eyes.

'You haven't been sleeping?'

He looked up at her and said, 'Not a lot.' Then pulled a wry face, and tugged at his moustache anxiously. 'Forgive me, I don't mean to worry you.'

She shook her head, and a strand of dark blonde hair fell forward. She was wearing one of Marguerite's cosy cardigans, it was emerald green and rather baggy, but even that could not disguise her very swollen stomach. 'You haven't made me worry, I've been worrying about that for a long time,' she admitted. 'But sleep is hard even without the worry.'

He smiled then, and it lightened their mood as they thought

of the child to come. It would be good to have something to look forward to.

Spring seemed to arrive early in Provence. In February, Elodie helped Sister Augustine plant seedlings and bulbs in the abbey's greenhouse. The nun wore a gardening smock over her habit and wedged her feet in wellingtons. The sight amused Elodie.

With the cold weather, Sister Augustine made them a pot of English tea, Earl Grey, which was Elodie's favourite. Freddie always sent over boxes of the stuff for her, and she had brought some for Sister Augustine one year to try and now she was hooked on the stuff.

They sipped their tea from big green tin mugs, Elodie taking a seat at a planting table, while Sister Augustine dropped an old blanket over her knees to keep her and the baby warm.

They planted seeds for the potage, basil, cauliflower and aubergine, and flowers for the nuns' home-made remedies, perfumes, soaps and tinctures, like ageratum and geranium. Some of the seedlings they planted included things like sunflowers, tomatoes, squash and strawberries, plants that one would only sow under glass much later in England, according to Sister Augustine.

Elodie was grateful for the work and enjoyed listening to the nun as she explained some of the properties of the plants. It was distracting. Perhaps she still looked anxious, because the nun commented when she looked at her as she wrote a label for the geranium seeds she'd planted.

'You know, the oil from geraniums has been used throughout the centuries by some for the treatment of anxiety and even depression.'

'Really? Does it work?'

Sister Augustine shrugged. 'I find it to be calming, even just sniffing the scent. I'll get you a bottle.'

'Thank you,' said Elodie gratefully. 'I'll tell Monsieur Blanchet to put some drops on his pillow too.'

Sister Augustine nodded, then placed a hand on the younger woman's shoulder. 'He's still worried for Jacques?'

Elodie nodded. 'Yes. I think we'll both rest easier when he's home.'

Sister Augustine's eyes were sympathetic. 'I'll pray on that tonight.'

'Thank you,' said Elodie.

Jacques' letters were increasingly about the presence of the Nazi naval officers, and his latest one in the second week of April caused her some distress.

> For the most part they have been polite, respecting our research areas and even going so far as to show an interest in what we're trying to accomplish. However, this week there was some tension when they disturbed some of the breeding sites of northern gannets as well as the dwindling razorbills. One of our teammates, Herman, got into a heated discussion with a junior officer about it. In fairness to the Germans, it's difficult to do their work without disturbing the nature around them, and we are trying to be appreciative of that, but it is such a sensitive time, as Herman's and my research is on the meticulous study of the breeding patterns of all of these migratory birds.
>
> I've reminded him to keep a cool head. In June, we will be able to wrap up our findings, though we do worry about what will happen to the island once we're gone...

Elodie's heart quickened as she read. She didn't like the sound of this. It was starting to seem as if the polite façade between the researchers and the navy was beginning to slip.

She fished out a piece of paper from her grandmother's writing desk and began to respond with a frown.

I'm worried, Jacques. I don't like the sound of this... come home. I'm sorry to be so direct but I think, let's rather be safe than sorry here... please, I know you love me, and I wouldn't ask if I didn't absolutely believe in my bones that you need to get out and now. Your father agrees with me, just come home to us. The island will look after itself, let us keep you safe now.

Elodie

She waited anxiously for the post the following week, half-expecting to see either the postman or Jacques walking up the gravel path. Either one would be welcome. She knew that Jacques would not ignore her request. Wary of being a demanding wife, she almost never put her foot down on anything, but she absolutely had to insist and she knew that he would respect that and would agree.

But when Wednesday came – the day her letter from Heligoland usually arrived – and no letter came, she began to worry.

Monsieur Blanchet came past early that afternoon, just after she'd closed the restaurant for the day.

'Anything?' she asked him. He shook his head, tugging at his moustache in his anxiety.

They made their way back to her farmhouse and Monsieur Blanchet said, 'It's probably because he decided to leave straightaway after you sent your letter.'

She had, of course, told Jacques' father what she'd written

and he'd nodded, giving a hollow laugh as he said to her amazement, 'I wrote the same thing.'

Elodie reached over and squeezed the old man's hand now.
'I think you're right.' She smiled in relief. 'It's late because he is
on his way.'

He nodded, and smiled too, but the worry was still in his
dark eyes, even as he suggested a game of chess to calm their
nerves.

By the following week Jacques still hadn't arrived, and neither
had any post.

Elodie sent a telegram asking for any news, but nothing
came.

'I don't like this,' she said. 'Someone should have answered
that at least.'

Monsieur Blanchet agreed. 'Send another,' he suggested. So
she did. She sent four more.

Nothing came.

She telephoned Freddie hoping that with his position in
government – he was now working as a senior secretary for the
prime minister, Neville Chamberlain – he would be able to find
out what was happening.

'I'll try my best, El. I noticed that the letters stopped too, but
I was hoping it was because he'd done the sensible thing and
come home. But let's not panic, it could be something as simple
as a storm delaying the mailing ship.'

Elodie let out a breath. 'Oh, Freddie, I hope that's the case.'

'It may well be. Try not to panic, El. I'll get back to you as
soon as I know what's happening – give me a few days, it might
take some digging.'

She nodded, but of course he couldn't see her, and when she hung up, she told Monsieur Blanchet who was standing nearby what Freddie had said. In answer, he made the sign of the cross and began to pray.

She closed her eyes and did the same.

31

PROVENCE, 1938

Elodie was making bread, fists pummelling the dough, before she rolled it back up again then slapped it onto the table covered in flour and began the process once more. It was the only thing that seemed to help ease her mind.

Monsieur Blanchet was tending his vines, which at least seemed to be offering some distraction for him.

The kitchen window was open, letting in a cooling breeze, despite the warmth of the early spring sunshine. The roses and lavender had begun to bloom, and she had barely taken any notice. She'd had to close the restaurant because she just couldn't focus.

She heard a car approaching and looked up in surprise, dropping the dough, and frowning.

It was a very posh-looking black-and-white car and it was slowly making its way up the gravel drive.

She raced around the front, and opened the door, her heart skipping a beat as she saw a man get out.

The sun was in her eyes, as she hastened towards him, her

stomach doing flips. He straightened, and she paused. The first thing she noticed was his height. He was too tall. She frowned, shading her eyes, and then she saw it was Freddie.

She blinked, and at first, she almost smiled in welcome, and then she saw the look on his face. It was tight and bleak. She felt her knees begin to give way.

He raced towards her, clasping her by her elbows.

'Just tell me,' she begged, looking at his face, searching for anything that she could pin her hopes to. 'Has he been taken somewhere – captured perhaps?' Her lips trembled. They had been hearing all sorts of stories of people being sent off to detention centres, people who opposed their views, the Jews, anyone who wasn't deemed to fit with their view of the world... perhaps they had discovered Jacques' doctored paperwork. It had been the cold, dark thought at the bottom of her mind, and she had been trying her best not to bring it to the surface just in case it somehow rendered it into being.

Freddie closed his eyes for a moment, as if he were searching for the strength somehow to proceed. Elodie felt her legs give way again.

'Let's get you inside,' he begged.

Her face crumpled, and tears began to race down her cheeks. 'Freddie,' she begged.

There were tears in his dark blue eyes. 'He wasn't taken, no. Oh, El,' he whispered and she realised then that sometimes what life had to offer was worse than even your worst fears, and something inside her changed for ever in that moment. 'He's dead.'

32

PROVENCE, 1938

Monsieur Blanchet heard her screams from the vines and came running.

Somehow, she was led inside the kitchen, as she howled. She couldn't seem to get her legs to move, and they half carried her inside to a seat. All the while, through her haze of tears, she stared at Monsieur Blanchet.

'He – he is dead?' he asked, and Freddie confirmed it, while Elodie tried and failed to stifle the howls that were escaping her. She wanted – needed – to go to the old man and comfort him – but she was unable to move past the wall of pain and grief that had hit her.

He half fell onto his knees beside her chair, placing a fist into his mouth as he began to sob and wail. 'My son, my only son.'

Elodie at last managed to get off the chair, where she crawled towards him, reaching out a hand to lend him strength, then looking up at Freddie. 'How – how did it happen?' she asked her brother, through a voice that sounded strangled and unrecognisable as her own.

Monsieur Blanchet looked at him, begging him perhaps to say anything else.

Freddie swallowed and took a seat on her discarded chair, and he began to speak. She tried and failed to focus on Freddie's words. But all she could think was that Jacques was dead. It seemed impossible. He could not be. How could she be in a world where he was not in it? 'Are you sure – he's d-dead?'

Freddie blinked, as tears leaked from his eyes, and he nodded.

Elodie's lip began to wobble again and he carried on.

'It seems that there was an altercation of some kind. Something to do with his research. The navy had decided to extend their facilities on the island, to expand installations for their North Sea operations, so that it could become a major naval and air base – part of this was a major land reclamation project. Apparently, tensions between one of the research teams and a junior officer had grown when they disturbed some of the nesting sites.'

Monsieur Blanchet bit his knuckle, and nodded. 'Y-yes, he wrote to us about that.'

Elodie nodded. 'Yes, but he said it was one of his teammates that had had words with one of the Nazi officers, not Jacques, he told him to keep a cool head.'

'Herman Ludho, yes, that's what I was told too. It appears, though, that when Herman lost his temper, it ended what had been up till that point a tense but polite state of operations between the ornithologists and the officers. The officer who Herman shouted at took great offence at his tone, and things came to head between them a few days later. Jacques intervened while they were fighting and he got caught in the crossfire.'

Elodie blinked. 'He was shot.'

'The officer said that it was an accident. That he was in the way but—' He broke off, like he didn't want to say anymore.

'But what?' asked Monsieur Blanchet.

'I spoke to Jacques' boss, and it seems as if there were witnesses. It wasn't as the officer described it – as a kind of accident. It was deliberate. He turned the gun first on Herman and then on Jacques. It was an execution.'

Elodie began to keen. Monsieur Blanchet, however, became furious, stuttering in his pain and outrage.

'B-b-but if they saw that,' he said, 'couldn't they go to the authorities and tell them?'

Freddie shook his head. 'Not when they are the ones in charge. They all turned a blind eye. The official report that was filed said it was an accident. It seems that this officer is someone thought to be on the rise. Jacques' boss said that even if they could fight it, the fact is that they have broken the law. If they pursued the Nazis they would soon find out that Jacques had Jewish heritage, something that his team – along with my help – forged the paperwork to disguise. If the Nazis found out that they had illegally employed a Jew they could all be detained, or worse, suffer the same treatment as Herman and Jacques.'

Elodie fought for air.

'Thank you for telling us,' said Monsieur Blanchet.

Freddie nodded.

Elodie stared at the floor for a long moment, thinking of this man who had taken a husband, a son, who had wiped out two lives as if it were nothing, for the mere crime of annoying him.

'What is his name?'

'Who?'

'The man who killed him. What is his name?'

'What difference does it make?' said Freddie.

'Because they won't always be in power, and one day he may still face his crimes.'

Freddie replied, 'His name is Otto, Otto Busch.'

33

PARIS 1942

They were good legs, thought Otto Busch, as the woman before him spoke of her plans. Slim, yet shapely in their stacked brown brogue heels. The stockings looked new or well cared for and he appreciated that almost as much as he did the fine shape inside them. No pucker marks or runs – he hated that, thought it said something about character. Like the women who drew lines on their bare legs, it made him feel slightly ill for some reason, like it was indecent. He knew there was a bit of a shortage but still, you'd think that would just make them all the more careful with them. He despised sloppiness, especially in a woman.

She didn't seem to suffer from that affliction, and it made her presence all the more enjoyable for him.

She was speaking now, her voice girlish but not high, like there was a touch of whisky to it, delicious. He made sure to lean in close so that he could sample that perfume again. It was expensive. Some kind of floral scent. Light but not overly sweet. Smelled a bit like geraniums. They had them at the hotel he was staying in.

He looked up from his coffee and his blue eyes danced when she parted her red lips in a smile. It was not every day that you got to sit across from an attractive Frenchwoman who wore the kind of lipstick you wouldn't mind (too much) getting on your shirt. After all, he lived near an excellent laundromat.

The café was just around the corner from his hotel. The bistro chairs faced the pavement and everyone here knew how to dress. You might even forget for a moment that a war was being fought, even as they spoke. He didn't, though, wars weren't just for battlefields, the war he was fighting was on people's thoughts and ideas, getting them to see the world the way the Party wanted them to. It was slow and he had never been a patient man but progress was being made every day.

But sometimes progress happened quickly and easily and it made him grateful for his new role. Like now.

Her blonde curls shone in the sunshine, done in the latest style, and her eyes were such a rich blue, like the flowers that used to grow in his mother's garden every spring.

The business proposal that she had prepared was detailed, and convincing. Efficiently typed up and showing a real understanding of how to run a successful restaurant, she clearly knew what she was speaking about. Busch wouldn't have to do much to convince anyone to support her.

She had a bit of her own money to add to the project, nothing substantial but enough to prove she was serious.

It made the goal of collaboration child's play.

They would be pleased if he pulled this off, he was sure of it. A feather in his cap – actually helping to open a new restaurant? It was exactly what they wanted – to show that German-French collaboration could be to everyone's benefit. And the fact that he had brought it about should help the one small stain on his reputation considerably. He was thought as tough, even by Nazi standards, something he was proud of. What he wasn't proud of, though, was the belief, whispered behind closed doors, that he was something of a loose cannon. It had served him well in the beginning, helping him to rise quickly, because the Party knew they could trust him to do what needed to get done, no questions asked. Still, what had happened in Heligoland had left a mark.

He'd been sent to work with the navy as they fortified the island and restored the military base, important work that Hitler, personally, was interested in, so the post was especially significant for Busch who longed to gain the Fuhrer's trust and respect.

The official directive was that their work took precedence but they should be mindful of being respectful of the islanders, and the researchers stationed there who were studying the patterns of the bird population.

He tried, he truly had. He even went so far as to show an interest in seeing what they were doing in the hopes that he could better understand. He was shown around their research facility by an enthusiastic man who confused politeness with interest and shared anecdotes and statistics from their studies, his eyes lighting up as he told Busch what they had discovered and how important the area was for the breeding populations of so many bird species. By the end of his tour, Busch's frustration with their presence on the island had grown into irritation. These were grown men spending their days watching birds, leaving others to do the vitally important work their country needed to restore their standing as a proud and productive nation – rebuilding their military, factories, agriculture, family and social values and restoring the reichsmark to be a currency worth more than the paper it was printed on. And yet as he watched them, these able-bodied men wasting their time ogling birds... something in him started to snap. They may as well have wasted away their time in a pub for all the good they were to the Fatherland. And then there was that Frenchie, who looked almost Jewish in his colouring, despite the paperwork that said otherwise, whose eyes seemed to bore into his own as if he could tell what Busch was thinking, and worse, judge him for it, it was all just tinder.

When one of them, a young man, younger even than he, named Herman Ludho, flew at him one morning, wagging a finger at him for disturbing a few birds' nests while he was laying cable, the spark ignited, and the rage grew inside his soul at their total disrespect as he carried out the real work that needed to be done. Still, Busch might have been able to bring himself back from the brink, if Ludho had had any sense and not confronted him again. Then the Frenchie had got involved and it was just too much, he'd just seen red. He wasn't proud of his actions, the regret he felt was more to do with the fact that he'd let them get to him – what he should have done was proven his authority by having them shut down and that damned Ludho shipped off to a detention centre.

That was the lecture he was given by his superior officer, Harald Vlig. 'You're an asset to us, and loyal to a fault, those men should never have been allowed to stay on, but next time you have to learn to control the beast within – right now, we have a lot of work to do, my boy. And we can't afford getting embroiled in international affairs. There was even some government Englishman poking his nose around, after the Frenchman was killed, we can't have that... officially it's on record as an accident – but you need to make sure that no such accidents occur again. Do you hear?'

He had, loud and clear.

His new role as a cultural liaison officer was partly an attempt to change that wild-cannon impression. His family friend, district leader of Berlin, Joseph Goebbels had put in a good word for him personally, but this too had come with a warning. 'Otto, diplomacy is the knife hidden in the velvet glove. If you can convince us that you have what it takes you could go far but if you let your emotions control you, you will peak soon.'

So this was his punishment and also his reward.

He didn't expect it to be quite this enjoyable, if he were honest.

He picked up the business proposal again, and downed the last dregs of his coffee.

'Madame, I am impressed. It is not far from my base – lots of important men are visiting this city, and I can tell you a restaurant with this kind of menu, in this slightly more discreet location would be just what we need.'

'Oh, do you think so?' she said with a smile. Her large blue eyes were full of hope. That was what respect looked like, he thought, as she seemed to wait for his approval, which he was happy to give.

'I hope that it could be useful to you and your men, you all work so hard. The food is good for the soul, and it's something very close to my heart; simple, yet nourishing country fare. Like my grandmother used to make.'

He smiled, he really did like the sound of this.

'You are married, Madame Blanchet?'

'Not anymore.'

His eyes flared with interest.

'You leave this with me, madame, I can tell you already I look forward to working with you, I am pleased you got in contact with me.'

'Call me Marianne, please,' she said, with a smile, 'and I assure you, monsieur, the pleasure is all mine.'

PART THREE

34

SABINE

She was so relieved to discover the Abbey de Saint-Michel was still in operation.

After seeing the convent listed on Sabine's mother's birth and adoption certificates they had decided it was worth it to see if someone there perhaps remembered something about it.

Sabine was a little shocked when she dialled information and was then connected through to the convent. It seemed odd, somehow, to imagine an abbey, deep in the Provençal countryside, having a telephone.

Modern times, she thought, with some awe.

A minute later a polite, gravelly sort of voice with an air of efficiency answered.

'Bonjour, the Abbey de Saint-Michel, Sister Agnes speaking.'

'Good day, Sister,' said Sabine. 'I was wondering if you might be able to help.'

'Certainly. Is it about the lavender production? We are open for tours, Monday to Saturday from 8 a.m. to 1 p.m. and we serve lunch in the gardens as part of the package.'

This sounded a bit more modern than she was bargaining for.

'Oh, er no, actually. Um... I was wondering if there was anyone who could help provide some information about a child that was born in the abbey in the late 30s, just before the war. I believe that the nuns also handled the adoption.'

'Oh?' said the sister in some surprise. 'Well, I was not aware of such an undertaking, but it is possible, especially in those times. I can make some enquiries if you like. If you leave your name and number I can get back to you.'

'Yes, that would be fine, thank you,' said Sabine, giving her details and feeling oddly disappointed, though she wasn't sure why – perhaps it was just that until they spoke to someone who remembered those times, they were just going around in circles with the information they already had.

She popped by Monsieur Géroux's antiquarian bookstore on the way home from the library, where he made her a mug full of the tar-like black coffee he enjoyed. They drank it next to his old-fashioned desk. Monsieur Géroux looked tired; there were deep shadows beneath his eyes. 'I didn't sleep well,' he admitted. 'I kept going over the possibility that out there, someone might remember something about your mother's adoption and offer some kind of a clue as to who Marianne was... but then I stop myself, knowing that I'm reaching. It's possible she simply abandoned the child, your mother, shortly after giving birth and no real questions were asked...'

Sabine sighed. 'I've been tormenting myself with the same thoughts. When I phoned today, I was so hoping someone would just be like, *Oh yes, of course she will be listed on the adoption papers, let me go check our records...* I waited all day for someone to call back, hardly got a thing done properly at work...'

'I can imagine,' said Monsieur Géroux, showing her the pile of work that was on his desk. There was new stock that needed protective jackets as well as calls to be made to interested collectors but his heart hadn't been in it.

'I even – for the first time in at least a decade – had someone show interest in the Nabokov,' he said, putting his head in his hands and groaning softly. 'And I blew it.'

'The Nabokov?' Sabine asked, curious, a tug of sympathy going out to him.

'*Lolita* – American edition – it's in that cabinet there, the one with that ghastly cover,' he said, pointing.

She stood up to go and look. It was indeed not attractive as far as covers went, though she wouldn't go so far as to call it ghastly. To be fair she'd never really liked the story of Lolita; she knew it was meant to be progressive and all of that, but it had given her the creeps.

'I've been trying to sell that copy for thirty years,' he admitted.

'Oh no, I'm so sorry,' she gasped, realising how distracted he must have been. She felt a twinge of guilt... 'If it wasn't for me dredging all this up...'

'Don't be silly, if it wasn't for you I would not have known that she warned Henri to stay away. Or that there might have been more to this story. I am grateful to you, truly. It is like a weight has started to lift.'

She reached over and squeezed his hand. 'As I am to you, monsieur.'

He smiled and his freckles were more prominent, making him look younger.

'Don't you think it's time, Sabine, that you started calling me Gilbert?' he said, patting her hand, which had an ink smudge from where she'd been stamping book returns.

Her lips twitched. 'I'll try,' she said.

Two days passed before Sabine heard back from the abbey.

'Good afternoon,' said the same voice that she'd spoken to before. 'I am looking for Sabine Dupris.'

'Speaking!' she replied, breathless.

'Ah, yes. This is Sister Agnes from the Abbey de Saint-Michel, calling about your enquiry?'

'Yes,' she responded quickly, sitting up straight, and ignoring the customer who was patiently waiting for her to check out his book. She signalled for one of the other librarians to take over. She didn't even notice when the customer shot her an affronted look.

'Well,' said Sister Agnes, 'I apologise for taking so long to get back to you. But the sister who was here when the child you mentioned was born is on a silent week – this is when the nuns take a vow of silence for a period. She has managed to indicate, however, that should you wish to speak with her about it, she will do when her vow is over, next week on Wednesday.'

'Should I call her then?'

'I think it is best that you come here if you can.'

Sabine blinked. Yes, actually, she thought, that probably would be best.

'I'll be there then,' she said in some surprise to herself.

'Very well,' said the nun. 'Sister Augustine will see you then.'

35

PROVENCE, 1987

The Abbey de Saint-Michel was a beautiful old building surrounded by gardens and lavender fields. It sat on a rocky promontory, a few miles away from the hilltop village of Lamarin which dated back to Roman times. It was part of the northern area of outstanding natural beauty that was the Luberon.

Sabine and Gilbert had hired a car and made the drive from Paris, which had taken them just over nine hours. It had been years since she'd driven, but she found that though rusty, it all came back. The same could not be said for Monsieur Géroux, who had wanted to share the burden of driving, and gamely offered to do the first half of the trip. After he kept putting the wrong gear in place and grinding the clutch, she had had to lie and tell him how much she enjoyed driving. In relief he'd allowed her to take over, confessing it had never been one of his passions.

When he pulled to the side, she'd given the car a pat of apology and had gamely pretended it was one of hers.

They stopped only twice for the lavatory and for a quick baguette – ham and wedge of cheese – which they ate as a mini picnic on the side of a road overlooking a field of poppies, needing to take off their jumpers from the heat. They were definitely not in Paris anymore.

When at last, they arrived, she pulled into a parking area where a noticeboard advertised tours of the garden. The garden, so the informative sign said, had been in operation for the local community since medieval times, the flowers used for homeopathy, aromatherapy and the lavender supplying some of the perfume trade.

As they made their way up the path, they were given a tantalising glimpse of vast rose gardens, as well as beds of other beautiful summer blooms, like hollyhocks, snapdragons, and dahlias, not to mention the breathtaking views of lavender that surrounded it all.

Despite the beauty before them, they were both nervous now they were here. Monsieur Géroux's hands shook and Sabine's mouth had turned incredibly dry in her anxiety.

They took a moment to calm their nerves, and take a sip of water from the bottle they'd bought when they had their impromptu roadside picnic, before making their way to the tall, arched entranceway to the abbey.

Inside the thick walls, their footsteps were noisy on the flagstone floor. A nun was sitting behind a vast oak desk, dispensing tickets for the lavender tours. A group of six people was queuing in front of her.

When Sabine, at last, stepped forward, and asked for Sister Augustine, the sister hit a buzzer, and soon afterwards another nun, tall with dark eyes and a wide smile, came out of a concealed entrance behind her. The first nun whispered something to her, and she smiled and then indicated that their guests should follow her. They went around the corner and then up a flight of stairs. The journey took them along a passage deep in the abbey. Along one of the walls was a tapestry depicting the apostles; another had various baskets as well as other old-fashioned-looking farming equipment.

'These are some of the old tools that we used to use to collect and distil the lavender,' the tall nun explained, seeing Sabine's curious expression.

'Oh,' was all Sabine and Monsieur Géroux said in response.

'Things have changed a bit since then,' said the nun with a smile.

They all managed a laugh.

They were then led from the passageway to another building, by crossing a small courtyard which was full of large potted ferns, and a table and chairs. From there they were taken not into the building that led on from the courtyard, but outside to a gravel path that led them to a rose garden around the side. They were led to a table where another nun was standing in wait.

She appeared curious, like a small blue-and-white bird, in her habit, with her head cocked to the side. She had dark eyes, and a kindly looking face, edged by deep lines. But it was difficult to determine her age – she could have been in her sixties or eighties, it was impossible to say, but if it were the latter she was in remarkably good health, and seemed spry and wiry.

She stared at them for a moment, and then came forward holding out a small, slim hand to Sabine. The fingers were swollen with age, and slightly reddened. The skin, however, was soft, and cared for.

'Sister Augustine?' guessed Sabine.

'Forgive me for staring, but it was – for a moment – like getting a glimpse of the past. You look so much like her. The eyes – the shape of the face even. It is disconcerting.'

Sabine drew in a breath.

'Y-you knew Marianne?' uttered Gilbert.

'Marianne?' said the nun, raising her brows. 'Yes, later she called herself that, of course, but to me she was always Elodie.'

Sabine shared a look of amazement with Gilbert. 'Was that her real name – Elodie?'

'Oh yes. It was her given name. I knew her from when she was a child, not long after she came to stay with her grandmother every summer. We were friends, you see.'

'Friends?' said Sabine.

Sister Augustine's revelation had been a shock for Sabine. Somehow, in her imagination, she had been convinced that Marianne had given birth in the abbey as a matter of convenience, perhaps in an effort to disguise her true identity, but this was something else entirely. The nun had known her. She looked at Gilbert and he looked just as floored as she did. It was more than they could have hoped.

Sister Augustine looked thoughtful. 'Yes.'

'Can you tell us about her?' ·

The nun stared at them for a while. 'Is that why you're here, to find out who she was? Or is it to find out why she did what she did?'

36

PROVENCE, 1987

They stared at her, utterly floored.

'You know about the restaurant – about the people that she killed?' said Sabine.

'I do. Is that why you're here? To satisfy some curiosity of yours?'

Gilbert and Sabine shared a look. The nun was surprisingly feisty.

'No, it's not like that. I want to know who my grandmother was – it's not some mild curiosity for me, it's more than that.'

Gilbert nodded. 'Me too.'

The nun stared back at them and nodded. 'Take a seat. I will ask for some refreshments, and then I will tell you what I know.'

They both pulled out heavy steel chairs and watched as she went back inside.

The garden was beautiful. The roses offered a profusion of pale lemon, salmon pink, and frothy white blooms that cascaded over walls, climbed trellises and bowed arches.

When Sister Augustine returned, moments later, it was with a wooden tray laden with rose-flavoured lemonade and several large glasses. She set it down carefully, and for a moment Sabine saw her fingers shake.

She wondered if it were a sign of age, or of nerves. Her words, when at last they came, confirmed for Sabine the latter.

She took a seat, then poured them each a glass of lemonade, spilling some on the table, muttering a soft, '*merde*,' which while about as tame as it came to cursing was still a surprise from a nun. 'I apologise, I'm nervous, now that it is finally happening – that someone is here for her.'

Sabine shared a look with Monsieur Géroux.

'You knew someone would come here?' he asked in some surprise.

'Marianne did. I think it was why she put the abbey on all the documentation; even though we had never handled anything like that before, she wanted to make sure that if one day her daughter came to find out what happened, there would be someone who could tell her – someone who would remember her, and perhaps explain.'

'But – but what if you weren't here? What if someone came and you were—?'

The nun took a sip of lemonade. 'Dead? Well, I was beginning to think that would be the most likely outcome, as the years passed and no one called.'

'If she – well, if she wanted her daughter to know the truth, why didn't you contact my mother? It's not like the adoption records were sealed.'

Sabine left out the fact that her mother hadn't known she was adopted.

Sister Augustine shook her head. 'Elodie was clear – if her daughter or family wanted to know what happened, I was to tell them, but I wasn't to go looking for her child and to deliver her tale. It is, after all, not a happy one. She thought that if her child grew up never knowing of who she was and where she came from, while sad, wouldn't it be worse for her to impose such a history on her? I had to respect her wishes even though it pained me to think that so few people understood what happened. The sacrifice she made – or indeed the honour she displayed.'

'Honour?' said Sabine in some surprise.

'Yes, I believe so, in her own way.' She looked at them both. 'How much of her story do you know?'

Gilbert answered. 'I used to work for her when she first opened the restaurant. I was there, right up until the night she killed all those people, including my brother, Henri.'

Sister Augustine's eyes widened in shock. 'You are Gilbert, Henri's brother?'

Gilbert turned pale. Sabine reached for his hand.

'Y-you know of him – of me?'

'Only what she told me.'

Sabine gasped. 'She told you?'

'Yes – she came here afterwards, like she always did, when she wanted to confess.'

'Confess?' breathed Sabine.

'Yes.' Sister Augustine nodded. 'She didn't mean to kill Henri, this I can tell you straight away, and I must admit that when she came here and told me what she had done, I wished that she would have tried to explain to you what had happened '

Gilbert's lip wobbled. 'Why didn't she?'

'She wanted to – wanted to be absolved by you, but she thought that wouldn't be fair to ask. I believe she felt she deserved your anger, your hatred; after all, she might not have intended for him to die, but it was nonetheless caused by her own hand. I believe she felt no excuse could justify this, so she should be condemned as a murderer, a monster, for what she had allowed to happen.'

They stared at her in shock. Tracks of tear were slipping unbidden from Gilbert's eyes.

Sister Augustine dabbed her own eyes with a corner of her habit. She swallowed, and then said, 'I will tell you what I know, but I think to really understand her story, we must start at the beginning, so if you'll allow me, I would like to share it – or at least the parts of it she told me.'

'I'd like that,' said Sabine.

Gilbert nodded too.

Sister Augustine took a sip of lemonade, like a fortification. 'In 1926, when Elodie was nine her mother died from tuberculosis in front of her and the shock of it turned the young child mute. Her father was a wealthy aristocrat living in England and it was decided that for the time being she would be taken to live with her grandmother, Marguerite, in Provence.

'Marguerite was delighted to have her grandchild back in her life, as the two had been kept apart because Elodie's mother Brigitte and Marguerite had a falling out when she ran away with a married man. A man who while he assured Brigitte he would care for her and the child, Marguerite knew would not leave his first wife for her, and when this proved true, it only seemed to fuel Brigitte's desire to stay away from her mother. A sad resentment that kept them apart till her death. No one regretted this more than Marguerite and she was determined to pour all the love she had on her grandchild. Which she did.' At this she smiled. 'Though it wasn't actually Marguerite that made Elodie finally begin to talk. That was your grandfather, Jacques Blanchet.'

When she spoke of Jacques Sister Augustine's voice caught.

'Did you know him too?' breathed Sabine.

'Yes. Not far from here was the Blanchet vineyard. It bordered your great-grandmother's – she owned a small parcel of land and he looked after her vines too. Jacques was a wonderful child; deep, introspective, he stayed away from most other children his age but he sought Elodie out when he heard that she had lost her voice and her mother, something he could relate to, having lost his mother not long before. I think he thought of her as a kind of wounded bird, one he could fix.' She smiled softly, her dark eyes looking into the past. 'And you know, for a while, he really did.'

She regarded her guests. 'As a nun, I'm not really meant to keep possessions, but I have a photograph of their wedding.' To their dismay, tears edged the corner of her eyes. 'Would you like to see it?'

'Yes, please,' said Sabine, sitting forward eagerly.

Sister Augustine nodded, then she reached inside the pocket of her habit, and brought out a thick envelope. She opened it, and took out a small black-and-white photograph with decorative edges.

Sabine recognised Elodie immediately. She looked young and pretty, her dark blonde hair in waves around her shoulders. There was a chain of flowers on her head. She was standing in the middle of a vineyard with a farmhouse in the background. On her left was an older woman with white hair and almost the same smile as her. Their faces were close together, and on Elodie's right, looking down slightly, his face away from the camera as he smiled, was a handsome man with dark eyes and dark curly hair.

'This was Marguerite?' Sabine guessed, touching the picture. 'And my grandfather. He was handsome. He looks so happy.'

Sister Augustine nodded. 'They were. It's hard to imagine that just a few years after this he would be murdered by that horrible man.'

Sabine stared at the nun in shock. 'Murdered?'

'Yes. By a person whose name I have never been able to

forget in all these years, though there were times I wished – prayed, really – that we had never been told it. How different her life might have been – how different all your lives might have been, then.

'His name was Otto Busch.'

37

PROVENCE, 1987

Gilbert knocked over his lemonade as he stood up full of anxiety.

'Are you certain, Jacques Blanchet – Marianne's husband, I mean, Elodie's husband –was killed by a man named Otto Busch?'

Sister Augustine took a deep breath. She looked at Gilbert with concerned eyes, and nodded.

'Yes – I gather you knew him.'

Sabine frowned. Even she knew the name, from all of Gilbert's stories.

Gilbert sat back down in his chair with a heavy thud. 'It was no coincidence – was it, that she chose to work with him, so that she could kill him?'

Sabine blinked.

Sister Augustine sighed. 'No, it was not,' she agreed. 'Though at first she didn't set out to kill him or anyone. She just wanted to meet him.'

'So after Jacques died, she set off – what? To find him?'

The nun frowned as she rubbed her fingers together like they were causing her some pain, though perhaps it was the memory that ailed her, as a shadow fell across her face.

'No, not at first. In the beginning, she really did try to put her life back together. She was to become a mother, and that was incredibly important to her. She loved baby Marguerite from the minute she fell pregnant with her and it was the only thing that kept her going after Jacques died.

'But then after war broke out, and Paris became occupied by the enemy, she came across an article from the gloating victors about a Nazi who was delighted with his new promotion, and his role as Paris's new cultural liaison. Seeing him – this man who had taken everything from her – being rewarded, well, something just sort of snapped inside her.'

38

PROVENCE, 1939

For Elodie grief weighed down all her senses. She glimpsed the world behind a veil of grey.

When she cooked, she did not put the radio on, or stop to listen as she once had to the stories of gossip filtering out from the front of the restaurant. No longer would she pause and smile, as she heard tales of romance, of intrigue, and of petty arguments that had waged for years... she was numb to it all, and it showed in her cooking, as without realising it, she had begun to repeat herself, making the same dish every few days, and most of them tasting pretty much identical.

The customers were loyal, and none complained.

But after several weeks of this, the good sister, Sister Augustine, stopped by the restaurant to visit her, something she had never done before.

'I hear it is ratatouille again,' she said.

Elodie glanced up, surprised.

'Sister?' she said, mustering her first smile in weeks.

'I came to see how you are doing, since you haven't been around.'

Elodie frowned, then carried on chopping vegetables. 'I've been busy, I'm sorry.'

'I can see that.'

Elodie put down the knife, then looked up at the older woman. They stared at each other without speaking for a while.

'I – I just didn't feel like speaking.' She sighed. She wasn't the only one. Monsieur Blanchet had stopped coming around. She'd given up asking him to visit, a few weeks after they found out about Jacques' death. They'd tried to play a game of chess that last time, but after a few minutes, he'd knocked over his knight, his hands in his hair, and saying, 'I can't do this, I'm sorry.'

She had sat in her chair opposite and cried after he'd left. She didn't blame him. Over the weeks that passed she watched him as he haunted his own vineyard like a ghost. She missed him.

Sometimes when she fell asleep at night, when the numbness left, and the grief made itself felt, when the tears began to wrack her body, she felt like she was in mourning for everyone she had ever loved. But then on other nights the grief didn't find her. Anger did. That was when she dreamed of an island she'd never seen before, and the man who had taken everything from her. When she awoke from one of those dreams, it felt like the rage that warred within her might choke her.

She cycled through feeling numb and angry most days. Neither made her good company to be around.

Sister Augustine seemed to sense some of this. 'These things take time. We don't have to speak. But you know you can come see me, and just be with me; I miss your face. The roses are in bloom. You could help with them, if you want to stay busy.'

Elodie surreptitiously wiped away a tear. 'I miss you too,'

she admitted. The loneliness she felt was overwhelming. 'I'd like that,' she admitted.

When she went home that night, she opened up one of Jacques' sketchbooks from when he was a child, one of many that were now in the little study he'd used after Grand-mère had passed. A heavy tear splodged onto a page which she wiped away, making the paper warp slightly, smudging a note he'd made about a blue tit.

Pattou, the old cat, came forward to nudge her leg. She felt so flooded with anger she screamed and the cat made a hasty retreat, making her sob all the harder.

She imagined herself doing to that Nazi officer what he had done to Jacques and Herman Ludho. She imagined finding him and making him kneel before her, looking into his eyes and her pulling the trigger. Sometimes she imagined doing the same to all the other officers who were stationed there and simply lied, all those people who denied Jacques and Herman their justice.

When Freddie phoned for his weekly catch-up, he was mortified to hear her speak like that.

'It's just... I feel so helpless. No one is stopping Hitler, they're all so afraid of a war and in the meantime, it all means that the horrible Nazi thugs he has employed to do his bidding for him, get away with murder.'

'Oh, El, don't torment yourself with that.'

She sucked in air, as she began to sob. 'It's hard not to, Fred. I just. I just wish we could bring his body back.'

There was a sigh on the end of the line. 'I know, El. But you know why we can't.'

She closed her eyes, and nodded, she would be putting other lives at risk if she did.

What she wanted was for him to be buried here but Freddy had said that would be incredibly difficult as then his paperwork might not match what they had on record. 'El, I helped to get him false papers, as you know, and it was supported by the other researchers on the team; if the officials saw his true identity it would endanger the researchers he worked with, they could be sent to prison – especially now, given how tense things are.'

'I know,' she said softly, but that only aggravated her more. This awful feeling of powerlessness – that there was nothing to be done – tormented her. That Otto Busch had just simply got away with killing her husband and she couldn't even bring his body home without risking other people's lives.

'Sometimes I can't bear it,' she whispered.

There was a swallowing sound. 'Oh, El, I'm sorry – you have to find a way somehow, you have a child to consider, and right now there is nothing that can be done. While the German government is run by Nazis and with things so tense, this is just how things are, one day that might change, but until then we just have to accept that this is how it is.'

'Yes,' she agreed, 'until then,' but it was the latter that calmed her down slightly. The belief that one day things might change.

39

PROVENCE, 1938

Sister Augustine kept to her word when Elodie came to visit
her. She took her to the greenhouse to plant seeds or to the
perfumery where they harvested essential oils, and she didn't
press her to speak unless she wanted to.

Instead, she distracted her with the plants. Elodie had
always found the healing properties of plants fascinating, and
the nun knew this and tempted her out of her grief by fuelling
her curiosity.

One afternoon, while she was helping Sister Augustine
weed the serenity garden, the nun pointed out one of the plants
she pulled up. 'Did you know that plant was often associated
with witches?'

'What, really?' asked Elodie, surprised, looking at the peri-
winkle flowers.

'It is aconite, commonly referred to as wolfsbane or
witch's bane, a deadly garden plant that seeded here many
years ago that can cause paralysis of the respiratory system,
resulting in death within moments. Women who fashioned

themselves as witches in the Middle Ages used these as part of love potions but they ended up killing the intended love interest instead.'

'Why would you have that here?' said Elodie, shocked.

'It's a weed, and we make a point of pulling it out whenever we find them, but I think it was planted here in the medieval period as in small doses many dangerous plants are thought to have medicinal effects, though to be honest we haven't really found that to be the case with this – and so we weed.'

Elodie grinned, but it did give her an appreciation for how toxic some plants were which most people were unaware of. She had seen those in other gardens too.

Later, the nun showed her another poisonous one. 'This is belladonna, I'm sure you've heard of it?'

Elodie had. 'I'm not surprised, even a small, chewed leaf can kill an adult. The flowers on the other hand aren't toxic. What's interesting with belladonna is that it grows as a decorative shrub, and people who have ingested it don't always feel the effects straight away; it can come on days before the side effects – like a coma or convulsions.'

Elodie stared at the plant as Sister Augustine weeded it out, thinking of how the nuns had the knowledge to do harm as much as heal. Was it any wonder people used to associate these sorts of plants, and the women who knew how to use them, with witchcraft?

In late May, when the roses started to bloom, Sister Augustine put her to work with the garden shears. 'You can help me dead-head them.'

Elodie was now heavily pregnant and she was feeling it. The mild sun felt like hot pokers. Her feet were painfully swollen and she felt irritable; seeing her red face, Sister Augustine quickly called it a day.

They took a break and sat beneath the shade of a tree, and Sister Augustine went to fetch her a jug of her rose lemonade.

Elodie gave the briefest of smiles when she saw it. 'Whenever I have lemonade I always think of you,' she said.

The nun smiled. 'It's one of the few recipes I have from my mother. It's a way to remember her, I suppose, whenever I make it. She loved her gardens, too, perhaps that's why I feel so at home here.'

Elodie took a sip. 'I wonder when that will happen for me?' she asked.

'What?'

'When the memories will be happy again. Even with Grand-mère, sometimes it's still hard to think of the happy times, without crying. With Jacques...' she bit her lip and it began to wobble, and she spoke through a suddenly constricted throat, 'it's impossible to do anything else.'

'Oh, my dear,' said Sister Augustine, reaching for her hand. 'I'm sorry. It's the advice we all hate to hear, but it's the only thing that does help with loss – time. It will never not be tinged with sadness, but someday it will be less painful, you'll see.'

Elodie didn't say anything. She didn't think that would be the case for her.

Then, after a while a tear fell from her eye, and she dashed it away angrily.

Sister Augustine looked at her, concerned. 'What is it?'

'I – I'm just so angry, Sister. It's been months and it's just there – this, this, useless, impotent anger. Every day more stories come through of what is happening in Europe as a result of the Nazis. And every day I realise that no one will ever answer for what happened to Jacques. It fills me with rage,' she admitted. 'Everyone here has been so kind, so supportive...' Her face wobbled as she thought of the patient locals at the restaurant and she gave a half laugh, half sob.

'Half the time I end up making the same thing every couple

of days. My grandmother rarely, if ever, repeated herself; it was always somehow slightly different to whatever she might have made previously. It was all part of the charm of visiting her. Two weeks ago, I made the same dish three times and didn't even realise it.'

'I heard,' said Sister Augustine with a smile.

News spread fast in small towns.

Elodie closed her eyes in shame.

The nun reached forward and patted her hand. 'They understand, *cherie*, and I promise you, they don't mind. Besides, it's got better – last month you made ratatouille almost every day for two weeks.'

Elodie half sobbed, half laughed again, then dashed away a tear. 'Is it better? I hope so, they're all so wonderful, and I feel like maybe I could deserve their kindness, their support if I was just simply... sad. Sometimes, I can't sleep because the rage consumes me, making me envision hurting that man who took Jacques from me, torturing him.'

To her surprise Sister Augustine nodded. 'Grief isn't just despair, *cherie*, it's this too, the anger we feel, it's a part of the process. Trust me, it's natural to question one's faith at such times...'

'It's not that, it's not God I'm angry with, perhaps I should be... for what he allowed... but I feel my rage directed at the man who got away with killing Jacques, Otto Busch. Sometimes I wish Freddie had never told me his name. It feels seared into my skull. This name for this faceless person that I wouldn't be able to spot in the street even if my life depended on it, who stole Jacques from me, stole the father from my unborn child, and changed Monsieur Blanchet into a shadow of himself.'

It was at that point she began to sob.

'He will be all right, Monsieur Blanchet, already he seems a bit better to me.'

'Does he?' Elodie was doubtful. 'It's like he's wasting away.

He's half his size, rarely if ever comes around, not since the memorial.' Elodie closed her eyes. 'It's that that probably hurts the most – that I couldn't bring Jacques home, I couldn't have a funeral, just a memorial,' she said, as hot tears slipped down her cheeks.

Sister Augustine had attended the service, so she was well aware.

'It torments me that no one said his last rites,' sobbed Elodie. 'I keep thinking that his soul can't be at rest.'

Sister Augustine shook her head. 'No, child, don't think of it like that. You don't know that. I'm sure his friends would have said something. He was buried by friends – good friends, loyal ones who cared deeply for him, so much so that they helped to protect him and disguise his nationality, and they chose to bury him on one of his favourite parts of the island, correct?'

Tears were leaking down Elodie's face. She hadn't thought of it that way. She nodded. She had told the nun what Freddie had told her about Jacques' death and burial on the island, but she hadn't thought of it the way Sister Augustine was now inviting her to – that he was buried with love. It helped more than she could say to think of that.

Sister Augustine continued. 'I have never believed as some do that without a clergy present one's soul is in limbo – that may be blasphemous but it is what I think. Before we had churches, there was God, he is in all things. He would not abandon Jacques, never fear that. Perhaps, someday, you can see his grave and have his rites performed then, if that would help you.'

Elodie stared at the nun, whose words offered a small glimmer of solace, like daylight through a crack in a window. 'Yes,' she said. 'Maybe after the baby is born, when things settle down in Germany, perhaps.'

. . .

Little by little Elodie began to put her life back together, as Grand-mère had advised her back when she'd suffered her first miscarriage. Every day she set herself one goal: to make a new dish at the restaurant or to visit the river again. To tend Jacques' mother's meadow. To get out and to see Sister Augustine.

All of these helped and when the lavender bloomed in the second week of June, while she was visiting her friend, she went into labour.

'*Ma cherie*,' cried Sister Augustine as Elodie clutched her stomach, bent over in pain. 'Is it the baby?'

'Yes,' panted Elodie, recognising the pains from her miscarriages; this time, though, she hoped and prayed on all the heavens above to bear a living child. 'Fetch someone!' she cried.

Sister Augustine rushed inside the abbey and returned shortly with another nun. She was tall, with thick, straight black brows and sharp features.

'Sister Grace has helped to deliver many children,' said Sister Augustine.

'Oh, thank goodness,' said Elodie as the nun reached out to take her hand.

'Let's meet this child then,' she said.

Elodie nodded, gratefully, taking her hand, and smiling through a shimmer of tears before another contraction ripped through her and she bent over again and cried out.

'Come on, let's get you inside,' said Sister Grace and the nuns helped her to walk into a courtyard and then to another building, where they staggered down a corridor, with Elodie's face contorted with pain, and finally into an empty cell that had a single cot and a painting of Mary with the baby Jesus on the wall opposite. Two other nuns were there already, their arms filled with linen and towels.

She was helped carefully onto the bed, once the pain subsided momentarily.

The sister began to examine her, helping to remove her

undergarments, timing the moments for when the pain did not rip through her.

'It won't be long now,' she said. 'Perhaps another hour or two.'

'Two more hours,' cried Elodie. 'I can't do this for two more hours!'

'You can. It might be quicker, though.'

It wasn't. It took four. Marguerite Blanchet came slithering into the world, fists balling, face screwed up in rage as she howled, calming only when she was wrapped up and placed in Elodie's arms.

Elodie, who was half delirious with pain and fatigue, stared at her daughter in wonder, seeing Jacques' face looking up at her in miniature.

Sister Augustine came to sit by her side, bringing her a glass of water, and leaning forward to stroke the soft skin of the baby's cheek. 'We like to use the word miracle a lot in our line of work,' she said with a grin, nodding at the painting on the wall opposite of the virgin mother, then softly touching the baby's head. 'But this definitely feels like one.'

'Yes,' agreed Elodie.

'What are you going to call her?' she asked.

'Marguerite,' she said, without hesitation. 'After Grand-mère, I feel like she helped to bring the baby into the world safely somehow.'

Sister Augustine smiled. 'That's perfect. It is a lovely name, and she would be very honoured. Sister Grace has gone to fetch the birth certificate; we'll need to fill out the forms later. But there's no rush.'

Elodie frowned, staring at the painting on the wall opposite. 'You can put down that her mother's name is Marianne Blanchet.'

'Marianne?' said Sister Augustine.

She nodded. 'Didn't you tell me that when you took your

vows you took a new name? I think I'd like that too, as we start a new life. Grand-mère's second name was Marianne, a version of Mary, the mother. Well, today I felt that giving birth here, under her gaze, that perhaps she was watching over us. Perhaps it was a sign for a new beginning.'

The sister patted her hand, she understood.

40

PROVENCE, 1938-40

The world her daughter was born into seemed on the brink of war. In the months that followed everyone seemed to be doing their best to appease Hitler and everything he wanted. In September, Hitler had demanded that the Sudetenland – a border area that contained an ethnic German population area in Czechoslovakia – be returned to Germany. He vowed to unleash war if this did not happen. In a bid to appease him and prevent another war, the leaders of Britain, France, Italy and Germany met at a conference in Munich and they agreed to the annexation of Sudetenland in exchange for peace.

It wasn't just Germany. In April of 1939, emboldened by Hitler's success with the territories he'd captured, Mussolini followed a similar path and annexed Albania. France and Britain had joined forces, vowing to protect Poland's borders – an area known to be on Hitler's target list.

Everyone seemed to be holding their breath and trying not to rock the boat and in the meantime it meant that they were allowing the most horrendous things to occur in the name of peace ...

Every day she wrote a one-line sentence to document baby Marguerite's progress and over the first year of her daughter's life, Marianne found it wasn't always the big moments that caused her joy or pain when she thought of everything Jacques would never get to see, like the first time she smiled or laughed, it was all those other endless days that bled into the next that gave the ones after meaning.

Then Germany broke their agreement and invaded Poland. Britain and France declared war. On the same day that the news broke out, Monsieur Blanchet suffered a heart attack. He'd been worrying about it for months. He feared the loss of his nephews and what another war would do to their country.

'We barely survived the last one,' he kept saying.

His death hit Marianne hard. Apart from baby Marguerite, he was the last of her family here in France. This time, when she mourned, it was like the world did too. Widows from the first war wore black. Fathers looked at their sons with hopeless expressions, no one had an answer as to why it was happening again.

Like before, she spent as much time as she could with Sister Augustine.

Freddie phoned regularly asking her to consider moving to Britain, to raise her child there, but she couldn't understand why he thought they would be safer there. She felt like she had given up so much over the last few years, she didn't want to lose her home too.

Their time over the next few months was taken up with preparations. People began to stockpile food, and while the government assessed its borders and thought of their strategies, closer to home families were given drills on what to do in case of poisonous gas attacks. They were given masks and for those rst few months, everywhere she went she took a mask for her and the baby. Carrying them as she walked through their beautiful hilltop village, she felt like she had entered some strange new world.

At the restaurant she heard tales of students preparing by hiding beneath their desks, which felt to Marianne so much so like closing one's eyes and hoping someone else couldn't see you. Wherever she walked, people looked up to the skies, worried that bombs might start raining down on their heads. But when nothing at first happened, everyone carried on as usual, and Marianne continued running the restaurant and raising her child.

Some days, despite having a child to focus on, she felt like she was a ghost, like Monsieur Blanchet had been like a ghost before he passed, stuck, unable to find hope in the future while he roamed his vines without seeing them, unable to join back into life. Marianne tried to do a small thing every day, the way she had in the past, to push herself to get out of the house or out of her routine, like seeing the nuns, and spending time with Sister Augustine.

But the haunted feeling lingered. The only thing that helped was Marguerite.

Every week she tended to Grand-mère and Monsieur Blanchet's graves. She brought flowers for Grand-mère, and sometimes a new spice she decided to try out as part of her aim to do new things, though new spices were getting increasingly hard to come by.

With Monsieur Blanchet she spoke as if no time had passed and they were finally able to say the things they may have wanted to say but couldn't before he died, like how much they had missed each other, but had struggled to be around one other because it hurt too much without Jacques. Though perhaps this wasn't something either of them had needed to say, it had just been understood, and forgiven. She wished that she had told him while he was alive that he had filled that part of her that had longed for a father since the age of nine, and that when she'd thought of what a father was, he was what came to mind.

She had taken to playing a game of chess with him, and every week she brought one of the pieces, as if she was inviting him to make a move.

Sometimes when she returned she would find that the castle piece she had left had fallen or a knight piece had been blown elsewhere by the wind. But when she left a queen it stayed exactly where it was, and she wondered about that, as if somehow he was saying something to her.

Something about strength perhaps or courage.

41

PROVENCE, 1940

In May, a month before Marguerite turned two, what became known as 'the Phoney War' came to an end as across the sea, Germany battled the skies to conquer Britain and in June, France, joined the battle.

It seemed strange that the lavender would bloom as it always had when so many people feared for their lives, like it should have bowed its not-yet-purple shoulders and halted in protest.

But it did not, the world continued as it always had.

Mothers and fathers said their goodbyes to their sons, before they went to join the army. When Timothee and Giles, Jacques' cousins, had left a few weeks before, stopping past the farm-house in their new uniforms to say their farewells, it all felt so very real.

She hugged each one. Both had worked with her at various times in the restaurant. They were the last males of the Blanchet line. 'Please keep safe,' she begged.

'We will,' promised Timothee, giving her a last hug goodbye. Giles winked at her. 'We'll be back before you know it – before the next harvest.'

Marianne had watched them go helplessly, knowing it was foolish to make such promises.

At Monsieur Blanchet's grave, she put a castle piece down, and said, 'Now you are up there, hopefully you'll be able to protect them.'

When she returned a week later and the castle piece was still standing, she took it as a sign that he would.

On Marguerite's birthday the nuns had a party for her in the rose gardens. Marianne made a chocolate cake with the last of her sugar icing, and Sister Augustine made her rose lemonade.

Marguerite laughed as some of the nuns played a chasing game with her, her little hands clapping in delight as tall Sister Grace, the nun who'd helped guide her into the world, giggled and said, 'I'm going to catch you, I'm going to catch you,' and held her hands out in a tickle pose.

Marianne smiled, then turned to give Sister Augustine's hand a squeeze.

It was hard to imagine, on such a beautiful day, while the sun shone on them, that along the country's borders, their friends, neighbours, and cousins were trying to fight for this – their freedom. Along France's borders, other sister countries had already ceded to Germany. The one comfort they had was that France would never surrender.

They were sure of that at least.

Freddie sent her a package with a note.

'Just in case – Fred.'

Inside was a wad of money as well as a British passport. She didn't know where he'd got the picture of her. The name was her old one.

Elodie Clairmont.

It made her wonder if there was something he knew that she didn't and it made her worry, even though she was grateful to him for the gesture.

Days later, the unimaginable happened. After a series of disastrous battles the government ceded to Nazi Germany.

The news sent shock waves around the world. Marianne listened to it on her radio in the farm restaurant, the food she had been making lay only half prepared, and many of her customers crowded around the entrance to the kitchen, not for their lunch, but to listen too, as the broadcaster announced that the government had left Paris.

'It can't be true, they wouldn't do that!' said an old woman with long grey hair in a chignon and a slight hunch to her back. She wore a long black dress, having taken to wearing mourning as soon as France declared war, despite the fact that all her sons had been killed in the previous one; or probably because of it, thought Marianne, biting her lip.

'I think it is. Come in,' she beckoned, and they all crept in, their faces solemn, eyes fixed on the radio.

'*The Germans are marching in on the capital now*,' came the crackling voice over the waves.

Marianne gasped, clapping a hand over her mouth. 'Paris? *No*,' she breathed, looking back at her customers, her friends, who had all come closer to huddle inside the kitchen, gasping too.

A hubbub followed, fuelled by fear and anger as voices began to rise while men and women shouted at the radio.

An ageing farmer threw his beret on the floor and stood on it. 'March or die, not this,' he raged. 'Never this,' he repeated, fists balled uselessly at his side. A woman near him tried to comfort him.

'They must have had no choice.'

He didn't answer her, he just turned on his heel and left.

He wasn't the only one, as the tears began to flow amid the panic, and soon the restaurant was empty, as they all left to find their loved ones and to prepare for a changing world.

In the weeks that followed, in the same railway car where twenty-two years earlier Germany had signed the armistice to end the First World War, Hitler delivered his own ceasefire terms to the French, a deliberate act intended to humiliate. Their former war hero, Marshal Philippe Pétain, was now to head up the new Vichy Regime, where the government had fled, leaving the Germans to occupy Paris. The country was divided into a 'Free' and an 'Occupied' zone, but both were to collaborate heavily with the Germans, particularly in its anti-semitic treatment of the Jews. Later, the armistice document would become known to many throughout France as the 'Article of Shame'.

Provence was to be part of the Free Zone. People fled the cities in their droves, taking with them all they could carry. Mothers, children, grandparents, arms aching, laden with suitcases full of clothes and whatever had been left in their pantries, headed to the Free Zone, where they hoped to escape.

Marianne watched as, days and weeks later, some of them arrived in Lamarin. She opened up her restaurant, and made big batches of soup. The villagers did what they could, opening up their homes; Marianne was no different. She overheard a tired and anxious young mother with two young boys tell an old man who'd come to Lamarin to live with his sister, that she too had come here to find her family: a distant relation, one of the few that was living, who was thought to live in their village. 'But he left years ago, his neighbour said.' As she spoke, tears leaked down her face that was covered in dust from her long walk. The older man patted her back as her boys began to run around and play and she broke down in sobs, her hand clutching the soup spoon like it was her only lifeline.

'I have a place you can stay,' she told the woman, coming forward and touching her shoulder. The woman looked up at her in shock. She had straggly light brown hair, her eyes were brilliant and green, shimmering with tears.

'Y-you do?'

'Yes. Your boys will like it there – lots of room to run around. Come, don't cry. Eat your soup, and afterwards I'll take you there.'

'But you don't even know my name?' said the woman.

'What is it?'

'Melodie Bonnier.'

'I am Marianne Blanchet. Now, see, we know each other.'

Melodie gave her a watery, grateful smile. 'Yes. Thank you.'

Many people who came to live in the Free Zone, like Melodie Bonnier, found that life there wasn't much better than in the Occupied Zone, since the Vichy Government increasingly toed the Nazi line, and the bulk of their food was sent to feed the German army.

Marianne watched in horror as new laws quickly came into effect, heavily supported by the collaborationist government, to demote Jews to second class citizens. Soon they were not allowed to work in certain areas like law, medicine, administration and education.

It turned her stomach. She looked at her beautiful baby girl and the anger that had been suppressed since Jacques was murdered – since he'd been forced to disguise his true identity because of this awful, pointless hatred for some imagined difference – began to boil. That the authorities could endorse any of these laws that would blight her daughter's future made her clench her jaw at night, unable to sleep.

When she found a pamphlet designed to educate others on the 'threat' of the Jews, she crumpled it into a ball, only to uncrumple it and with her lipstick draw a large 'X' on it, then nail the pamphlet to the door of her restaurant.

When Melodie, who had begun to help out in the restaurant, enquired about it later that day, Marianne's eyes were blazing, her expression like marble, and the woman took an involuntary step backwards, shocked. 'If anyone believes that – they are not welcome here, do you understand?'

Melodie nodded.

'Spread the word,' said Marianne, who went back to chopping vegetables, her knife moving fast.

Melodie nodded. 'I will tell them.'

Later one of her customers, Madame Lennoux, the old woman who had taken to wearing mourning garb, tentatively told Marianne that the town's mayor wanted her to take the red-lined pamphlet down.

Marianne stared at Madame Lennoux, and the old woman narrowed her eyes. 'Don't worry, I told him where to go.'

Marianne raised a brow, and the old woman pointed down. 'Straight to hell.'

They shared a smile.

42

PROVENCE, 1941

Every night that winter, before she put Marguerite to sleep, she read her daughter the stories of the strong Jewish women in the bible. Her favourite and the one that came to mean the most to Marianne was that of Miriam, who had seen such tragedy from Egyptian slavery and the death of so many children from the Pharaoh's decree. Her father, Amram, despairing at the idea of rebuilding a nation after this and wanting to end the suffering of his people, leaves his wife, urging other men to do the same. Miriam tells him that his decision was worse than Pharaoh's as it affects not just this life but the next and she convinces him to look past the here and now and to the future.

'We will be like Miriam, my child, looking to the future, to a world beyond this one. A future that is bright,' she promised, as the seed of bitterness at what the Nazis were trying to accomplish grew, along with her determination to do whatever she could to prevent it.

. . .

If the government were going to distribute pamphlets then so was she. Only hers were not going to be filled with hateful lies.

She had heard of a resistance operation, in Gourdes, one of the bigger towns not far from her, and she set out to join.

The only person she told was Sister Augustine, who tried at first to prevent her. They spoke in hushed voices in the abbey's greenhouse, their regular springtime haunt. Their mugs of Earl Grey were left to grow cold.

The nun looked worried. 'Think of your child, Marianne. This was meant to be a new start for her and you.'

'I am, Sister – and this is how I will make sure she has a real start. I can't just sit back and let this happen.'

'You think that's what everyone is doing?'

'No, not everyone. But then perhaps I know more than some about what is at stake if we truly give in. I believe what they're saying in these resistance cells to be true.'

'Which is what?'

'This war will be won from within, just as much as from the allies fighting across the borders. We all need to do our part. Jacques was forced in the end to live his life in secret. That decision to falsify his papers meant that even in death he was forced to carry on with a lie. I won't have that for my daughter. Not if I can help it.'

Sister Augustine nodded. 'There is a time for all things,' she agreed, quoting the book of Ecclesiastes. 'There is a time to be silent and a time to speak. A time to love and a time to hate, a time for war and a time for peace.'

Marianne nodded, adding, 'A time to kill and a time to heal.'

Sister Marguerite sighed. 'That too.'

In Gourdes, in the cellar of an abandoned restaurant that was filled with sofas and long tables full of pamphlets, Marianne was introduced to a visiting member who was part of a Paris resistance organisation; a handsome, wiry man with tanned skin, black eyes and hair, whose name was Sebastien Bastille. He walked with a slight limp, which later revealed itself to be caused by a prosthetic leg. He lifted up his trouser leg to show her: 'They thought they could keep me out of the war, because of this, but no one can stop me now,' he said with a grin, holding out a hand and shaking hers.

She smiled in return.

'My uncle Fabrice lives in Gourdes, so I'm here for a few weeks,' he explained. Fabrice was the leader of their particular chapter.

'What's it like in Paris?' asked Marianne.

They took a seat on one of the sofas while he smoked a cigarette.

He sighed, 'Worse than you can imagine. Crawling with Nazis, everywhere. They think they are there on bloody holiday, attending theatres and restaurants with great big smiles on their faces—'

Marianne gasped. 'The restaurants all serve them?'

He looked at her. 'Who else could afford to go? The owner still has to make a living.' She frowned, and he continued. 'It's easier for the French to keep up the pretence. But it's hard, people are practically starving, it's a city of women, children and the old – they were left to fend for themselves – the rations are even worse there than down here.'

Marianne clenched her jaw. 'While the Germans have the time of their lives.'

He stared at the hatred in her eyes, and nodded.

'Here,' he said, reaching into a leather bag at his side. 'Take a look at this – we get a local paper, it comes out daily in German. Then there's a weekly one translated in French for the rest of us chumps.'

Marianne took the copy of *Pariser Zeitung* from him, and began to read the stories in some fascination. Sebastien was called to discuss something with Fabrice, and she turned to give him back the paper. 'Keep it,' he told her.

'Thanks,' she said, folding it and placing it in her own satchel, as she was called by another member to collect that week's supply of resistance material. She filled her satchel with the stack of pamphlets and then made her way out of the building, collected her bicycle and rode home. Later, two girls from the village would circulate the pamphlets, fetching them from Marianne at the restaurant, which had become a key distribution centre for the area.

That night while baby Marguerite was asleep, she took out the newspaper Sebastien had given her, and began to read the articles, frowning as she discovered how saccharine it was, full of praise for the French for their wonderful collaboration efforts. Each piece was designed to highlight this. Then, on the second page, she came across an article that made her blood turn cold.

At first it was a seemingly innocuous story about the appointment of a new cultural liaison officer in Paris, whose job it was to ensure that cultural centres and Parisian businesses were kept operational.

There was a picture of a blond officer smiling as he shook hands with the owner of a bakery, a stocky man with haunted black eyes. The caption said, '"Bread is a cornerstone of French culture and so our bakeries need to be kept open. We must restore Paris as the centre of French culture, and we will do that by keeping businesses like these flourishing," says Otto Busch, the new cultural liaison officer for Paris.'

She forgot to breathe.

It was *him*.

He was here in France.

And he was *smiling*.

. . .

She sat in the dark, consumed with rage. She shed hot, angry tears but they brought no release.

Otto Busch was thriving. He dared to speak of French culture. French culture was rooted in liberty, equality and fraternity, not bread.

It was like he was mocking them. It was too much.

The man who had snuffed out her husband's life like a candle had suffered no consequences for his actions. She stared at the paper and re-read the article once more. It said he had been promoted. Somehow, after all he'd done, he had been rewarded. She didn't know how, but she vowed with every fibre of her being that she would find a way to change that.

Marianne gave Melodie Bonnier the keys to her restaurant. 'I'll be leaving for a while. If you can, keep it going.'

'But I can't cook, not like you,' protested Melodie.

'You can make soups and stews, that's all anyone needs,' she said, and then she showed her the secret place beneath the floorboards where she kept the pamphlets. 'Tomorrow two young girls will come for these.'

'Marianne?' breathed Melodie, staring at them in shock.

'Can I trust you to give them to them?'

Melodie sucked air into her cheeks, clutched her chest and nodded. 'Of course. I owe you everything, madame.'

'Keep safe,' said Marianne giving the young mother a hug before she left.

She took Marguerite to Sister Augustine next, having packed a large suitcase for her.

'I need you to look after her for me, until I can come fetch her.'

'That's fine – when do you think you'll be back?' asked the sister.

'I don't know. It might be a few months.'

Sister Augustine gasped, 'Months?'

'Yes.'

'But then why won't you take Marguerite?'

'Because it might not be safe. Things are getting worse by the day for Jewish children. I don't know how far they plan to go but I need to know she is in good hands, hidden if necessary.'

Sister Augustine wasn't blind to what was happening. She too had heard the stories. There were lots of Jewish people who were trying to leave the country to escape. 'I will. I promise. But where are you going – is it safe for you?'

'Paris.'

Sister Augustine's eyes widened. 'What?'

For a moment Marianne hesitated, unsure if she should show her. But then she took out the newspaper that Sebastien Bastille had given her. 'I found him, Sister. I found Otto Busch.'

43

Sebastien Bastille offered her a lift to Paris. Marianne had made contact with him shortly before she left Provence. She was in luck, as he was planning to return that afternoon.

She met him and a group of women who were travelling to the city, all of whom were being transported in the back of a livestock van.

She sat next to him, alongside a clutch of chickens, and in the hours that stretched before them they got to know one another.

'Why the sudden need to move to Paris?' he asked, above the rumble of the engine, the sound of the tyres, and the clucks of the hens.

'There's someone I'd like to meet.'

At his look of confusion, she took out the newspaper he'd given her just two days before. His black eyes widened as she tapped the picture of Otto Busch. 'Him? Why do you want to meet him?' She didn't answer. 'Maybe I can help.'

She looked at him. 'Maybe?'

'It depends on why you want to meet him.'

She stared ahead, and her jaw was tight. 'Honestly?' she asked.

'Yes.'

'I haven't decided just yet.'

'Decided what?'

'If I want to look him in the eyes and see if he is as truly evil as I believe he is. Or—'

'Or?'

She breathed in, then looked Sebastien in the eyes. 'If I just want to kill him.'

His eyes widened. 'In that case, I will see what I can do.'

44

Sebastien Bastille had been as good as his word and within a few months had helped Marianne to get an appointment to meet Otto Busch, using a contact from within the organisation.

Sebastien conducted surveillance of the cultural liaison officer on her behalf as well, watching him as he met with potential clients – those in need of help with German finances and collaboration.

He watched and he listened, making notes.

Marianne was to meet him in a week at a café in Montparnasse.

She had found an apartment in the Batignolles village, just above an abandoned clothing shop, and she began to cement in her mind how she was going to approach him – with a new business in mind.

At first, she was invested only in having the meeting – to look into his eyes – but then Sebastien prodded her, asking her one night, 'And then what – after you've looked him in the eye? You let him turn around and go?'

Her answer, when it came, shocked her. 'No!'

He nodded, then lit a cigarette, and smiled. 'Good.'

She blinked. She didn't know if that was good.

'So then you know what we need to do?'

She frowned. 'It means that somehow I'm going to have to go through with this,' she said, looking at the proposal she had worked on day and night, buying a cheap typewriter and painstakingly typing it. She hadn't been sure that she actually would. She'd half convinced herself she was only preparing the proposal in order to take the meeting, but Sebastien had made her see that wasn't true. She wasn't going to be satisfied watching Otto Busch just leave.

What she wanted was to be close to him. So that she could find a way to bring him down.

She spent a fortune on her outfit, a forest green suit with a black trim. The skirt was figure-hugging but not overly tight, and fell below the knee. The stockings, with black piping down the centre, were expensive even for the black market. But it was worth it to see the burgeoning smile on the officer's wide Germanic face.

Sebastien's surveillance of Otto Busch had revealed that he was a complex man. He was gregarious, and agreeable, but quick to temper if he was not given the respect he thought he was owed. He seemed put off by disorder of any kind, and would not sit at a table that had not been wiped down and cleared; the cutlery had to be buffed in his presence. He appeared to prefer taking meetings with potential new clients in the restaurant, mainly so he could judge their table manners.

It was all useful.

He stood up as she smiled, 'Herr Busch?'

'Madame Blanchet?' he enquired, holding out his hand for her to shake.

Marianne's heart was thudding in her chest. She couldn't believe that he was sitting right there across from her, that the hand he was holding out in front of her might have been the one that squeezed the trigger, ending Jacques' life.

'Oh, madame, you're shaking – there's no need to be scared. I'm not the big bad wolf, I promise you,' he said, giving her a wide smile.

He seemed to enjoy the effect, though.

From deep within her she summoned one in return.

'Here, let me help, you,' he said, coming to help her take a seat.

'Th-thank you,' she replied.

'Would you like a coffee?' he asked, pulling out her chair for her.

'I would, yes, thank you,' she said, picking up a napkin and cleaning the cutlery before her.

He smiled, a look of puzzled delight coming across his face, then held up his hand to order.

By the time they had ordered their coffees she had started to talk about her business proposal. She handed him the detailed folder, and he bent his head as he read through it, nodding as he flipped over the pages, seeming to like what he saw.

She caught him staring at her legs. She pretended not to notice.

Soon he had shifted closer to her, and she tried not to flinch. When she got home she would have to have a shower, though she didn't know if she would ever get clean enough after this.

'So tell me about the kind of food you make?'

Marianne did.

He picked up the business proposal again, and downed the last dregs of his coffee.

'Madame, I am impressed. It is not far from my base, lots of important men visit this city, and I can tell you a restaurant with this kind of menu, in this location – slightly more discreet – would be just what we need.'

'Oh, do you think so?' she said, forcing another smile, squeezing her legs tightly together as she really tried to sell it. 'I hope that it could be useful to you and your men, you all work so hard. The food is good for the soul, and it's something very close to my heart, simple, yet nourishing country fare. Like my grandmother used to make.'

His smile widened.

'You are married, Madame Blanchet?'

For a moment, she forgot to breathe. She thought for a second of ending it right there and then with the knife at her side. She looked down and realised she didn't just have to sell the restaurant but herself as well.

'Not anymore.'

His eyes flared with interest.

She had him.

She felt like she might throw up.

'You leave this with me, madame. I can tell you already I look forward to working with you, I am pleased you got in contact with me.'

'Call me Marianne, please,' she said, with a smile. 'And I assure you, monsieur, the pleasure is all mine.'

45

PARIS, 1942

Marianne couldn't believe she'd pulled it off.

It took just three weeks and she had permission as well as an injection of capital from the Nazis in order to open up a restaurant. An official letter arrived letting her know that they would be delighted to help her open this restaurant.

Sebastien was gleeful as he read it. He took a drag of his cigarette and then looked at her over the top of the paper. 'They're helping to fund their own downfall. It's poetic, almost.'

She smiled at him, then took a drag of his cigarette to calm her nerves.

'But now is when it gets hard.'

His black eyes turned serious. 'You're in, *cherie*. But now is when we need a strategy,' he agreed, 'and while I know you're tempted to just lay him flat, the fact that you want to play the long game on this means you want to try and do it properly, correct?'

She nodded. 'Yes.'

Eventually she had told Sebastien why she wanted to take

Otto Busch, in particular, down. It was a few weeks after she'd moved to Paris. The two had become friends: as he was her only contact at that time in the city, he was also the only person she'd told her plan to find the cultural liaison officer.

There was something about Sebastien that bred trust. Perhaps it was his manner. He was unfailingly direct. He was not the kind of person who minced words or tried to be polite. But due to his disability, there was an empathy in him that ran deep, as well as a steely resolve, hardened by years of people underestimating him. 'Growing up, some people would either be cruel about my leg, or treat me as if I was amazing and brave just for existing. The ones who couldn't see past it I ignored but it always annoyed me people thinking I was special when I hadn't done anything. Now I get to do something, to sabotage the Nazis from within. It helps that their opinion of people with disabilities is about as bad as their opinion of Jews.' Then he laughed.

'Why is that funny?' she'd asked, appalled.

'Because I've got Jewish blood too. My grandfather,' he said.

They shared a grin, but it was then that she told him about Jacques and how he'd been murdered and how because of his Jewish ancestry – which his research team had helped to disguise – she hadn't been able to even attempt to get Jacques justice.

He'd stared at her and blew out his cheeks. 'No wonder you want to do this,' he'd said at last. 'But that's the kind of anger that can poison you if you're not careful.'

She'd nodded. 'I know.'

He hadn't quite said as such, but she soon gathered that he was rather high up in the Resistance organisation because when he needed something to happen – whether that was a flat for a friend, or to speed up a meeting – it happened, fast.

Without him, she was sure she would never have got quite as far so quickly.

'There's a senior member of the Resistance who wants to meet you, and soon. He's the only one who knows who you are – and I think it's best if we keep it that way. For the time being he and I will be your contacts. After tonight it will be safer for us to not meet here.'

'Oh no,' said Marianne, who was sad to think that this might be the last time he came over.

'We have to think that quite soon they will begin to monitor you. I have eyes and ears on your door, to make sure no one followed me, but realistically now that they have agreed to help you with the restaurant, things are going to change and we will need to be more careful.'

She nodded.

'From now on we will meet at the Saturday market. I will find you. Your position is going to be a vital one for the Resistance. You'll be perfectly placed to acquire as much information as possible from leading members of the Nazi Party, while they are relaxed and at leisure, and possibly, we hope, revealing more than they would in more formal settings. This will help us dismantle their power from within – but your situation is a precarious one too. We don't know how much you will be able to glean from them, but the potential is limitless. We will have to be careful, though, deciding what we choose to act upon.'

She blinked. 'What do you mean?'

'I mean that what might be hardest, Marianne, is the information we will have to sit on in order to keep you safe, so that they don't figure out that you are an informant. We may need to allow some things to pass – dark things, evil, even – in order to stop bigger crimes.'

She stared at him in horror. She hadn't thought of that.

'I don't mind risking myself. It's my choice.'

He shook his head. 'It isn't, though, because what we – the Resistance – act upon could mean it comes back to you as the source, so it's on all of us. We have to agree on that now, or we cannot proceed. It's not pretty, Marianne, what we're doing. Or neat. It's not a fairy tale where we slay the beast and everyone lives happily ever after. Things might get muddy on our way to killing this beast. We'll have to be strategic.'

She sat thinking for a long time: what he said made sense, but it was awful too. Could she look the other way if they found out something horrid that the Nazis were planning so that she could live another day or go on to fight the bigger fight? She hoped so. She knew there was no turning back now.

She nodded.

'Good,' he said. 'So, as you know, your mission will be top secret – we cannot afford anyone to know about you. Do you understand? It will be crucial that for all intents and purposes the Nazis continue to believe that you are one of their best collaborators. You cannot tell anyone, apart from myself and this contact: we need to keep the chain as small as possible.'

She was given a name, Geoff, and an address. It was a butcher's down the street. 'The code will be as follows. He will say, "I hear that oxtail is as fine as brisket in a stew," and you will reply, "Yes, though the brisket is more tender." From there you will use your code name – which is Anne – and he will radio whatever intelligence you find.'

'Radio?'

'To the British.'

Marianne's eyes widened.

'We are not as alone as we thought, trust me.'

She was glad to hear of it.

'I understand,' said Marianne.

The sale of the shop below her apartment was completed and it was officially now in Marianne's name. She used the money that Freddie had sent her when the war broke out to buy it. She smiled, thinking of what Sebastien had said about how the

British were helping; sometimes they were helping like Freddie had now, without even realising it. But she was grateful – she wasn't sure she would have been able to do it otherwise. Even with the help from Otto it wasn't enough to secure the building and she had been adamant that she wanted to own it.

She wanted to put the Blanchet name on that purchase as an act of defiance after Jacques had been forced to give up his name.

She knew that she wouldn't need a lot of staff – she hadn't needed much in the restaurant in Provence – but she knew she couldn't do it alone, and so she placed an advertisement in the local paper and had a handful of respondents who she interviewed in the empty shop below. Most of the people who applied weren't a good fit, however, like the bitter, tired woman with dirty blonde hair and very large, almost bug-like blue eyes, who had lost her husband and was so full of blind hatred she spent fifteen minutes telling Marianne how evil she was for opening up a restaurant, how awful it was that she was collaborating like this. 'How do you sleep at night?'

Marianne just raised a brow. 'I don't sleep much,' she answered mildly, yet truthfully.

The woman shrugged. 'Yeah, well me neither, not with the baby,' she confessed, reluctantly. Then she looked at Marianne. 'So are you going to give me the job or what?'

It was like looking at a distorted reflection of herself.

When Marianne demurred, saying that she was still interviewing other candidates, she narrowed her eyes and then spat on the floor.

'I'll get back to you,' said Marianne, with a half laugh.

Someone else joined in. She looked past the woman who was leaving with thunder on her face and saw a teenage boy with red hair and freckles.

'Are you Madame Blanchet?' he asked. 'I'm here about the

job as a kitchen assistant, and I er... promise not to spit on the floor if that will help my chances.' And he grinned.

She laughed. 'You must be Gilbert Géroux?'

He nodded. He was the last person on her list and she sighed in relief; to be honest, he was the best thing that had happened all morning. Every other person she had interviewed acted as if they were being led to the gallows, apart from this bright-eyed freckled boy, who appeared to have brought some sun.

This boy would do very well, she thought.

A week later, she met her contact at the butcher's. He was perusing the near-empty shelves. He was in his mid-thirties or so and walked with a cane, he had dark hair that was neatly combed back, and was very tall and thin. He wore a long black overcoat, with a matching hat, and he had twinkling blue eyes.

As she made her way over, he said, 'I hear that oxtail is as fine as brisket in a stew.'

She detected an English accent, rather posh.

She smiled in reply. 'Yes, though the brisket is more tender.'

'Anne?' he asked.

'Geoff?'

He nodded. 'Bonjour, monsieur, Can I have some lamb chops?' he asked the butcher, who came in from the back, wiping his hands on his stained apron. The butcher nodded, then looked at Marianne, who said, 'The same, please.'

'Two each,' said Geoff, handing over ration cards.

As the butcher began to prepare the meat, Geoff looked at her. 'You're all set to open?'

'Won't be long now.'

He nodded. 'There's going to be a fair bit of publicity, do you think you can handle it? They'll need to see this as a feather in their caps.'

'Yes, I can imagine. I've hired someone, Gilbert Géroux, he's great – an innocent. I need to ensure he stays safe.'

'That can be arranged.'

'Only—'

'Only?'

'Only he has a face that hides absolutely nothing, especially his loathing for the Germans. I can guess that it won't be long before he tries to join' – here she lowered her voice – 'our organisation, but we will have to keep an eye on that.'

He nodded. 'I know someone, a girl – I'll get her to recruit him in a few months. She can keep an eye and an ear out.'

'Sounds good.'

Then they left with their lamb chops, and went their separate ways.

46

BATIGNOLLES, PARIS, 1942

In just two weeks the new restaurant would open its doors. The hand-painted sign, reading 'Luberon', sparkled in the late-summer sun.

Marianne and Gilbert had just returned from trawling a local brocante market where they had got an excellent deal on some old restaurant's pots and pans. They had been about to leave when Gilbert spotted several funny posters. They were illustrations of cats who were cooking. One poster had a cat with a moustache and a chef's hat. He started to laugh and he showed it to her.

She laughed, seeing it. 'It's perfect – we'll put that in the kitchen,' she said.

'Really?'

'Yeah, can you imagine the Germans' faces when they see that?'

He'd laughed all the more.

She was hanging one of the posters up, along the front wall in the entrance, where Gilbert was sweeping the front step. She saw him stop as a pair of women outside began to whisper loudly. They wanted him to notice, so it appeared.

She heard one of them whine, 'They say *she* had a special dispensation, to turn it into a restaurant.'

The other replied, 'Yes, everyone else is starving, their businesses going under and she's opening up – it's little wonder how she achieved *that*.'

The first one sniffed. 'Shameful, shameful. And the fact that she's going to serve provincial fare, here, it's like a double insult.'

Marianne tuned them out, focusing only on Gilbert, whose fists were balling at his sides. But she overheard:

'Oh yes. She should have just saved herself the trouble and called it The Happy Collaborator.'

The two laughed, and then finally walked on.

Marianne could have laughed herself – it was exactly what she needed everyone to think if this was going to work.

Gilbert, however, was another matter. She'd come to care for the boy over the past few weeks. He was such a hard worker, and the fact that they were almost ready to open their doors was largely thanks to him. She really didn't want him to get hurt in the process of working here. Sometimes, if she did feel any guilt at all, it was about him, what she might be putting him through.

As Gilbert threw his broom onto the floor and stepped onto the street, his mission was quite clear: to give those women a piece of his mind. Marianne grabbed his hand to stop him.

She smiled at him. 'It's not worth it, Gilbert. We need them to come around – and you can't force that.'

'But how can they "come around" if they don't understand?' he said with a frown, his freckles disappearing as his face turned red in annoyance.

'They will, just give it time – something like this,' she said, pointing to the building behind her, 'well, it's not an easy thing to just accept overnight. Not when everyone is facing such hardship. It looks suspicious, and we need to acknowledge that. Our job is to win their trust, slowly. We need patience,' she said, with a wink.

Then she frowned. 'You look tired, Gilbert. Your eyes have big circles underneath them – when was the last time you took a break?' She knew his mother had been ill and that had been a big worry for him.

He shrugged, then gave her a crooked smile. 'When was the last time you did?'

'Touché. Tell you what – help me paint the last two skirting boards, and then we'll have some coffee and maybe even an early day? Sound good?'

'If you want?'

Just then, the sound of booted feet beat a tattoo, and involuntarily he flinched knowing it belonged to approaching Germans. They turned slowly to find a group of Nazi officers marching towards them.

Marianne's throat turned dry. She would never get used to seeing Otto Busch coming towards her, even though he'd been making a point of stopping off almost every day since they'd begun work on making the shop presentable.

She knew that she had to work on this too, on being around him. On trying to pretend that being near him was the most wonderful part of her day. Sebastien had told her much the same thing when she'd seen him last, at the Saturday farmer's market, where he'd bagged her a tomato and an onion, his disguise being that of a greengrocer.

After they'd had a quick catch-up, and he'd commented on how tired she looked, his eyes had turned sympathetic. 'Are you up for this, Marianne? It's not too late to back out.'

She blinked. 'It is for me.'

He'd raised a black brow. 'OK. But you know how to make this work – to ensure that they want to be there as often as possible. You'll have to make him fall for you, you know that, right?'

She sighed, but nodded. 'I know.'

'So that means *sleep*. You have to always look your best.'

She pulled a face, but she'd known he was right.

After that, she made sure she was always well-presented, and when in doubt, armed with concealer for the shadows beneath her eyes.

'Madame,' greeted Busch with his fresh-faced, farm-boy smile. 'You've moved fast, I'm impressed – just look at this beautiful sign.'

'Well, that was young Gilbert's work – he's an artist – if it wasn't for—' she hesitated, 'his mother's illness, he would have gone away to art school. I'm lucky to have him,' she said, touching Busch's arm. His eyes flared in interest.

'That's good work,' said Busch, turning to the boy, and enquiring about his mother's health.

Marianne was pleased when he arranged to have a doctor be sent to look at Madame Géroux. She had hoped he would try to act the gentleman for her – Gilbert was risking a lot working here without even realising it. If she could find a way to help him too, she would.

As Busch began giving the other men orders, which they were quick to respond to, she made a show of looking impressed. 'Oh, Herr Busch, that is so kind of you.'

He dismissed it but she could tell that he was pleased that she was happy. His cheeks were flushed. Soon he was praising her again and marvelling at all she and Gilbert had accomplished from the freshly painted exterior to flower baskets filled with pink geraniums.

She smiled wide. 'Well, we couldn't have done it without your help,' she said.

He waved his hands. 'It's nothing,' said Busch, dismissing her thanks, 'I just signed a few papers, spoke to some colleagues, it was easy to convince them that a new restaurant was needed here. Madame, you are just what we need, agreed?'

There were enthusiastic utterances from the group.

Busch left his large hand on Marianne's shoulder, and she touched his bicep, smiling even as she stared into his loathsome eyes.

'Well, I am in your debt. You will always have our best table,' she said.

He clapped his hands in delight. 'Well, that sounds like a good deal to me.'

Soon Busch was offering to assist with the rest of the work in order to help them open quicker.

'Just tell us what you need, madame,' said Busch.

Marianne and Gilbert shared a quick look – there went their early afternoon. But she cheerfully turned back to him and began to tell him what she needed done. Soon several officers were trooping inside, rolling up their sleeves and beginning work.

Several passers-by stopped to watch. There was a hacking sound and an old man in a dirty coat spat on the ground. He held up two fingers with the back of his hand, then walked on.

Marianne watched the old man and then looked at Gilbert, who stared after him looking despondent. She knew what he was most likely thinking, that this restaurant wasn't likely to be a success, but it already was. Their customers were already there, and while they were hard at work trying to help her, she was going to do everything she could to try and destroy them. The thought made her calm before she turned to go inside once more.

47

PARIS, 1942

Marianne had a basket ready to be filled and Sebastien was waiting to serve her, coming over to help her pick the best tomatoes, carrots and aubergines. As he pointed out several that were good for stews, she quickly told him how things were going. The restaurant had now been open for a month and she finally had something valuable to share. It was the name of an important General named Karl Fuegler, who was known to be a key figure involved in the deportation of people the Nazis deemed 'undesirable' east to the concentration camps they had begun to build en masse. He was arriving from Berlin, and she overheard the route and time they were expected to meet him. She gave Sebastien the name and what she had overheard on a slip of paper along with her ration card when she made to pay.

Nothing happened with Fuegler, and she heard no news of sabotage. In fact, when several days had passed, Otto Busch told her that he wanted to invite someone special to dine there and she realised that it was the same person. She smiled, and said, 'Of course.'

When she met Geoff, her contact at the butcher's, they were able to speak slightly more freely. 'It was too risky to do anything with your information,' he explained. 'There were officers crawling everywhere. I figure, well, it might have been a test.'

'A test?' she asked, eyes wide.

He nodded. 'Think about it – after a month this was the first bit of real information you gathered and it was huge. If we'd taken Fuegler out, they would have been able to trace it back to you. But even if we had wanted to, he was too protected. It was like they were waiting for us to do something.'

Marianne swallowed.

'But it is good news.'

'It is?'

'Yes, because now, well, we know he likes you – but now he's starting to trust you. We just need to ramp that up a little more.'

She frowned. 'How?'

'There's going to be a small, targeted attack on the restaurant.'

Her eyes widened.

He continued. 'It will give him a moment to be your hero, to offer you comfort.'

She closed her eyes in revulsion, pulling a face.

Then nodded.

They didn't waste time. Just three days later a man threw a brick into the restaurant window and then climbed through it.

Gilbert and Marianne were in the kitchen when they heard the noise. They raced to the hatch and saw a man breaking up furniture. Gilbert shouted at him to stop, but Marianne held him back. The man had covered his face with a black scarf – but he wasn't someone Marianne recognised. He reached inside his trouser pocket and withdrew a knife, which he flicked open. She swallowed. Even though she'd been warned, this seemed worse than what Geoff had described. The man jumped through the hatch and she and Gilbert stepped backwards. Gilbert cried out, 'What do you want?'

'Me?' said the man. 'I want you scum to die for what you're doing here.' He lunged, slashing the knife against Marianne's arm, as she jumped in front of Gilbert. Then he turned and ran.

Marianne didn't need to feign her distress. Her hands shook as she began to tend to her cut. Gilbert raged against the intruder even as he helped her bandage her arm.

Afterwards, she felt in desperate need for a whisky and to be anywhere but there and she sent Gilbert home. He left reluctantly.

'You'll be all right? What if he comes back?'

'He won't press his luck. It won't be long before the Germans start arriving. Perhaps you could just leave a sign outside saying we're closed for now?' she asked.

He nodded.

When Busch found out what happened that afternoon, he raced to find her at her apartment upstairs.

'Madame,' he cried, knocking on her door with heavy impatient fists.

Marianne took a deep breath before she opened up. Then she allowed the tears to fall.

'Oh, Herr Busch, you are here,' she said, and then she began to cry.

'Oh, madame, I got so worried – I saw your window. Gilbert said that some madman attacked you! Are you all right? Why didn't you send for me? What did he look like – we will find him, trust me, he will pay for this.'

'And then another will just take his place,' she said with a sigh. Then her lip wobbled. 'I don't understand why they are so hateful. I am just trying to help feed them good wholesome food.'

It was true, actually. While she did want desperately to find a way to sabotage the Germans – which was her main goal – she was and always would be in her heart a cook, and she knew that cooking simple, nourishing meals for the locals would be a small act of defiance too. Every mouth she was able to feed, to keep alive, was another person who defied the order of things. To live to fight another day.

She allowed herself a small, final tear which she quickly wiped away. Then she looked at him. 'Why can't they see that? It really is better for us all to work together.'

'Yes,' he said, coming forward, and pulling her into his arms. 'It is, and we will help with that. We will try harder to get them to see that.'

'You will?' she asked. 'Oh, Herr Busch, thank you.'

When he kissed her it was all she could do to not scream. But thankfully it was over quickly, and it was worth it to see the tender expression in his eyes.

48

Once Busch had convinced and *threatened* Madame Géroux, Gilbert's mother, and her neighbour, Fleur Lambert, to visit the restaurant things began to change, and the locals began to flock in.

It had the odd effect of helping the Germans to begin, in time, to drop their guard.

Busch – who had made it his habit to visit at least a few times a week – was now there almost every night, partly because he could be sure that Marianne would welcome whatever guest of honour he might be entertaining in the correct and gracious manner, and partly because he was beginning to feel that a romance with her was on the cards.

Marianne did her best to try and manage this expectation, walking the tightrope of wanting to curry favour and keep his interest, but also not wanting to give in to too easily. As Sebastien said one morning when she was running errands, such as picking up cigarettes for the Germans in case they ran out in the restaurant, 'Men like the chase – especially men like that.'

She gathered from this exchange that they had somehow been watching them.

He also told her that her suspicions about Gilbert joining the Resistance had proved right, but that a friend of his was looking out for him, and reporting any of the information he gleaned back to him. 'We're worried that there is an informant in that group, but we can't be sure yet. Right now, he doesn't really speak German so that's a help, but you may want to keep an eye out yourself.'

'Thank you, I will.'

It was good seeing Sebastien; she missed spending time with him like she had before. Right now, apart from Gilbert, he felt like her only friend.

He seemed to read her mind, because he touched her hand lightly and sighed. 'Stay strong, *cherie*. I'll check in again soon. Geoff will be moving on to a new location. I'll update you here, same time next week.'

Now that the restaurant was busier than ever, it was getting too much for just Marianne and Gilbert, and she suggested that they hire his little brother, Henri. Marianne had met him a few times and she liked him.

Gilbert wasn't sure at first if it would be a good idea, saying that Henri was a bit of a wild card. 'He says such stupid things sometimes, Marianne, like he wants to knock the Nazis off their bicycles, or throw a brick through their car windows. I worry he might do or say something stupid.'

Marianne could understand that.

'He's a teenager, Gilbert, full of hormones. The one thing I can tell you is that the best thing for that is to be busy and also to be under a watchful eye – at least here we can watch over him. Besides, he's not stupid, he might be impetuous but he won't say anything that could get him into serious trouble.'

It took Gilbert a while to convince not Henri, but his mother, but when Henri started to work with them, he brought a real dash of fun.

His first night there was a busy one with very important guests for Otto Busch – guests who were getting steadily drunker as the night wore on.

They heard one of the Germans singing in a very strained falsetto and they both started to laugh. They laughed even harder after Henri produced a near pitch perfect imitation of the German singing while hugging a bottle of wine to his chest – but in Henri's case with a large bottle of washing-up liquid.

Marianne saw Gilbert come in, and carried on laughing, but when Busch entered she stood to attention, turning pale. Unfortunately, Henri didn't notice and carried on with his impression.

When Busch asked, 'Are you mocking my singing?' the room grew quiet and Marianne tried to think of something – anything – to say, cursing herself for being an idiot, and not listening to Gilbert's warning, and risking this young man by hiring him, when she of all people knew what kind of a person Busch was. What he was capable of when he got angry.

She felt like she might throw up.

Henri, however, was a champion charmer. 'Not yours, sir,' said Henri, including him in on the joke. He beckoned Busch over to the hatch where they could just see one of the other officers, with a red face, deep in his cups, holding on to a bottle of wine while he sang rather out of key along to 'La Vie en Rose' on the gramophone that they had set up in the restaurant.

Busch stared. Then he began ever so slowly to laugh, uproariously. 'Oh, you are a *dummkopf,* your accent is impeccable. I think we have done well to have you here. Well done, madame.' He raised a finger and smiled. 'This is exactly what we need – more fun, yes,' and he placed a gentle hand on Henri's shoulders, and winked at him.

After that night, Henri was a firm favourite. He was invited to do regular impressions of the officers, and was delighted to do so. Marianne wasn't sure if this was a good idea. She liked the boy enormously but the guilt at having put him in this predicament gnawed at her.

She tried to keep him away, squirrelled at the back, but Busch wanted him out front, amusing the others and insisted that he was better suited as a waiter, at the front of the restaurant rather than in the back, and Gilbert traded places with his brother. As time went by, Henri was often invited on slower evenings to join them in playing cards. Marianne and Gilbert, however, breathed easier when he was away from them.

One evening while the restaurant was busy, Henri was serving the table of officers and was running himself ragged with requests. Busch had told her that a new and important guest was arriving that evening. 'His name is Harald Vlig and he's a very senior member of the party, so we have to go all out to impress him. He's not a fan of fussy French food but he did say he'd had the best French meal of his life in Alsace, it was a *coq au riesling.* Do you know of it?'

'I do. I can prepare that especially.'

Busch breathed a big sigh of relief. 'Thank you, madame.'

Marianne, Gilbert and Henri took this instruction seriously. As even Busch, who was ordinarily the picture of charm, seemed on edge.

The next evening, after their visitor was welcomed in, and Marianne was preparing the final stages of the dish, she listened as their voices rose in heated discussion.

She heard one of them say, 'You sure he can't speak German?'

'Definitely not. He's a hot-head, and I'm quite sure if he knew my nickname for him meant half-wit, he wouldn't be all that happy.'

At the word '*dummkopf*' Henri raised a brow and said, 'Sir?'

Vlig and the others stifled their laughter behind their cards. 'Very well.'

Soon Busch and Vlig began discussing plans for what sounded like a covert operation.

Marianne watched as Gilbert looked up when they mentioned a map. Standing on tiptoes, he crept closer to the hatch and watched as Vlig and Busch bent their heads together.

Marianne heard them discuss Jewish children who were being hidden in a Catholic school. Her heart started to pound, and she watched as Gilbert took an order slip and began to write something down. Marianne snatched the slip out of his hand and then set fire to it on the gas stove.

'What the hell are you doing?' he hissed, whispering.

'Saving your life – don't be an idiot,' she said, smacking him on the side of his head.

He stared at her with so much pain in his eyes it hurt.

'Marianne – you don't understand. They're planning some-thing – something to do with children. It could be Jewish kids.'

She was furious. He could jeopardise everything – her whole operation, their lives and those of the children – she had to get this information to the right people. It couldn't just go through the local Resistance chapter. The last time she'd seen Sebastien he'd said that the group Gilbert had joined may have an informant, she absolutely couldn't take that chance. She didn't even know if Sebastien and the others would act on this information. She prayed they would. But she was beginning to think of something else that she might do, to ensure Vlig didn't carry on missions such as these.

Marianne shook her head. 'Listen to me. It is unforgivable what they are doing – monstrous.' Her face flashed for a moment with such hatred that he actually recoiled. 'But you will get yourself killed, like that,' she said, snapping her fingers, 'if you deliver that information to the Resistance.'

He blinked. 'You know I am working for them?'

She went to turn up the radio. Then said in a fake, cheery voice. 'Oh, I love this one.' It was Maurice Chevalier's *'Paris sera toujours Paris'*. She swayed her hips. 'You're right, I think a nice summer stew with courgettes tomorrow would be lovely.'

She waited until the Nazi officer who'd turned to look at them through the hatch turned back to the others.

Marianne waited, and when the coast was clear she told Gilbert, 'What you heard earlier – this is the only place they would have discussed it. Which means we'd be the prime suspects if the information came out. Especially you, as he saw you standing by the hatch.'

'I'm sure he didn't.'

'He did. Don't be *stupid*. As much as Otto Busch and the rest of the boots play at being gentlemen, they are deadly soldiers, first and foremost – and the first thing they would do is watch out for listeners.'

'They don't know I can speak German.'

'They don't know you don't. Promise me this stays here.'

It took a long time, but eventually he nodded.

Marianne was able to get the information to Sebastien quickly when he came past the newsagent's early the next morning. 'I'll go to the school myself,' he promised. 'It will be quicker. I'll ask them to evacuate the Jewish children they are keeping hidden.'

Marianne started to cry. Breaking protocol, Sebastien gave her a quick hug. She sank into his arms and wished to never leave. He gave her a quick kiss on the head. 'I'm going to ask them to do something awful, but it's the only way to keep you safe.'

She looked up at him and frowned. 'What do you mean?'

'I don't know, but somehow I'm going to have to get them to cover their tracks – they can't just simply move, it'll be too suspicious.'

'Please be careful.'

'Always, *cherie*,' he said and then kissed the top of her head. 'That goes for you too. Carry on as normal.'

'Yes.'

It was two days before the planned move on the school, and Harald Vlig was visiting the restaurant once more. The decision she'd made the night before sat like a stone inside her belly. But she knew it had to be done. This time Vlig wanted to try something else, something really French. She had prepared a ratatouille just for him.

When she dished up his plate of stew, she was careful to shred a tiny leaf of belladonna inside – the nuns had said it could take two days to take effect, and that was what she was counting on. She took it out to him personally, as she had done the evening before. He seemed to enjoy that he was the only one with a special meal; Busch had told her to really make him feel like an honoured guest so that was what she did, even coming out to pour his wine.

'Here you go, General. One ratatouille.' She gave him a wide smile, as he set it down before him.

He smiled in return. 'I'm looking forward to it. Busch really did well by discovering this gem. I can see why he likes to dine here so often.'

She touched her heart, as if she was flattered, murmured, 'Thank you,' and went to pour one of the other officers' wine, waiting with bated breath as Vlig finally put a forkful in his mouth. Then he turned to her and pressed his fingers to his lips. She beamed in response.

49

PARIS, 1943

In the new year, she found out that Harald Vlig had suffered a heart attack. When Busch told her, she was careful to sound concerned. 'Oh no...' But her heart thundered in her ears. Part of her had been waiting on tenterhooks, almost half convinced it hadn't worked. She had killed a man. It made her feel ill to think about.

'That's so sad,' she managed.

'Terribly said, especially as he'd only just begun to live a little – eating French cuisine at last. Perhaps that's what finished him off.'

For a moment she forgot to breathe.

Then he laughed. 'Look at your face, you'd almost think you had killed him yourself. Don't look so worried, you're like my mother, she was always worried she'd give us food poisoning. She was phobic about meat and rice.'

Marianne blinked. 'Oh, I suppose I am a bit too.'

'Don't worry,' he repeated, giving her arm a squeeze, 'the

doctor said he was at that age – high risk and he had a very stressful job.'

That night it was just a few regulars for dinner, Busch and some of his men. They spent the evening playing cards and drinking wine, and Henri was invited to join in. Busch was in a contemplative mood, perhaps due to the sudden death of his mentor, Harald Vlig. 'Let's toast the old man, in the manner he would have liked.' Then he smiled. 'He wasn't a fan of their cuisine but he did love their wine,' and he called out to Marianne, asking her for a bottle of Bordeaux Lafite 1925.

Busch's deputy swirled the wine in his glass and took a sip, then sighed in pleasure. 'You always know the best wine to order, you must have grown up rather differently to me.'

Busch raised a brow. 'Oh, I doubt it. For a little while my father _____ ___b in Hanover, and I paid attention to what was t___

_____ ___d. 'That must have been great, growing up ___ __s whenever you wanted them?'

___nged. 'No, well, it might have been, he died ___ _y mother passed when I was baby, after that ___ system.'

___red at Busch; she couldn't believe they shared ___mon. The loss of a parent so young, it also made ___v different he might have been had his father lived. ___od had turned sombre and Busch shrugged it off. ___ good German beer to cleanse us of all of that,' he ___e others roared with laughter.

___ a further three weeks before she caught sight of Sebastien. He walked past her and said mildly, 'Fine day today

isn't it, madame?' Though it was raining, she smiled as brightly
as if the sun was shining.

Her knees almost buckled in relief.

It was only later that night after she had locked up for the
night, that she allowed herself to cry, great sobbing tears of
relief.

She missed Marguerite so much it was an open wound, but
this, what they had achieved, made her sure that what she was
doing was worth it.

'One day,' she promised her absent child, safe at the abbey
with Sister Augustine, 'one day you will understand, I hope.'

Marianne wished that she could tell Gilbert about the children.
She could see it in his eyes, the guilt he felt at not relaying what
he knew to the Resistance.

But it was what had kept him alive.

He was distracted from his guilt by the sudden decline in
the health of his mother. The doctor said it didn't seem likely
that she was going to live much longer. Marianne told him and
Henri that they needed to spend this time with her. Henri
seemed to want to be anywhere but at home. 'It's just so hard,'
he admitted, 'over the past few weeks she's got so thin, it's like
she's starting to wither away, I hate seeing her like that.'

Marianne's heart bled for them, she knew how hard it was
to lose a mother, and with Grand-mère, who had been like a
second mother to her, it was like she'd lost two.

'Henri, you don't know how long she has left.'

There was a sound from behind and Busch came in, making
straight for Marianne, touching her back gently, and then seeing
Henri's troubled face, he asked, 'What's this? What happened?'
His expression grew concerned as he came forward to touch the
boy's shoulders.

'I'm fine,' lied the boy.

'It's Berthe,' said Marianne. 'She hasn't been doing very well.'

'Oh, son,' said Busch, and he looked at the boy in sympathy. 'I'm sorry to hear that.'

Henri quickly dashed away a tear, then looked at the floor. 'The doctor is coming tomorrow morning, he's given her some new tablets; he said they might help.'

'You should go now, Henri, I can manage without you,' said Marianne. 'It's quieter now, with the new year.'

'Not that quiet, you still need help, I'll be fine, it's better if I'm busy.'

Marianne looked at Busch for support, touching his arm. 'You lost your father, when you were young, Herr Busch, tell him he needs to spend this time with his mother.'

Busch looked at her curiously for a moment, a frown on his face.

Marianne didn't notice, she only had eyes for the boy, 'Trust me, Henri, one day you'll have wished you had spent every moment with her.'

'Don't force the boy if he doesn't want to,' snapped Busch, 'not everyone feels the same things.'

Marianne frowned.

Henri looked up at Busch and then he nodded.

Later that evening, Busch was drinking beer, and he was barely engaging in conversation with his other men who were playing cards. When she came in, he called for her to bring another bottle.

'I don't recall telling you that my father died,' he whispered, when she put it near his elbow.

She looked at him, and her heart began to thud.

'Oh, I'm sure you did. Perhaps when we were speaking about my grandmother...'

He took the bottle of beer and held it between his hands, his brows gathering into a deep contemplative frown as he stared at the label.

'No, no, I don't think that was it.'

'It must have been at some point, I forget when. I mean, we have spent a lot of time together over the past year,' she said, touching his arm and giving it a squeeze.

His hand clamped onto hers tightly. Much more so than was necessary. She swallowed.

He looked up from the bottle, his voice low. 'I recall exactly when I mentioned that my father had died. It was right here,' he said, tapping the table with the index finger of his other hand, the other still clamping hers in a vice-grip.

'Oh, um... yes,' said Marianne. 'I must have just overheard you.'

Her heart was starting to roar in her ears.

He nodded slowly, then took a sip from the bottle, releasing her hand at last, his eyes once more on the bottle in front of him. Usually, he always made sure to decant it into a glass.

Marianne snatched her hand back, too afraid to move.

'I also recall that that was a conversation I had in private, and in German.' He looked up at her. 'All this time, I didn't know you could speak it.'

Marianne's mouth was dry.

'I – just a little, you know, over time.'

He nodded. Then shrugged. 'Yes, I suppose that makes sense.' Then he gave her a tight smile, 'Thank you, madame, that will be all,' and he dismissed her

When Marianne went back to the kitchen she found it hard to breathe.

Was he onto her?

Or just surprised?

She didn't like how this felt. It would be safer, all around, if Henri stayed away from now on, despite how much he wanted to escape his mother's sick bed. He was still playing cards with the men, so she wrote a message for him on a slip, telling him to spend tomorrow with his mother, and that it was an order.

He might listen to Busch but she was his employer.

Later, when Henri came through bringing beer bottles and plates which he'd stacked inside a big storage bin, he saw the order note and then raised his brow at Marianne. She looked up from where she was scrubbing the oven. 'I don't want an argument – spend tomorrow with her.'

He put the slip on the counter and sighed, then nodded.

After he finished cleaning the plates and putting them away, Marianne sent him home early. 'You look worn out, go on, get a good night's rest.'

He nodded. 'Thanks, madame.'

She was wiping down the counters when Busch stopped past the kitchen as normal to say farewell. His manner wasn't as cold as it had been just hours before and she was relieved.

'As you know, tomorrow evening will be a private affair, closed to locals,' said Busch. 'I have another senior officer I need to impress, Karl Lange. Do you think you could make something special?'

'Yes, of course, any particular dishes?'

'No, you can just make whatever you like, I trust you.'

The relief she felt was enormous. She smiled and he came forward to touch her shoulders, drawn to it like a crackling fire.

'I'll say goodnight, then,' he whispered, and gave her a soft kiss on the lips. He didn't linger, though, as he normally would.

His breath stank of beer, and every fibre in her wanted to push him away but part of her was also incredibly relieved that he was acting more normally again. Maybe he really had been surprised earlier. Either way, she knew she had to do something – usually he was very reluctant to leave in the evenings, wanting to have an extra coffee with her, just the two of them. He hadn't tried anything more than a few kisses, but still she was exhausted by the time he finally left.

She touched his face and turned the kiss into something a bit deeper. His eyes flared in interest, and he pulled her closer.

When they broke apart, he touched her hair, putting a strand behind her ear. 'Maybe tomorrow night I'll stay a little longer, spend some real time with you in private... tell you *all* my secrets.'

She stared back at him and a feeling of revulsion swept through her. Her legs started to shake but she smiled. 'I'd like that.'

He smiled widely at her, and then gave her one last kiss, before he took his leave.

When she was sure he had gone, she stood with her eyes closed trying to breathe. Her heart would not stop clamouring. She switched off the lights, and then went to lock up. Through the closed door she smelled smoke and she heard men speaking outside.

She pressed her ear against the door and heard one of them say, 'Louisa Tellier has a list. She's bringing it tomorrow at dinner.'

Busch's voice answered. 'Ah, good, soon we will find all the hidden rats.'

Marianne frowned. Hidden rats? She swallowed, did they mean... Jews? The people hiding them? Both?

She heard Busch's laugh. 'The little Frenchie was a good find. You did well to recruit her.'

'You know how it is, give them a little bit of jewellery, some lipstick and they eat out of the palm of your hand.'

There was some raucous laughter from the other side of the door.

Then Busch said, 'Soon we will smoke them all out.'

Marianne's heart thundered in her chest. Was this Louisa

Tellier an informant? Hadn't she heard that name somewhere before?

In the morning she met Geoff; his old haunt by the butcher's had moved on now to the wine shop around the corner and she told him what she'd overheard.

He looked shocked and angry. 'Sara, who used to head up Gilbert's Resistance chapter, said as much about Louisa but we all thought... well, we thought the two just didn't like one another.' He pinched the skin between his eyes. 'Jesus, she was right the whole time.' He clenched his jaw. 'We'll keep eyes on Louisa. It's important that the night goes as planned but see if you can get a look at that list,' he asked.

She nodded.

When she left the wine shop she saw an officer on the opposite side of the street. He was one of Busch's men, and she felt a chill begin to grow within her belly when he looked at her. He had small sunken eyes and they looked dark and forbidding.

Had she been compromised?

She walked along the street, and then up another, and when she looked back, the officer was there in the distance but he was now talking to another. They both turned to go back the way they had come, in the direction Geoff had gone.

She struggled to catch her breath. Had she just put his life in danger?

That evening, she prepared two separate pots of the same meal. One she laced with aconite, a poison that she knew to be fast-acting and deadly. She had found it growing in one of the parks, like a weed, and instinct had made her pick it a few days before.

When Busch had arrived at the restaurant half an hour later, he had his arm around Henri's shoulders.

'What's this about you saying that you don't need help tonight, Marianne – who is going to serve us drinks? I persuaded young Henri here that he was needed.'

Marianne paled. Her heart started to pound and it was all she could do not to scream at him to get out. She tried and failed to school her expression. 'Oh, monsieur, when you said you wanted a private restaurant I thought I would make sure it was truly so,' she protested in horror.

His eyes widened. 'Well, I do not need to be private from you or your staff, I am sure by now we can trust one another, right?' He smiled.

'Of course, monsieur.'

'Good.'

Marianne swallowed. 'Well, I will go check on the food.'

He nodded, and asked Henri to come and take their drinks order.

In the kitchen, Marianne was a mess of nerves. When Henri came in, some ten minutes later and began opening bottles of beer and pouring wine, she came to him in a rush. 'Why are you here?' she hissed.

He frowned. 'Madame, please, I just couldn't be there.'

'You shouldn't be here, Henri. Not tonight.'

'Please, madame, don't start.'

There was a call from the other side of the hatch for Henri. 'Where's my beer?' and Henri hurried to fill the order.

Marianne took a deep breath, tried and failed to steady her nerves.

Their special guest was Karl Lange, who was high up in the Nazi propaganda machine, which was doing overtime with Paris, and Louisa, the French informant, who was dressed in red, her sharp face softened by the glow of the candlelight.

When Marianne came out to pour the wine, Louisa shot her a defiant look.

Busch smiled at her. 'Do you know Louisa?' he asked her in German.

Marianne shook her head. But she'd heard of her and despised her on principle. She remembered Geoff's expression earlier, the shock and the surprise. For ages they had suspected they had an informant... this was her. Her blue eyes turned dark as she regarded the younger woman.

'Well, you should, you have so much in common. She too has seen the value of collaboration.'

'Has she?' asked Marianne, fixing the other woman with a tight smile.

'Oh yes,' said Louisa. 'Well, we all have to pick sides at some point. I just bet on the winning horse.'

'I like to bet on the rider personally,' said Marianne. 'They are the ones who end up surprising you.'

'I don't like surprises,' said Busch, giving her a pointed look. Marianne swallowed.

When Marianne went back inside the kitchen she struggled to calm her shaking limbs.

From the hatch she heard the talk turn towards Louisa's list and the forced removals of Jews hiding across the city. She heard Busch's voice carrying loudly; they were no longer trying to disguise or muffle their voices. She stood on tiptoe to try and get a glimpse of the list but their arms were in the way. She'd have to try and get it later, somehow.

When Henri served the meal, he came back with a puzzled look on his face. He came to fetch another bottle of wine. 'Madame, Busch says he wants to speak to you about the stew.'

Marianne felt a wave of anxiety threaten to engulf her.

'Oh yes. Does it need salt?' she said loud enough for anyone to hear. Then she put on her sunniest face, and took the bottle from Henri. 'I'll pour,' she said, going out to see what he wanted.

No one had touched their food. She saw that straight away. She went to Busch's side. 'Henri said you wanted to speak to me?'

'Yes, we just thought perhaps you would like to join us tonight?'

She swallowed. 'Oh. Um, thank you. I'll go get a plate,' she said, smiling. His hand shot out to stop her, once more she was caught in a vice-like grip.

'No, no bother, you can have half of mine,' he said, mildly, letting her arm go, and then slopping half of his stew onto a side plate for her.

'That is very generous,' she said. She held the bottle in front of her, then reached for the bottle opener that Henri had left on the table. 'Shall I pour?'

There were several nods.

'Eat up, gentlemen, don't let it get cold,' she said with a smile as she began to fill their glasses.

One of the men was about to when Busch held up his hand, a half smile on his face.

'Why the rush to feed us, madame?'

She looked at him, forced on a big easy smile. 'No rush.'

He stared at her and she forgot to breathe.

'You know, I have never seen you eat your own food,' he said, with a frown.

'Oh,' she said, 'well, it's not usually good for... for the cook to eat with everyone, but I always have a good taste,' she said, winking at the others, 'but if you insist.' She came to the place he'd set for her, and took a seat. She picked up a fork and filled it from the side plate he'd set out for her, ready to put it in her mouth.

She wouldn't mind dying if it meant they did too. If that meant that she could help prevent the forced removal of hundreds of people who were already afraid for their lives.

Busch watched her, a frown on his face, and then just before she was about to put it in her mouth he shook his head. 'Henri,' he called, 'make yourself a plate too. You can join us too – tonight is a celebration.'

'Oh no, monsieur, Henri...'

'You don't want him to eat this food?'

'It's all right, madame, I'm happy to join,' said Henri.

She felt like she was drowning.

'I don't think that's right, you have important guests,' she said, looking at Karl Lange.

'Oh no, I don't mind,' said Lange.

'Come here,' said Busch, taking the plate from her, 'come sit, Henri. Try some of Marianne's stew. Marianne, go get yourself a proper plate.'

Marianne's mouth turned dry.

Henri nodded, good-naturedly, waiting for her to leave her chair and then he took her place. Before she could do or say anything he'd shovelled a big forkful into his mouth, closing his eyes in bliss. 'Oh my gosh, it's delicious. I was starving,' he said.

Marianne felt like the world was falling away from her feet, she wanted to knock the plate out of his hands, tell him to run, but it was hopeless, they'd both be killed on the spot, and she needed that list from Louisa. From somewhere she managed to mutter and smile, 'I'm glad you like it.'

Something about this perhaps calmed Busch and he began to eat too.

'Look at the boy,' laughed one of the others. 'He is enjoying himself.'

'Good,' said Busch, patting him on his back.

Marianne got up. 'I'll go get one for myself,' she said, and made her way to the kitchen to get another plate and to stop her eyes from filling in front of Busch.

When she returned everyone was eating.

One of the soldiers called for another bottle of wine. 'Please, before you join us.'

She nodded, but by the time she brought it, the effects of the poison were already beginning to take effect. She watched in horror as they all began to convulse; there was the sound of chairs falling over, and gasping.

Busch was staring at her, his expression turning from shock to hatred as he gasped his last breath. Marianne tore her gaze away, knowing that the look he'd given her would haunt her nightmares, even though he'd deserved it. When the time had come for him to die, she didn't even get to tell him why she'd killed him or to feel any vindication, she just rushed to Henri, hoping that somehow she could get him to vomit, or get him to a doctor, but it was too late. He was already gone.

She fell onto her knees and held his body in hers. She looked at his young face, with its smattering of freckles so like his brother, and hot tears slid down her neck, the guilt crushing her like a tidal wave. The sound she made was like something wild, as she keened, holding him close. She said, over and over again, 'Oh Henri, what did I do? It should have been me. I'm so sorry...'

50

PARIS, 1943

Sebastien had been skulking in the shadows all evening, waiting, and when Marianne raced out of the restaurant, her hair a tangled mess, her eyes stained by tears, lips bloodless, he hurried towards her.

'Geoff told me about tonight, about the list, and Louisa.'

Marianne's chin wobbled. She was holding the list, clutching it. He took it from her, and said, 'Don't speak here, someone might hear.'

She shook her head and her eyes were wild and she began to gasp for air like she was having a panic attack. 'They're all dead.'

His eyes widened in horror. 'What?'

'I... killed them.'

He turned to go inside the restaurant, and when he came out a minute later, his face was pale, his black eyes filled with shock. He walked slowly, almost reluctantly back to her.

'But...the boy?'

Her face crumpled and she fell onto the street and began to

keen. He rushed to her to get her to quieten. 'It was an accident
– I didn't mean for him to eat it.'

Sebastien nodded, then held her in his arms, lifting her to
her feet, but she was a dead weight. 'Come on, you can't be
here!'

She didn't help and he half dragged her up the street.
Tracks of tears coursed down her face, as she sobbed, loud,
painful sobs. Henri's face was etched inside her brain.

'Come on,' he said, unwrapping the scarf around his neck
and pressing it against her mouth to stifle the sound. Through
glazed eyes she followed him to a flat a few blocks away, her feet
leaden and uncooperative. Somehow he got her inside. It was
just a studio, with a bed. 'I can try to get you out the country,' he
said. 'Just stay here, I'll need to make arrangements.'

'No,' she said. 'I n-need to face it... I can't run.'

He ignored her. If she faced them, she'd be killed instantly.
He turned to pour her a large glass of whisky and then went to
fetch a pill. But he couldn't trust her on her own, not like this.

'Take this.'

'What is it?'

'Just trust me.'

They were heavy sleeping pills he took in order to stop his
nightmares. While he believed in everything he was doing to
help the Resistance, it came with a price. The lines blurred and
sometimes it was hard to face who he'd become. The same
would no doubt be true for Marianne. *Poison.* Jesus, that
poor boy.

She swallowed the pill he gave her and drank the whisky
which burned as it slid down her throat. Nothing helped to
numb what she had just done.

Soon, though, her eyes turned heavy from whatever he'd
given her, and when she fell asleep several minutes later,
Sebastien pulled a blanket around her.

.   .   .

Sebastien watched her sleep, then he looked at the list and sighed; it was what they suspected. When Geoff had escaped, and came to tell him what happened: he had his suspicions that his escape was too easy. That there was a reason for it. The list was full of names of famous people, movie stars and singers. If there had been a real list, it had no doubt been put into action already. This was something they had put together in order to test if Marianne was actually informing against them – they had begun to suspect her. It was all a ruse.

He dreaded telling her when she woke up.

But he would. He didn't believe in lying.

It took five days to get to the Abbey de Saint-Michel. Sebastien helped her to get out of the city, by arranging transport on a cheese truck bound south. She stayed beneath a blanket for eighteen hours and then got another ride from a farmer headed towards Gourdes. She dyed her hair brown and wore the clothes of a boy. She was so slim and slight that from a distance she could almost pass for one.

When she arrived it was just after nine in the morning. She slipped inside the gardens, where the roses were in bloom, and found Marguerite sitting on a picnic blanket with Sister Augustine. Birds were pecking at the seed they had scattered.

The nun shaded her eyes as she looked into the distance. Hearing her approach, she seemed to tense, but then after a while she stood, frowned and breathed, 'Marianne?'

Marianne took a step forward only to pause as she saw her daughter. The child's hair was down to her shoulders now, dark like Jacques' and her eyes were so much like his too.

'Cherie, it's your maman,' said Sister Augustine and the child stood up confused.

'Maman?' she whispered.

Marianne rushed forward and embraced her, closing her eyes as she breathed her in.

Perhaps Sister Augustine understood, because she stayed back for a while, as Marianne played with Marguerite chasing after her, hugging and kissing her, committing every inch of her face to memory.

After some time, Marguerite retired to the blanket looking tired, and Marianne gave her one last kiss, trying to keep the tears from falling onto her child's face.

Marianne went to the nun. Sister Augustine's smile faltered when she saw her. It was written there.

Sister Augustine sighed. 'So you did it, then.'

She was speaking, of course, of Otto Busch.

Marianne nodded, and she began to sob quietly as she told the nun everything. Afterwards she said, 'I – I'll need your help.'

Sister Augustine nodded. 'Yes. We can try to hide you.'

Marianne shook her head. 'Not that. I made a promise to Jacques that I would have a priest come say the rites to place a headstone there. Do you think – perhaps one day when this is all over you could do it?'

Sister Augustine's lip wobbled. 'I would be honoured, *cherie*. But,' and that's when the tears began to fall fast, 'y-you could just stay, Marianne. God will forgive you, child.'

Marianne looked at her, then looked back at her now sleeping daughter and wished she could. But she couldn't. She knew she couldn't. 'They left out a part in Ecclesiastes, I feel.'

The nun frowned. 'What do you mean?' She remembered that they'd spoken of that passage before.

'There is a time for vengeance and a time for justice, too.'

Marianne turned to leave, as she squared her shoulders and prepared to return to Paris to meet hers.

51

PROVENCE, 1987

Gilbert wasn't the only one with tears streaming down his face as Sister Augustine told them of what had happened. The afternoon had turned to evening, and still they sat in the same chairs, listening to the nun as she told the story of her friend.

'She told me that if her daughter ever came I was to tell her what she had done, and why. She asked that I look for a family to adopt her, someone local who would love her and treat her with kindness and raise her as a Frenchwoman. After she left that day she returned to Paris and turned herself in to the authorities. It was many years later that I got the chance finally to go to Heligoland to find Jacques' grave and perform the rites. One of his old research mates was still there and he showed me where he was buried. When we commissioned the headstone we put a Star of David on it too.'

Sabine's lip wobbled as she listened to the nun.

'And the rest you know,' finished Sister Augustine.

Gilbert nodded. 'But I still don't understand, why did she

do that – turn herself in like that and not come back here for her daughter?'

'I don't think she believed that she deserved that. It was the same reason why she felt she couldn't come to you afterwards – she had made a choice in that moment not to interfere, not to tell Henri to not eat the food and it cost Henri his life. She didn't think that was something she would ever want you to have to rationalise.'

Gilbert nodded, wiping his eyes. It was a horrible thing, but he could appreciate she might have seen it that way. 'She was going to eat the poisoned food; she wanted it to be her, not him,' he said.

'Yes.'

Gilbert broke down then and through his sobs he heard the nun say, 'Yes, she always meant to face her sins. I think there are many people who would hear her story and see only the monstrous thing she did. But there was justice too. I believe in the end she saved many lives, with the children who managed to flee as a result of her intervention, and she did what she did thinking she was going to save others too.'

'And yet no one knows that.'

'Maybe you could change that.'

Sabine looked at Gilbert and he nodded.

'That is something we could do,' she said.

52

THREE YEARS LATER – PARIS, 1990

When the wind changes and you are standing on the corner of Rue Cardinet and Lumercier, the scent of cooking stops passers-by in their tracks: rich cream and port and roast chicken. Whispers swell of how well the new restaurant is doing, and about the woman who once owned it during the Occupation.

There was a group of people standing outside, speaking about it, just as Gilbert made his way onto the street. He caught snatches of their conversation and shook his head.

'They say she single-handedly took down a whole group of Nazis.'

'Sacrificed herself to a firing squad, so I heard.'

'Infiltrated Hitler's private circle – and it was poison that finished him off in his bunker...'

This last was new, and was, of course, ridiculous. The rumours had begun to grow again, but they were different now. This time they didn't anger him.

He made his way to the clean window; the glass was clear now. The words that been scratched into the glass – *collaborator and murderer* – were long gone. He went inside to savour the smell of fresh paint mixed with the mouth-watering aroma of roast chicken.

In the kitchen, he could hear Antoine humming.

He'd brought the champagne from '68 that he'd been saving for the day he sold the ugly American first edition of *Lolita*, which he finally had, but that wasn't what he wanted to celebrate – it was this.

He saw Sabine at the back, dusting a row of framed photographs, her hair in her customary top knot. As he neared, she turned to him and smiled, and he saw the now familiar subjects in the pictures – the ordinary men and women who had helped to sabotage the efforts of the Nazis. One stood in pride of place, with a framed article about the restaurant that they now were in – Marianne Blanchet – along with other photos of her and of Henri and Gilbert that they had managed to find when they decided to re-open the restaurant to cook her grandmother's recipes.

As Sabine came forward to embrace him, he caught a glimpse of the restaurant's new sign reflected in the glass of the frame.

Even backwards he could make it out.

It brought a lump to his throat. But this time it was because of pride.

Café de Resistance.

A LETTER FROM LILY

Thank you so much for reading *The Last Restaurant in Paris*. I really hope you enjoyed it. If you did, and want to keep up to date with all my latest releases, just sign up at the following link. Your email address will never be shared and you can unsubscribe at any time.

www.bookouture.com/lily-graham

If you did enjoy *The Last Restaurant in Paris*, I would be very grateful if you could write a review. It really makes such a difference helping new readers to discover my books. Also, if you'd like to get in touch or find out more about my other books, visit my website at https://lilygraham.net.

 facebook.com/LilyRoseGrahamAuthor

instagram.com/lilygrahamauthor

AUTHOR'S NOTE

Unfortunately, the beautiful village of Lamarin is fictional, but it was, in part inspired by Simiane-la-Rotonde, a commune in Haute-Provence, where the lavender rolls out its purple carpet every year.

The Last Restaurant in Paris was inspired by all the incredible stories I read about the ordinary men and women who helped to resist the occupation of the Nazis across Europe, as well as the film *A Call to Spy* which follows the true-life accounts of remarkable women who were recruited and trained by the British government to help sabotage German operations from within the Occupation. Their bravery and courage was incredibly inspiring, and I knew that my next novel would likely feature a spy as a result. But when I read an article in the *New York Post* about two young Dutch sisters, Truus and Freddie Oversteegen, and their friend, Hannie Schaft (https://nypost.-com/2019/12/14/meet-the-dutch-girls-who-seduced-nazis-and-lured-them-to-their-deaths), who took up arms against the Germans in the Netherlands by luring Nazis away from bars and inviting them to go on walks where they would shoot them, the seed was planted for a more morally ambiguous story about the price someone might pay for justice.

Victory comes at a price, and sometimes that price, as Truss told Sophie Poldermans, her biographer in the book, *Seducing and Killing Nazis: Hannie, Truus and Freddie: Dutch Resistance Heroines of WWII,* is on one's soul. 'I wasn't born to kill. Do you know what that does to your soul?'

After each attack, she often fainted or broke down in tears and years later they all suffered from depression, while Hannie Schaft was executed by the Nazis. However, their legacy lives on, a story of incredible personal sacrifice and courage as together they helped sabotage military installations, bombing munitions shipments and power lines, killing many Nazis.

ACKNOWLEDGEMENTS

This was an incredibly tricky novel to write, at a very difficult time in my life, and if it wasn't for my editor Lydia Vassar-Smith, it honestly wouldn't have happened. Thank you so much for your patience, support and kindness; you truly are one of the most wonderful humans out there, the world is a better place for having you in it.

My deepest thanks to the Bookouture team for their hard work and support, for the gorgeous covers, and everything you do.

Thank you as ever to my husband, Rui, who always believes even, and especially, when I don't, that the words will come.

Last and definitely not least, thank you to you – the reader; thank you so much for picking up this book, and to all the readers and bloggers who have reached out to me and been so kind and supportive, it means the world.

Made in the USA
Las Vegas, NV
26 February 2023